GREG JACKSON has been a writing fellow at the Fine Arts Work Center, MacDowell Colony, and the University of Virginia's MFA programme. A winner of the Balch and Henfield Prizes and a finalist for the 2014 National Magazine Award in Fiction, his short stories have appeared in, among others, the New _____ ta, and *VQR*.

More praise for *Prodigals*:

'Jackson's funny, vibrant and insi_____ ytelling, highs and lows included, makes you wish you were there . . . He's a terrific writer and *Prodigals* deserves to be on your reading list' *Esquire*

'This debut collection ponders how we come of age today, now that the old signifiers – marriage, career, kids – are by no means guaranteed. It shines a spotlight on a privileged 1 per cent to whom everything seemed possible until it wasn't' *New Statesman*

'This hotly tipped American writer proves himself to be the heir of Bret Easton Ellis with the opening story in this excellent collection [depicting] the foundering, drugged-out lives of a group of privileged knowing thirty-somethings with a brilliance not seen in American writing since Ellis's epoch-defining collection *Less Than Zero*. Jackson is a good degree more compassionate than Ellis, though, and a juicier writer' *Metro*

'Greg Jackson's stories are deft, compact, intelligent, and beautifully aimed. The short story, in our accelerating present, has advantages over its bulkier and slower-moving rival, the novel. Greg Jackson exploits such advantages in these fractal-like captures of moments and sequences from our current disorders' Norman Rush, author of *Subtle Bodies* and *Mating*

'[A] deeply felt and sparklingly erudite collection . . . Jackson's exquisite prose calls to mind David Foster Wallace and Ben Lerner, but his preoccupation with the demise of romance, wonderment and spirituality in our hyper-knowing age seems entirely his own' *Publishers Weekly*

'Unique – and often very funny too. "Wagner in the Desert" is both hilarious and unsettling, as is the incredibly witty and surprisingly sad reflection on loneliness in "Epithalamium" . . . Jackson at his best [is] able to veer between hilarity and soul-crushing sadness in a matter of words, while also building a sense of unease throughout' *Sunday Independent* (Dublin)

'As the eponymous prodigals squander their emotions and passions, their recklessness reveals hilarious and agonizing insights into the lost dreams of youthful ambition. Jackson proves himself a dexterous, compelling new talent . . . [A] daring and innovative collection' *Booklist*

'This is the best fiction debut [the *New Yorker*] has published in years' Lorin Stein of the *Paris Review* on Greg Jackson's story 'Wagner in the Desert'

'The sharpness of human observation – the bare-naked honesty on display here – is eye-watering . . . Jackson is style conscious – he not only wants to tell a good tale but titillate with its construction. Others will similarly experiment and fail but Jackson pulls it off . . . To witness the arrival of a new voice – one that rises above the cacophony on merit alone – is a rare privilege. And without doubt, Greg Jackson is just that – the real thing' *Bookmunch*

'*Prodigals* is that rare treat: a narrative inquiry into the nature of narrative that is neither tedious nor tired, that takes itself just seriously enough. His lyric virtuosity is thrilling, his sensibility acute and nuanced, but it was something deeper than either of these things that ultimately compelled me in these stories: It was a genuine sense of searching – without irony or apology, with fierce intelligence – for what might constitute a meaningful life' Leslie Jamison, author of *The Empathy Exams*

'[Jackson] trains his eye on millennials, addicted to social media, too drug-deadened to be neurotic, caught somewhere between satire and glorification' *Daily Telegraph*

'*Prodigals* is elegant and unpredictable. These stories of bewilderment, heartbreak and psychotropics will charm you with their humor and stun you with wisdom that's both rigorous and compassionate' Catherine Lacey, author of *Nobody is Ever Missing*

'Greg Jackson is the latest virtuoso on the US literary scene, writing stylistically self-conscious stories [where] the characters inevitably end up reflecting on the futility of their existence . . . *Prodigals* represents the most fashionable form of the short story, nibbling at its own limits like a frantic addict' *Spectator*

'This ultra-contemporary collection evokes a rarefied world of hyper-educated, over-stimulated people caught in the grip of their own privileged consciousness. Jackson writes with terrific fluency, wielding Fitzgeraldian phrases as he presses through to endings full of feeling' Matthew Thomas, *New York Times*-bestselling author of *We Are Not Ourselves*

'This is a whirring joyride of short stories. Jackson's debut collection is a satirical portrait of the elite, the aspirationally bookish types likely to be reading these stories . . . This brilliant book is like dating a clever boy with a prodigious vocabulary, you sometimes feel left behind, but are ultimately gratified for being invited along in the first place' *Tank*

'Greg Jackson is an uncommonly good writer – wickedly funny and deeply perceptive – and *Prodigals* is one of the most absorbing, intelligent, and unnervingly dead-on collections I've read in ages. I loved it' Molly Antopol, author of *The UnAmericans*

'These are tales about how we try to escape [our] identities, to fulfil the sense of ourselves as special by experimenting with drugs, hedonism, bohemianism, sex and role-play' *TLS*

'Inventive, daring, and exhilarating, the stories in *Prodigals* offer a vital, volatile mix of style and heart, slyness and candor. Read these stories and find yourself newly awake, thin-skinned to the world' Maggie Shipstead, author of *Astonish Me*

'With humour, cut-throat dialogue and drug-fuelled escapades gripping the reader from the off . . . Comparisons have understandably been made to the writing of Martin Amis and Ian McEwan, but there's also an ultra-modern, American feel to these stories that aligns them to writers such as David Foster Wallace and Gary Shteyngart' *Irish Times*

Prodigals

STORIES

Greg Jackson

GRANTA

Granta Publications, 12 Addison Avenue, London W11 4QR

First published in Great Britain by Granta Books in 2016
This edition published by Granta Books in 2016

First published in the United States by in 2016 by
Farrar, Straus and Giroux, New York.

These stories previously appeared, in slightly different form, in the following
publications: the *New Yorker* ('Wagner in the Desert'), *VQR* ('Serve-and-Volley,
Near Vichy'), and *Granta* ('Epithalamium').

Grateful acknowledgment is made for permission to reprint an excerpt from *The
Marriage of Cadmus and Harmony* by Roberto Calasso, translated by Tim Parks,
copyright © 1993 by Alfred A. Knopf, a division of Penguin Random House LLC.
Used by permission of Alfred A. Knopf, an imprint of the Knopf Doubleday
Publishing Group, a division of Penguin Random House LLC. All rights reserved.

A CIP catalogue record for this book is available from the British Library.

1 3 5 7 9 10 8 6 4 2

ISBN 978 1 78378 201 7 (paperback)
ISBN 978 1 78378 200 0 (ebook)

Designed by Jonathan D. Lippincott

Offset by Avon DataSet Ltd, Bidford on Avon, B50 4JH

Printed and bound by CPI Group (UK) Ltd, Croydon, CR0 4YY

www.grantabooks.com

For my parents, Katherine and Tony

I am always going home, always to my father's house.

—Novalis

Contents

Prodigals

Wagner in the Desert

First we did molly, lay on the thick carpet touching the pile, ourselves, one another. We did edibles, bathed dumbly in the sun, took naps on suede couches. Later we did blow off the keys to ecologically responsible cars. We powdered glass tables and bathroom fixtures. We ate mushrooms—ate and waited, ate and waited. Then we just ate, emptied Ziplocs into our mouths like chip bags. We smoked cigarettes and joints, sucked on lozenges lacquered in hash oil. We tried one another's benzos and antivirals, Restoril, Avodart, Yaz, and Dexedrine, looking for contraindications. We ate well: cassoulets, steak frites, squid-ink risotto with porcini, spices from Andhra Pradesh, Kyoto, Antwerp. Of course we drank: pure agaves, rye whiskeys, St-Germain, old Scotch. We spent our hot December afternoons next to the custom saltwater pool or below the parasols of palm fronds, waiting, I suppose, to feel at peace, to baptize our minds in an enforced nullity, to return to a place from which we could begin again.

This was a few years ago in Palm Springs, at the end of a very forgettable year.

•

When I say that I was visiting old friends, friends from whom my life and my sense of life had diverged, I am not trying to set myself apart. Marta and Eli had lived in L.A. for a number of years, long enough, I suppose, that whatever logic married immediate impulse to near-term goal to life plan to identity had slipped below conscious awareness and become simply a part of them. I was by no means innocent, either, of the slow supplanting drift by which the means to our most cherished and noble ends become the ends themselves—so that, for instance, writing something to change the world becomes writing something that matters to you becomes publishing something halfway decent becomes writing something publishable; or, to give another arbitrary example, finding everlasting love becomes finding somewhat lasting love becomes finding a reasonable mix of tolerance and lust becomes finding a sensible social teammate. And of course with each recalibration you think not that you are trading down or betraying your values but that you are becoming more *mature*. And maybe you are. Maybe you are doing the best you can. But what is true is that one day you wake up dead.

In any case I *was* writing a book, one that I hoped would make my contemporaries see how petty and misguided their lives were, how worthwhile my sacrifices, how refreshing my repudiations, how heroic my stubbornness, et cetera. Eli and Marta were trying to have a baby. They would spend the ensuing year attempting to get pregnant, and eventually they would, and later this baby, and their second baby, would grant them some reprieve from the confusion we were all afflicted by in those years. But before they had their baby, during the week when this story takes place, they had decided to do every last thing that a baby precludes, every last irresponsible thing, so as, I guess, to be able to say, Yes, I have lived, I have done the things that mean you have lived, brushed shoulders with the lurid genie Dionysus, who counsels recklessness and abandon, decadence, self-destruction, and waste. The Baby Bucket List, they were calling it.

And I was game. Although I was not planning to have a child anytime soon, I thought we could all stand to chemically unfasten our fingers from their death grips on our careers and wardrobes and topiarian social lives and ne plus ultra vacations in tropical Asia. The words "we" and "our" are a bit figurative here, as I remain unsure whether I rounded out our group's eclecticism or stood in contrast to it. But we were, in any case, a particular sort of modern hustler: filmmakers and writers (screen, Web, magazine) who periodically worked as narrative consultants on ad campaigns, sustainability experts, PR lifers, designers or design consultants, Commonwealth transplants living in the borderless monoculture of global corporatism, social entrepreneurs, and that strange species of human being who has invented an app. We rubbed elbows with media moguls and Hollywood actors and the lesser-known but still powerful strata that include producers and directors and COOs and the half-famous relatives of the more famous. We preferred vintage cars to new but drove hybrids (because the environment), took shopping to be an urbane witticism, and were conscious enough of our materialism to mock it. We listened to U2 and Morrissey and Kylie Minogue post-ironically, which is not to say, exactly, sincerely. We donated to charity, served on the boards of not-for-profits, and shepherded socially responsible enterprises for work. We were not bad people, we thought. Not the best, a bit spoiled, maybe, but pleasant, insouciantly decent. We paid a tax on the lives we lived in order to say in public, I have sacrificed, tithed, given back. A system of pre-Lutheran indulgences. Of carbon offsets. A green-washing of our sins. We were affiliated. We had access.

I was by far the poorest of our group. There was no doubt about it, although I was not poor for principled reasons. I am not sure *why* I was so poor. Laziness, perhaps. I didn't have much energy or imagination when it came to monetizing my talents, such as they were. And I think, to be honest, I had a bad conscience about getting paid to do what I loved and what seemed, on the face of it, self-indulgent. So in the Palm Springs house that week, where I stayed on need-blind sufferance, I had the dual consciousness of a Voltaire in the court of Frederick the Great or the Marxists who brood through high-society parties in Wyndham Lewis novels, which is to say I partook, mooched, sponged, *and* felt myself apart and nonimplicated.

From the start I had been set up as the counterpart to Lily, a pretty and neurotic executive-in-training who was also not there as half of a couple. Lily had brought a tote bag for her cosmetics, which numbered in the dozens and included machines I was not familiar with. Like all the women in the house, she had exceptional hair. Her hair had the tattered elegance of a *Rolling Stone* cover model's and I decided early on that one of my goals for the week would be to sleep with Lily, although this was less a decision, really, than the final figure in some back-of-the-envelope biological math.

Lily was in the habit of always needing things she didn't have: water, iced tea, spray-on sunscreen, her phone, Kindle, iPad, a hand, advice, Chablis. I remark on this because, given that my position in the group was as a secular boyfriend of sorts to Lily, it often fell to me to fetch her things or to hold things for her while she did stuff like pee. But I also think that her constant fidgeting neediness captured something we all felt: the ever-present urge to tweak or adjust the experience to make it a touch more perfect. "Can you just hold this?" Lily would say, or "Can you just do my back?" or "Can you just come look at something?" and I slowly understood what it is to be a man for a certain type of high-strung, successful, and thin woman: you are an avatar of capability, like a living Swiss Army knife. And when the child lock on her car door stuck, or the cocktail mixer fused shut, or a toilet ceased to flush properly, or we needed to adjust the propane supply to the grill or glass fire, I was the one called on. And I fixed things, and it felt good. And maybe anyone could have fixed them, maybe Lily only asked to flatter me, to give me a sense of purpose in a modern economy that had creatively destroyed men, but it worked, it allowed me to feel masculine and useful, and I experienced an uneasy gratification that Lily and I could confirm for each other this two-dimensional idea of who we were, who our genders made us, even as we recognized how stupid and outdated this idea was.

But this was a place to be old-fashioned, I guess. It was, after all, the town of Elvis and Charles Farrell, the Rat Pack, Richard Neutra, of Jack Benny's radio broadcasts from the desert, New Year's at Sunnylands with the Reagans, and drives hooking off the fifth tee like the Laffer curve—a place in thrall to an era when the impulse was to leave the lush coastline for a desert town as seedy and plotted as an Elmore Leonard paperback, where pills were prescribed *to* be abused, drinks took their names from Dean Martin taglines, and the wedge salad never died.

We found ourselves, one night early on, in a bar dedicated to just this legacy, a place called Sammy's with a clientele of corpulent besuited men deep into life's back nine and their girlfriends. The men perched on bar stools watching their girlfriends dance, sipping drinks, and giving off the captured firelight of time spent in the timbered lodges of Jackson Hole. To a man they wore the same unadventurous red tie and spoke of Toby Keith in the hushed tones of boyish veneration. They had the vital febrility of coronaries survived and seemed happy enough to sit there, letting their girlfriends brush up on their laps, untroubled by the jobs they'd shipped to Asia or the liability they'd dumped overboard in the clear, forgiving waters of the Caribbean. The women, their consorts, were all blondes in what I guessed to be their fifties or early sixties. Their ages were hard to judge because they'd had so much work done—high-quality work, I hazarded, although it had frozen their expressions, as though to hedge bets, halfway between smile and pettish complaint. It was a fun night. A tuxedoed ensemble of what I assume were pain-pill addicts played louche numbers like "All My Ex's Live in Texas," a song in which the narrator has fled to Tennessee, presumably for reasons of alimony or scansion. The women flirted with the sax player, a man rounding fifty with deep gelled furrows in his tow-colored hair and skin the color of wet drywall, and they sort of pawed the good-looking mixed-race lounge singer, not quite inappropriately, but close, while the men looked on equably, having made their peace with death, aureate in the power of knowing excellent tax lawyers.

Our Manhattans came in highballs the size of cereal bowls with enough ice to treat a bad sprain, and although I was pretty sure all these people would be dead by the time I turned forty, I thought we had been granted a Jazz Age vision, a benedictory mirage, one that said so long as the bills in your pocket were crisp enough, the lights dim, and the band played on, you could be twenty feet out over the canyon's edge with no one the wiser.

·

On the afternoon of day three, walking his dog, Lyle, Eli confessed to me that a good chunk of the financing for his new film had fallen through. One of the backers had pulled out, and now the production company attached to his script and the director and whatever hamlet-size retinue a more or less green-lit film accretes were all scrambling to gin up new money. Eli had it on good intelligence that a financier named Wagner was in Palm Springs that week, and so one of our running intrigues became Eli's attempt to casually intersect with him. The movie sounded like a hard sell to me, a biopic about the economist Albert O. Hirschman focused on his war years, but Eli assured me that Wagner was their man.

"This guy—" Eli put his hands together as if in prayer. "You know Richard Branson? Okay, this guy is like the Richard Branson of nature and environment music. His wife's cousin—or no, no, no. Here's what it is. His wife's mother's sister, his aunt-in-law"—Eli chuckled—"Hirschman helped get her out in forty-one."

It was not quite evening. The sun had fallen below San Jacinto as it did every afternoon, leaving us in a long penumbral dusk the color of a pinkish bruise. For the second straight day we'd missed the canyon hike we intended to take, arriving seven minutes after the cutoff, according to the park ranger, who took evident pleasure in disappointing us and had the air less of a park ranger than of an actor playing a park ranger—I doubted he did much "ranging." And so to salvage the excursion, we'd driven around the tony western edge of the city, taking in the walled-off, single-story period homes, including Elvis's strange bow window of a house, and we would have explored longer if we hadn't wandered into a postmortem garage sale and found, laid out like memento mori among old Steve Martin Betamaxes, an assortment of superannuated chemotherapy supplies, which so depressed us that we each immediately took a bump off the key to Lily's Nissan Leaf.

Walking now with Eli, feeling just a hair better, that whatever happened I would not die that night, that I could follow some twisting course of multivalent inebriation to the torchlit inner sanctum of the self-subsuming mood, where the need to make decisions would end, and the need to evaluate decisions just made would end, and I would exist in a sort of motiveless, ethereal *Dasein*, I was feeling a bristling love for my friend, who hadn't said a word to me in five minutes, showing, in the understated way of competitive men, that our friendship transcended his need to sell other people on a garish idea of his life, that we could be quiet together and find peace in each other for the simple reason that we could offer each other nothing else. I was hoping badly that Lyle would pee on the Ferrari hatchback we were passing, when I looked up to see a slight Hasidic man pacing a jogger down the middle of the street. The Hasid was in full getup, shuffle-walking to keep up with the jogging man and pointing something out to him insistently on a piece of paper. The jogger looked at us with a grin or a grimace that was perhaps self-excusing, but he needn't have. It became clear to us in the days following: Chabad-Lubavitch was everywhere, Crown Heights had emptied out into our corner of the California desert, bearded men in long black robes haunting our bacchanal, coy and twinkling with a great-avuncular look that seemed to say, You will understand in time, you will see—or maybe not.

But it's also possible that I was losing my mind. It was day three, as I said, and the wheels were beginning to come off. Lily and I had made out for a while in bed the night before, humping a bit half-heartedly before she sent me away to sleep by myself—and I had felt grateful, because this way I would actually sleep and wouldn't have to wake up next to her tired and noisome with a monomaniacal erection. But I'd also felt spurned, or confused, because whereas Eli had the goal of finding and wooing Wagner, and Marta had the goal of treating her body like a chemistry set, and Lily had the goal of having a man around to hold her purse, and the others in the group had various faintly boring goals that involved their partners and spa treatments, my only goal to that point had been to get laid in a state of near-primal cognitive decomposition. And so when I awoke that morning and realized just how seriously in jeopardy this goal was, I promptly ate an entire rainbow Rice Krispies treat of marijuana and lost track of everything but a premonition that the world was going to end.

I was lying motionless on the couch, under a protective throw that had become important to me, when Lily came over and started talking. She played with my hair while she talked, and I tried to think up one grammatical sentence to indicate that I was still a human being or would some day be one again. The only recognizable thought in my mind, however, was the sudden overpowering desire to have sex, and this wasn't even a thought as such. If I had been in any state to speak, let alone make an argument, I would have brought a Christian martyr's passion to the task of getting Lily spread-eagle and receptive, but all I managed to say, interrupting her arbitrarily to say it, was "I'm very stoned."

She looked at me curiously. "Really?" she said. I thought it was so obvious that I was briefly furious at her—that she was so wrapped up in telling me whatever shit, none of which I could translate into meaningful ideation anyway, that she had failed to notice I was demonstrating the vital signs of a Pet Rock. Eli walked over to ask if I wanted lunch, or anything, or what *did* I want, and I said "no," "maybe," "later" in some order, and then I realized that there *was* something I wanted, although it was not exactly a group activity, which was to lie on the bathroom floor and masturbate until I died.

"Excuse me," I said, getting up. I was not terribly steady on my feet and had to brace myself on furniture all the way to the bathroom, but I was excited, let's say ludicrously excited, at the prospect of masturbating, and more than that even *amazed* that I had forgotten the possibility of masturbation as a sort of compromise formation in my ongoing sham coupledom with Lily. And although I could barely breathe or stand, the sensitivity I felt to the world just then was a revelation. It was as though every surface of my body, inside and out, had thinned to the basis weight of tracing paper. I seemed to feel the blood in my body coursing along the inner banks of its vessels, a trembling life force lighting up my meridians like neon, and as I pushed off from the free-form couch by the fireplace, the lone thought surfacing within the indiscrete salmagundi of my brain was something like: *I* know what a chakra is.

In the bathroom I locked the doors and stripped to nothing, put the cold-water tap on low, and lay down on the bath mat. Something like fevered joy clenched in my abdomen. If there is an end point to the confessional mode it is surely the things we think about while masturbating, but here goes: I thought of the breasts of a woman who had been at dinner the night before, big, heavy breasts. I thought of her telling me to fuck them, or maybe having multiple dicks, or a kind of *Matrix*-like displacement of dicks, and fucking her and her tits at the same time. I thought of ass-fucking. I thought of someone wanting it, maybe begging for it, maybe Lily. There were mirrors all over the bathroom, and I thought of fucking Lily standing up, of gazing at the mirror and our eyes meeting in a look that said, Wow, we are fucking and it feels *awesome*. I thought, Mental note: return to question of mirrors, why we like watching ourselves fuck in mirrors— then I forgot this immediately. I thought, This feels *so* good, and when it is over I will die, but there won't be any reason to live anyway, so that's fine. And I thought, What am I doing with my life? And I thought, Am I a good person or a bad person or just a person? And I thought, Am I powerful or weak? And I thought, Now's maybe not the time . . . And I thought, Let's pretend powerful, just for now, let's pretend I'm powerful and Lily's powerful and I'm fucking her in the ass, and she's asking for it, pleading probably, and our eyes meet in the mirror in a look of concern or coital oneness or existential hurt or gratitude that something could feel this good. Yes, *that*. Let's pretend *that*.

And I came just then, for the first time in my life, before even getting hard.

•

At dinner that night I gave a drunken toast that couldn't have made much sense. After dinner we sat in front of the glass fire. To get it lit you had to open two separate valves, and even then it wasn't clear where the gas emerged from, so when the flame finally took, the whole fireplace, which by then had filled with gas, came alive suddenly with the whoosh or whoomp of a fireball combusting. I had learned at the expense of a great deal of forearm hair to be careful with the ghostly blaze, which finally settled to dance above its moraine of shattered glass, as though a flame could be entranced by a hearth of ice.

It was the night before New Year's Eve and we were playing games, full from another exquisite meal, sipping Sazeracs and eighteen-year-old single malts, looking for just that elusive shade of irony or absurdity to surprise even ourselves in laughter. We played Cards Against Humanity. "_____. Betcha can't have just one!" the prompt read, and Eli answered "Geese," which made me laugh, and my thoughts ran to Mary Oliver, as they always do when geese are mentioned, and I wondered why we couldn't just let the soft animals of our bodies love what they loved. Then I remembered that we were too busy being witty to have any idea what we loved. And if you closed one eye and found yourself in a moment of some perspective, I thought, maybe within the yet-uncracked genetics of the witticism, you could hear a hollow and performative laughter echoing down the swept streets, floating into Sammy's and out, tripping down the decades, the stone-wrinkled valleys of the San Jacinto, a sound constructed and dispersed on the Santa Ana wind, cleft by giant windmills turning in the lowlands, coming through on radios in Calipatria, in the kitchens of trailers and rusted-out meth labs, sparkling like the Salton Sea—that bright veneer happiness as flat and shimmering as the scales on a dead fish.

This was not a human landscape. None of California is, but this place especially, with mountains as bare and rubbled as Mars, days identical to one another and so bright they washed out. The wind farms blinked red through the light-spoiled nights. It was that particular California melancholy that is the perfect absence of the sacred.

•

I awoke on the morning of New Year's Eve on a deflated air mattress without any memory of having gone to sleep. It turned out I was *not* licking Julie Delpy, but holding Lyle in a kind of Pietà. When he saw I was awake he began chewing on my hair, and I thought about going and getting into bed with Lily, then decided to conserve goodwill. I don't mean to give the impression that sex is all I think about, but I am goal-oriented. I need goals. And I felt cheated out of something. Lily's car kept breaking, and so did her toilet, and she needed water and grapes like several dozen times a day. I was getting all the bad boyfriend jobs, I felt, and none of the good.

But in retrospect I know it wasn't really about Lily, this sense of being cheated. I needed something to *happen*. Something new and totalizing to push forward a dithering life or to put a seal on the departing year like an intaglio in wax. I needed to remember what it was to *live*. And drugs were not just handmaiden or enabler but part and parcel of the same impossible quest, which you could say was the search for the mythical point of most vivid existence, the El Dorado of aliveness, which I did not believe in but which tantalized me nonetheless, a point of mastering the moment in some perfect way, seeing all the power inside you rise up and coincide with itself, suspending life's give-and-take until you were only taking, claiming every last thing you ever needed or wanted—love, fear, kinship, respect—and experiencing it all at the very instant that every appetite within you was satisfied.

It is a stupid dream, but there it is. And not a bad agenda for a day, as agendas go, as days go.

Lily turned out to be up already. She was sitting in the patio sun, reading the latest *New York Review of Books*, which we talked about over my first smoke. It had articles about our bad Mideast policy and a pretty obscure seventeenth-century Italian painter and the comparative merits of Czesław Miłosz translations and a book that said technology was isolating us as it seemed to be connecting us, replacing the passions with wan counterparts, so that loving became liking, happiness fun, and friend ceased to refer to a person but to a thing you *did* to a person, the noun "friend" retired for a cultlike horde called "followers." Even a few years later, recalling this, I feel just how tired the complaints have become, but at the time it all seemed more poignant, not the conclusions, exactly, which were even then proto-clichés, but that *The New York Review of Books* existed at all, that it continued to devote such good minds and scholarship to what after five minutes in the desert sun, driving with the top down by imitation-adobe strip malls full of nail salons and smoothie shops and physical therapy outlets, was almost painfully irrelevant. And then I wondered, What is our fucking obsessions with *relevancy*?

I didn't follow this line of thinking quite so far until we were on our way to the hike that afternoon. It was another perfect day—each one was—and we had mobilized early, nearly two hours before the closing time, which by that point had been embossed forever on our psyches. The sun hung in the southern sky at the height of a double off the left-field wall, hot and pleasant and a whitish color, slipping at its edges into a pale powdered blue that had the particulate quality of noise in a photograph. I was glad we were going for the hike. It felt almost moral in the context, and even if it was a relatively level hike and only about an hour round-trip, and there was a waterfall at the end hidden among the sere folds of rock, I thought at least we will have to put *something* in, something of ourselves, to get whatever out.

Our friend the ranger was waiting for us at the gate, and this time we approached him with an air of triumph, as though he had doubted our resolve, but we had persevered and now things would be different.

"Hey," we said.

"Hello," he said, perhaps smiling a little.

We looked at one another for a minute.

"Trail's closed," he said. "Closes early today, on account of the holiday."

"Oh, come *on*," Eli said. "You realize we've been here every day this week."

The ranger actually had his hands on his hips, as if posing for a catalogue. The olive-green uniform hung on him so perfectly that I wondered whether he wasn't perhaps the fit model for the entire clothing line.

"Park reopens January second," he said. "Eight a.m. sharp."

"Is it because we're Jews?" Marta said.

The ranger's gaze, emerging from his tan and handsomely creased face, cast out to the distant escarpments on the far side of the valley.

"Same rules for everyone," he said.

"What if we hike really fast?" said Marta. "You just let that woman with a walker in. We're definitely going to be faster than her."

"Hike takes one hour, thirty minutes. We lock the gate in one hour, twenty minutes. You do the math."

"I feel like you're not getting my point," Marta said.

"Same rules for everyone," he repeated.

"What is this, *Brown versus Board of Education*?" Marta said under her breath.

"Your hike is a piece of shit," Eli informed the ranger.

"You can always hike the Sagebrush Trail," he said, pointing vaguely to a boulder-strewn slope in the distance that seemed to rise, precipitously, toward nothing.

"And the Sagebrush Trail has a waterfall?" I said.

"Ha, ha. No."

"Such bullshit," Marta said, laughing lightly, such warm placid annoyance in her tone that it seemed to me suddenly a master class in the management of emotions in a public capacity, the decoupling of an emotion's expression from its affective consequences. And it came to me then, as we hiked the Sagebrush Trail, just how public most people's lives were and how *un*public mine was, how unsuited to public acquittal I had become in this modern world of ours, this world of glass fires, where flames hovered over drifts of glass, playing on the idea that a fire consumes some fuel beneath.

We hiked the Sagebrush Trail until boredom overtook us. It seemed not to go anyplace or end, and at the top of a ridge, where we finally stopped, a Hasid in black robes stared out across the Coachella Valley, past the lush plot of Palm Springs, which sat in the dun funnel of mountains like a piece of sod on a field of dirt. I wondered what it would take to imagine my way into his mind. I tried to look out at the scene through his eyes and couldn't. I could only see it through my eyes: the grid of roads, the golf courses twined round their fancy houses, the brassy glow of the sun catching on the mountain faces to the south, the lights of convenience stores blinking on in the dusk. Another mellow California evening, where the idea of Sémillon and a cigarette in the velour air seemed a kind of permission—to be cosmically insignificant, maybe—an evening as lovely and forgiving as longing, as the line where we saw the shadow of the mountains end several miles to the east. I touched Lily to see if she felt it too.

•

Our steaks—the steaks we ate that night—had been cows that had eaten Lord knows how much grain, grain farmed using heavy machinery and fertilizer and then shipped on trucks, cows that had produced Lord knows how much waste and methane before they were slaughtered, before they were butchered and shipped to us on different trucks. It was a very special dinner, courtesy of the Maldives, Bangladesh, Venice. We were each supposed to say something, something meaningful or thankful, I suppose, that would begin to repay our debt to the cows and the people of Sumatra. I wanted to read a poem that had recently moved me. I had been trying to read it every night, as a prelude to dinner or a coda to dinner, but things kept getting in the way. The mood, for instance. It wasn't a very poem-y poem, but it was a poem, and I guess it had that against it. Still, it was funny and affecting, and I saw it as a moral Trojan horse, a coy and subtle rebuke to everything that was going on, which would, in the manner of all great art, make its case through no more than the appeal and persuasiveness of its sensibility. The others would hear it and sit there dumbfounded, I imagined, amazed at the shallowness of their lives, their capacity nonetheless to *apprehend* the sublime, and the fact that I had chosen a life in which I regularly made contact with this mood. Don't get me wrong. I didn't expect this state to last more than a minute. But the poem had become meaningful to me as I felt increasingly stifled, or stymied, or *something*, and I was about to read it when dinner was very suddenly ready, and then when dinner was over dessert appeared, and then there were post-dinner cigarettes, and then we got a call that our cabs were on the way and we had to hurry to clear the table so that we could all do a few lines before the party. We crushed the coke into still finer powder and spread it, thin and beautiful, on the glass coffee table. And by the time we were packed into two cabs any memory that I had been about to read a poem, or that poetry was a thing that existed, had vanished.

Eli had done a line or two himself and I could feel him growing tense in the way he did, which I had come to know years before when we were roommates in college. It was the tenseness of someone who gets almost everything he wants very easily actually wanting something he's not sure he can get. The thing Eli wanted, most proximately, was Wagner, who we'd heard was at the party to which we were en route, and yes, Eli wanted Wagner's money, wanted the financing so that his film about Albert O. Hirschman could be made and play the festival circuit and make a bid to be picked up by Focus or Searchlight or whatever, but more than that, I think, Eli wanted to know he could bag a fish as big as Wagner. To try to get his mind off things, I asked who he liked in the Cotton Bowl, but he must not have heard me because he said, "It's all the fucking drugs. Drink some water when we get there," and then I realized that we were shouting across six people from opposite ends of a taxi minivan.

By the time we got to the party I was compulsively, twitchily, taking hard sniffs through my nose. At the door we were greeted by a contingent of bashful children in party hats who blew party horns and kazoos at us. I crouched down, taking one of the horns, and said something like "Now-aren't-these-fun-and-who-are-you-don't-you-look-pretty-where's-the-bar?" and as I settled on the last word and realized I had addressed it to a six-year-old, it came to me that I probably shouldn't talk to children for a while. They ran off, in any case, for their own whimsical reasons (I told myself), and I went to the kitchen and poured half a bottle of Aperol into a Solo cup because—well, let's assume I had a reason at the time. I didn't know anyone, but I was feeling pretty great when Eli came over to me and whispered in my ear.

"Wagner's here," he said.

"Where?"

"Fuck if I know. This place is a catacomb."

I asked whether we should go looking.

"In a minute," he said. "Anyway, there's something I want to ask you."

I followed him to one of the living room's conversation pits—there were several—where we settled into the deep embrace of leather armchairs, resting our ankles on our knees, and had the following conversation while the seven or twelve other versions of us that appeared in the intricately mirrored wall had it too.

Me: So.
Eli (*after a beat*): Are people *happy*?

M: Like, *spiritually*? Like, which people?

E: Our friends, our group.

M: Like would Maslow—

E: Am I being a good host?

M: You're making me sleep on an air mattress.

E: I'm serious.

M: It sort of deflates every—

E: Is there more I could be doing?

M: I'm not sure I know what we're talking about. Are *you* happy?

E (*pausing for effect*): I am *so* happy.

M: Okay, now pretend you're not on tons of coke.

E: It's Marta, though. I mean, is this it? If we have kids, it's going to change everything, her life more than mine. I just want her to feel like she's done all the things she wanted to do.

M: Yeah, I don't think that's the way it works.

E: Meaning?

M: The bucket-list thing. I don't buy it. There's a hole in the bucket list!

E: What hole?

M: Life, tomorrow, the astonishing insufficiency of memory . . .

E: I don't want her to have any regrets.

M: Jesus, don't be insane. And look, it's not like there's some perfect moment of some perfect evening when you go: *That*. That was it. That was living, and it doesn't get any better, and now I can die. Or have kids.

E (*a little peevishly*): I know.

I was pretty out of it, but still it wasn't lost on me that what I had just denied the truth of was exactly the fantasy I had let myself entertain throughout the trip. And I felt, realizing this, neither wise

nor duplicitous but tired—tired of all the things that were equally true
and not true, which seemed to be just about everything right then.

"C'mon, let's go find Marta and Lily," Eli said, because we
hadn't seen them for a while and that could mean only one thing.
And sure enough, in the third bathroom we checked, there was Lily
speaking without punctuation, lining up lacy filaments of blow on
the porcelain tank of the toilet, while Marta did smoothing or plump-
ing things to her eyelashes that only girls understand. And somehow the four of us squeezed into that bathroom, which was the size
of a telephone booth, and did our lines and got most of the excess into
our teeth, and Eli scraped what was left very carefully over the
beveled edge and into a bag the size of one Cheez-It.

The good feeling rose in me with the gentle inexorable certainty
of a tide. "We're going to go find Wagner," Eli announced. And Lily
and I looked at each other, or our eyes met in the wall of mirror before us, and we both made a motion to speak before realizing there
was nothing we meant to say. And realizing this, we smiled, because maybe we weren't in love, and maybe love is a chemical sick-
ness anyway, one that blinds us to who the person we love really is, but
we were committed to each other, committed somehow to forgiving
each other every stupid, careless, needy, and unpleasant thing we
did or said that week. And forgiveness is a kind of love, I think.

It didn't take us long to find Wagner, although time had grown
a bit fishy at this point. We scrabbled through doors and rooms—I
don't know why we checked so many closets—and when we got to
the library a voice said, "Come in, come in," as if it had been expecting us. The voice belonged to a man of perhaps seventy who was
sitting low behind a desk, sipping from a snifter of what looked like
corrupted urine and talking on a large phone that for an instant I
took to be a kitten. He made such a striking figure that I almost
missed the Amazonian woman standing to the side in a studded black
leather bra and garters. I did a double take, but she didn't seem to
register my gaze, just looked off glassily with impassive disgust and
worked the tassels on her riding crop like a rosary.

"Satellite," Wagner said, covering the mouthpiece with his hand. Then: "Yeah, yeah, go fuck yourself, Fred. Ten a.m."

"Mustique," he said, putting the phone down, "I'm supposed to fly out tonight."

"Frank," Eli said and took a few larger-than-normal steps toward Wagner, putting out his hand and smiling like they were old war buddies.

"Do I know you?" Wagner said. "I don't think I know you."

Eli laughed his public laugh. "Eli. Eli Geller-Frucht," he said. "I'm the writer on the Hirschman film. *Philosopher's Whetstone*? Actually that title sucks, but Marley Jones at Buzzard told me her people talked to your people, said you had a personal connection to the story. Tell me if I'm making this up. Your wife's family? Right. So we're thinking sort of a John Nash in *The Good Shepherd* thing, but without all the schizophrenia, of course, and David's got this big fucking man-crush on Louis Malle, so we're doing kind of an *Au Revoir les Enfants* open, very faithful to the *spirit* of Hirschman's story, you know, but we think we can play up the Varian Fry angle—"

Wagner held up a hand as though in some vague pain. "Yeah, yeah, I get it. I talked to David—no, not Levinson, Gould. Look, I'm on board. I don't give a fuck about Hirschman, but my wife, Lydia? She won't shut up about 'Nana would have wanted to see her Albie as Zac Efron' or whatever. It's fucking ridiculous, but, well, you get to the point of certain understandings"—Wagner inclined his head to the half-dressed woman in the corner—"and so, yeah, you get the picture." He put his hands on the desk and raised himself, and he must have been sitting in a comically small chair, because when he stood, far from being the wizened troll I'd come to imagine, he loomed over both of us, six-four easy, with an elegant and gawky grace.

"Here," he said, "give me some of that blow you're on and I'll let you in on a secret." Eli reached into his pocket without taking his eyes off Wagner and passed him the bag. The man looked at us like we had to be joking, then produced a two-inch piece of straw from the breast pocket of his jacket and snorted everything that was left, right from the plastic. He thumbed his nose and sniffed a few times, gave a small shrug of disdain, and settled, half sitting, on the front of the desk. "That coke sucks, but I'll tell you anyway," he said. "Here's what I was going to say: Stop giving a shit."

We blinked at him. "What do you mean?" I said. I love that you can ask people what they mean right after they've said the most obvious things and almost invariably they'll think *they* are the ones who've failed to be clear and go to elaborate lengths to make themselves understood.

Wagner looked at me, then turned to Eli. "Is your friend retarded?" he said. "What I *mean* is, look, if you care about something, like horses, go raise horses. Go ride them and fuck them, or whatever people do with horses. Sell them to Arabs, I'd guess. But if you're going to stay in this crappy business, and they're *all* crappy, stop giving a shit. Because you're here for one reason and you should know what that reason is. Do you?"

He looked from one of us to the other, then barked "Sonia!" and we jumped, but Sonia didn't. She just walked over and spanked us each insanely hard on the ass with the riding crop.

"The reason you're here," Wagner said, "is that you already have the nice cars"—I didn't, but I went along with the spirit of his admonition—"and girlfriends with that taut skin, and decent rentals in the hills. Or maybe you own?" He looked at us doubtfully. "But you don't have the good stuff, do you, the *really* hard-to-come-by shit? You know what I'm talking about: *Envy*. Grade-A, un-stepped-on, Augusta-green . . . Serious, irrefutable reasons for people to envy you. And not just any sort of people of course. You need people well enough informed to understand just how enviable you are. And people clever enough to know how to show their envy without being sycophants. And worldly enough to be charming company while they're envying you . . . You need *courtiers*, see? And right now you *are* courtiers, that's why we pay you shit to hang around us. But if you play your cards right, one day you'll have your own. Oh, they're better and worse than friends. They don't care about you, sure, but they understand the *terms* of your success far better than a friend ever could. And so at last, when you forget why you did the shit you did, all you have to do is look at their greedy, envious, unlined faces and say, Ah, yes. *That's* why."

He stared out the sliding glass doors for a minute while Sonia cracked walnuts on a teak coffee table with the blunt end of a bowie knife, then he continued more softly. "And here's the really fucked-up thing," he said. "When you've bloated yourself on all the envy a person can take and you're still not satisfied, you'll see there's only one place left to go. You *have* everything that can be bought, all the blow jobs the people who covet your power can give, but what you don't have, you'll see, is *pain*. And that's where Sonia comes in. Sure, I *pay* her. But she would hate me just as much if I didn't. And that's real." He sipped his drink contemplatively. "It's the realest thing in the world."

He shook his head, as though to clear the cobwebs of this sentimentality, and it must have worked because he started again in a livelier tone. "It reminds me of when Nietzsche and I had our falling-out."

"Wait," I said. "Hold on. You're the *real* Wagner?"

He looked at me with what I think was hatred. "There is really something wrong with your friend," he said to Eli. "Of course I'm not the real Wagner. How much fucking blow did you do? I'm talking about David Nietzsche. The exec over at Iscariot?"

Well, I'm not going to dwell on this chapter of the night any longer. We got out as soon as we could. Sonia was bending Wagner over the Louis XV when we left. The change of year, we discovered, had come and gone; we had missed the countdown and the kisses. Marta put a silly hat on Eli, and Lily kissed me pretty chastely. I won't bore you with the rest: the long unaccountable conversation I had about Gaelic football in which I confused Michael Collins with Charles Parnell, or buying more coke in a bathroom at the Ace, or skinny-dipping at the Ace and getting kicked out, or sneaking back in and waking up among patio furniture, cuddling a metal vase full of flowers, or a strange interaction with someone who seemed to say "Lick my nipple" and "Hey, what are you doing?" in quick succession, though that may have been a dream, or the ghost of Bing Crosby saying something in my ear like, "You're a real prince of a guy, always were, always will be," and me saying something back like, "Bing, you always knew what time of day it was," and then I tried to pet a cactus, which—*bad idea*, and finally I found Lily asleep in the faux ship-rigging of a window arrangement, and after a while, when I got her untangled, we walked home, her tripping in high heels, me carrying a bag that turned out not to be hers (or a bag), then later carrying her, then climbing a wall to fetch her shoes after she threw them, in either joy or rage, into the koi pond of a meditation center.

At home we each peed while the other showered. Lily removed her contacts while I kissed her shoulders, then she applied three different lotions to her face.

When we finally lay down I said, "Look, we're here, we're happy, it's a new year, let's just . . ."

Lily sat up partway and looked at me. Her blemish-free face looked tired and sober all of a sudden, a bit how I picture the Greek Fates when I picture them—handsome, pristine, sadly knowing. "The thing is," Lily said, "we could and I'm sure it would feel good. And it's not like sex is any big deal. But we're old enough now to know some things, to know what happens next, to know that we have sex and then we text and e-mail for a bit, and then you come visit me or I come visit you, and we start to get a little excited and talk about the thing to our friends, and then we get a little bored because our friends don't really care, and we remember that we live in different places and think, Who the fuck are we kidding? and then we realize that we were *always* just a little bored, and the e-mails and text messages taper off, and the one of us who's a bit more invested feels hurt and starts giving the whole thing more weight than it deserves—because these things become referendums on our lives, right?—and so we drift apart and the thought of the other person arouses a slight bitterness or guilt, depending on who's who at this point, and when the topic of the other person comes up, we grit our teeth and say, 'Yeah, I know him,' or, 'Yeah, I know her'—and all that for a few fucks that aren't even very good because we're drunk and hardly know each other and aren't all that into it anyway."

"We could get married," I said.

"Don't be cute," Lily said. "I like you better when you're not cute."

I may have looked a little hurt because she said, "Hey, but don't feel bad. I really like you. I don't want you to feel rejected, that's not what this is."

Really? It wasn't? Well, yes and no. She didn't want me to *feel* rejected, but she did want to reject me. Still, Lily's reasoning was very sensible, and she was right that I was bored, I am often bored, and I felt a strange relief and, behind the relief, a faint sadness. It was sadness about a lot of things, but perhaps, most simply stated, it was regret that we had grown self-knowing enough to avoid our mistakes.

I left Lily's room and walked right into Eli and Marta's because I thought I should tell Eli what I had just understood, him being a screenwriter and all—that our lives had become scripts, that love had become a three-act formula worthy of Robert McKee—but then I saw that he and Marta were going at it, Eli fucking her from behind while they watched themselves in the mirrored doors of the wall closet. When they saw me they paused mid-thrust, and I said, "Oh, God, sorry," and Marta blinked and said, "It's fine, sweetie," and Eli kind of surreptitiously finished the suspended thrust and said, "Yeah, no biggie. What's up?"

•

We all felt amazingly good the next day. This seemed remarkable considering the night's program, but it's the truth. The coke had somehow burned off whatever residue encrusts on you throughout the year—free radicals, shame? We felt unashamed. We were done auditioning for one another and could now be friends, or not-friends, but ourselves. I speak for everyone. That's what you get to do when you're telling the story.

And here's a model for a modern story: *A prince met a princess but they both agreed they were too busy to explore a meaningful relationship.*

Everyone lived not unhappily after.

The end.

But this story doesn't end quite yet.

•

We left for Joshua Tree that morning. It was the same day it always was, but that day was beautiful, and the wind farms spun and the mountains gave up their passes and although the park was busy by the time we got there we didn't care. We climbed a rock pile, ate a sandwich bag of mushrooms, and lay contented in the sun. There were families around, white families and Latino families and Asian families, and everyone said "Happy New Year," all of us pleased, it seemed, that we had something to say to one another. There were people rock climbing and tightrope walking on a distant butte, and we hiked over to them as distances took on a subtle fun-house deception and the rocks grew more interesting and our bodies less reliable. The sun tore through the tissue of the sky. The stone-littered ocher valley below recalled a time when humans and dinosaurs shared the earth—not a real time, I'm not stupid, but the time in our collective imagination when we were the scrappy dreamers and they were the powerful monsters and we all had a lot more business with volcanoes.

The tightrope walkers had their lines stretched at the top of a bluff, we saw, thirty or forty yards across an open chasm. They were a group of Gen-Y hippies, most of them shirtless in rolled-up canvas pants, making coffee in AeroPresses and practicing qigong while an Alaskan Klee Kai ran from one cliff edge to the next. I sat because my balance was shot and watched in rapt dread as the bohemian boys and girls scooted out onto the ropes on their butts, stared at the horizon to find their point of balance or stability or Zen, and raised themselves, waving their hands back and forth above them in a sort of willed precession. I kept expecting them to fall, but they never did.

Half an hour later we were eating lunch on the low wall of a lookout. From where we were sitting you could see down into the Coachella Valley to the south, see the Salton Sea and the San Andreas Fault, which ran like a post-Impressionist margin in the landscape. I was mostly focused on my sandwich, though, the way the Gala apple and country-style mustard interacted with the sharp white cheddar and the arugula, how the tastes all came together and produced nuances in their interaction that I had never encountered before. I thought I had never been happier than eating this cheese-and-arugula sandwich.

I was tripping very deeply and beautifully, and I strolled to the top of a sightseeing hillock. It must have been the presence of another Hasid there that accounted for the turn my thoughts took, because I remember thinking, You and I are not so different. We are desert people, sons of a Trimalchio race. We come to places like this where there is nothing and don't *see* nothing. We see a long trailing history of wandering and persecution and the melancholic fruits of so much lineal sharpening. But then I remembered the truth, which was that I didn't really have a "people" or a "race," not as such; I was a mutt, like everyone, except Lyle, who is purebred and not a person, and whatever confluent strands produced me or anyone had their own chapters of persecution and oppression—or, to be less polite-society about it, of rape and forced labor and murder—and what we seemed always to forget is that our sense of what a person is rests on our latent sense of what a slave is, even today.

I felt a sort of sigh pass through me, and although I knew it would make up for exactly nothing, historically speaking, what seemed important to me just then was that everyone got his or her own cheese-and-arugula sandwich. "Pretty amazing," I said to my fellow gazer, and I was briefly proud of myself for coming up with something so appropriate to say, when the gazer turned and I saw he was not a Hasid after all, just a teenager in a black hoodie, and he looked at me and his eyes said, unmistakably, "You can do one of two things right now, and both of them are to go fuck yourself." And I thought, Well, okay. You're sixteen. I'd probably feel the same way. And then I thought I had to shit very badly, so I went to the single-occupancy bathroom and waited with a twelve-year-old boy while his mother shat inside. And that seemed poignant to me too, his waiting for his mother, our uneasy and yet companionable wait- ing, and for a second it occurred to me that perhaps I was traveling back to my own birth along a sequence of encounters with boys of diminishing ages. But no, I wasn't. And in the end it turned out I didn't even have to shit, I just had a stomachache.

The early evening was upon us, a dwindling and rapturous light invigorating the mountains as we debouched from the hills, descend- ing to the Cholla Cactus Garden and the smoldering twilit valley below. The cactuses themselves appeared to glow, as round and char- treuse as tennis balls, the air wholesome with a hovering feculence, the play of shadows on the far slopes giving them the cast of spalted wood. We stood together, smiling in goofy acquiescence at all we felt and lacked the words to speak. We ate the last caps and stems of the mushrooms. We were high, but we weren't courting death. We were just some nobody hustlers in the desert, trying to make a film about the economist Albert O. Hirschman, trying to read a poem and be present together and save the shards of hearts splintered many times in incautious romance from further comminution, try- ing to keep up with our Instagram and Twitter feeds and all the autodocumentary imperatives of the age, trying to keep checking items off our private bucket lists because pretty soon we would have babies and devote our lives to giving them the right prods and cush- ioning so that they could grow up to be about as bad and as careful as we were, and avoid stepping with too big a carbon footprint on our African and Asian brothers and sisters and the Dutch. We were looking for a moment, not a perfect moment but a moment in which the boundaries of ourselves and the world grew indistinct and began to overlap, to share an easement that in days past might have been called spirituality, so that we could see ourselves as dull integers before the mantissas of history and take refuge in a moment's togetherness, a kindness done in secret, in patient listening and unrequited oral sex. We were not heroes. We were trying to find ways not to be villains.

The sun was setting and we were rising—me, Marta, Eli, and Lily—the four of us in a Prius, experiencing a transcendental glee and hoping that the other half of life was gone for good. It wasn't, of course. In time it would return. But first I would wander around the plein-air Palm Springs airport that night with a vague sense that I was at a golf tournament, and watch the yellowed planes above the Denver airport hover as bright and still as fireflies. And I would wonder what they did with the burnt glass in our fireplace, whether they threw it out, replacing it with fresh glass, or if they just raked it under. And before even that we had the long ride back through Twentynine Palms and the towns of Joshua Tree and Yucca Valley, the whole thing one unbroken span of luminous development, or so it seemed, more beautiful than you can imagine.

We were listening to a late Beatles album very loud, finding folds within the music that seemed never to have been there before and unlikely to be there again. I could not get over the fact that what we were hearing were the actual hands of these men falling on their instruments half a century ago. Lily, every few minutes, burst out laughing wildly, I don't know why. We petted each other a little, sensually, asexually, then we passed into the Coachella Valley, swept down, down into the vast grid of lights, so many colors, all communicating with one another in a lattice of shifting and persistent harmony. And as we came down from the risen pass and returned to the valley floor, where the windmills blinked red and the stars through our open windows were small rounded jewels in the great velvet scrim of night, Lily spoke.

"It's like . . . it was all *choreographed* for me," she said, her voice hushed and marveling. "Like everything was arranged for *me*. To experience just like *this*."

It took me a second to realize what she was saying and what it meant, to gather my thoughts and say the only thing there was to say.

"But that's what it is," I said. "That's what being on drugs is."

Serve-and-Volley, Near Vichy

I was thirty-four when I met Léon Descoteaux, the famous tennis player, and stayed for a few days at his home in France, where he lived with his wife and children. I was traveling with my girlfriend of the time, Vicky, and she was old friends with Léon's wife, Marion, from when the two had been on the tour together. It had been ages since Vicky had last seen Marion, and she convinced me to stop in on the Descoteaux on our way to Rome, where the uptown magazine I was on assignment with wanted me to do a travel piece. "Rome to the Maxxi." "Beyond Trastevere." Something like that. I was toying with the idea of proposing to Vicky and thought that if I got up the nerve Rome was the place to do it.

It was an odd moment in my life. I no longer felt young, but I didn't feel exactly old. I felt, I suppose, that I was running out of time into which to keep pushing back the expectation that my life would simply sort itself out and come to resemble the standard model. Vicky and I had known each other from college, one of those prestigious East Coast schools whose graduates are cagey about where they went, and we had reconnected two years before. That was five years after she'd given up pro tennis and fallen, in her blithe, chipper way, into a job at a consulting firm. We were not the most natural fit, Vicky and I, but I had scaled back my ideas of romance and she must have too.

The Descoteaux were living in the countryside of the Auvergne, not far from Clermont-Ferrand but pretty far from everywhere else. This was why Vicky hadn't seen Marion for so long.

"Léo has her secreted away in middle-of-nowhere France," Vicky said. "I can't imagine how she can stand it. She was such a party girl on the tour."

I said maybe it was glamorous living in exile with a tennis legend, maybe people change.

"Not from Liberace to Thoreau," Vicky said with her great mischievous smile. When she smiled that way, I felt, just possibly, that I could spend a life with her.

"Léon Descoteaux," I said and shook my head.

I was excited about this part of our detour, I admit, the Léon Descoteaux part. It was why I had agreed to go with Vicky. I didn't think of myself as a person especially fascinated by celebrity, but that didn't mean I wasn't curious to meet the guy and peek in on his private life. It would be a story I could tell people, a casual small-talk currency. *Hey, did I tell you I spent a weekend at Léon Descoteaux's place in France last month? . . . a while back? . . . when I was in my thirties? . . . decades ago?*

There was a more personal reason too. I was no huge tennis fan, but I watched the Slams when I could, and once, about fifteen years before, I'd seen Léon play a gutsy five-set semifinal against some Scandinavian phenomenon. Léon was at the peak of his career, number six in the world, and though it was clear that his finesse game didn't stand a chance against this freakish Nordic power baseliner, Léon, with his becalmed court presence and upright bearing, played the Viking to a fifth set and a tiebreak too. I remember few tennis matches, but in the hours I spent watching this one I formed a bond with Léon Descoteaux and I rooted for him throughout the rest of his career. He had a slim body and moved lightly around the court with a kind of magic poise—the sort, I suppose, that you need to return a 125-mph serve. It may have been no more than this: I saw someone who moved with particular beauty or grace and the animal part of me responded. But in the story I told in my head, I admired his stoicism in the face of what seemed to me an occasion for despair. He was more skilled than his opponent but unable to compete with him physically. This hard-fought loss would be the best Léon could do, perhaps the best tennis he would ever play. So what I was watching, I felt, was someone *almost without peer* confront exactly the limit of his ability. Most of us don't ever get to be sixth best in the world at anything, fair enough. But then neither do most of us have to face such an objective, historical accounting of the upper limit of our talent.

On the plane over to France, above the dark nothing of the Atlantic before dawn, with the wing light blinking to my left and Vicky dozing against my right shoulder, I imagined that Léon and I might strike up a friendship, that after a few days I would tell him about watching the U.S. Open semifinal all those years before. I might say something like, "I fell in love with your game, Léon. I was living and dying with each of your points. And although you lost the match, I thought you played with terrific guts and poise." I had no illusion that I would actually say this, but I was in the habit of making these little speeches in my head. The vacant ocean passed beneath us. I was awake when the world began its too-early brightening.

•

We made our transfer in Paris and I finally sacked out on the domestic flight, only to be awoken what seemed minutes later by Vicky saying, "We're here," with annoying cheerfulness.

For a minute I had no idea what "here" she meant. A pall of exhaustion and physical misery enveloped my mood, and I thought suddenly that the trip had been a mistake, my fantasy of a warm friendship with Léon Descoteaux close to lunacy, and, most troubling of all, that I was following around a woman I barely knew and to whom, in the stark sobriety of daily life, I had almost made the mistake of proposing. I had these feelings about Vicky from time to time, and I think she must have had them about me too, because there were points at which we so thoroughly baffled each other that we were forced to confront the origin of our intimacy in college, when we were so young and drunk and hopeful that it was easy simply to adore other people as the mirror images of our own bright futures. There was more to me and Vicky than that, surely. But there was also a sense in which what held us together was having come to know each other before we knew ourselves and before, as a consequence, we knew how impossible it was going to be to know anybody else.

I can be a bit moody, and I certainly have that male thing where my bad mood is the world's problem. So a lot of what I was feeling just then, as I waited for my bags to not-arrive in Clermont-Ferrand Auvergne International, was dubious and melodramatic. I was trying to convince myself that new luggage was still being added to the carousel fifteen minutes later, when Marion showed up.

"Victoria!" she said, spotting us and raising a hand. She was an impossibly pretty woman of some wonderful, indefinite European age, who gave off an aggressive public comfort in her body that I took to be distinctly French.

"Marion, this is Daniel," Vicky said once they'd embraced. Marion looked me over like a rental billed a notch or two above its class.

"A pleasure," she said.

"Enchanté," I said and felt immediately like the sort of seamy flirt who says "enchanté."

"Poor Daniel," Vicky said. "He didn't sleep on the flight over and now his bags are lost." She rearranged my hair.

"Mais non," Marion said. She swept a hand across the scene. "They are all idiots here. *Consanguin*, you know? C'mon, we'll give you Léo's clothes."

My mood lifted as we drove beyond the outskirts of Clermont-Ferrand. Marion turned onto a rural highway and in a matter of minutes the land opened out into gorgeous hilly country. It may have been this beauty, or catching a second wind, realizing that I was okay and not teetering on the brink of inward collapse, or it may just have been one of those moments when, like a flipped switch, you go from thinking the world is conspiring against you to seeing that the world doesn't care and you are free to find your own happiness or sorrow.

"So what will we do while you're here?" Marion said. "You'll want to tour around, I suppose." She sighed. "It's funny, we live such isolated existences. I hardly know this place."

"That's not possible," Vicky said. "You've been here, what, five years? What about the kids, what do you guys *do*?"

"Yes, the poor kids," Marion said. "They are too young to care. And we have a woman, Madame Lévesque. I play tennis in the city some days and Léo—who knows what Léo does."

We were passing fields cleared for crops, wild slivers of un-cleared fields within the forests and hills. Fields with rocky outcrop-pings and stone farmhouses, quaint and picturesque, with linens and dresses sailing from clotheslines. It was a windy day and at points the sun would find a hole in the clouds and unload its cache of warmth on the champagne hood of Marion's BMW.

"What do you mean?" Vicky said, her voice as light and delicate as wind chimes.

"Léo . . . ," Marion said, "is peculiar these days. He spends ages in his workshop. He's always taking long walks in the forest. Maybe he's crazy."

She laughed, so we laughed too.

"Does he still play?" I asked.

"No," Marion said. She looked out the window and added softly, mostly to herself, "No, no, no."

We pulled up to their house not long after, a large but not im-modest country home, tidy on the outside and nicely fixed up, built in the French farmhouse style, with peach-colored terra-cotta roof tiles, small casement windows, stone masonry. An elegant and un-pretentious house set back a half mile from the road. To the right was a fenced-in tennis court with mounted lights for night play.

The net wasn't strung, but the clay surface was neatly rolled and swept.

Marion left us in the front room with Vicky's bags while she went to find the others. I drifted over to a desk with a visitor log and Vicky peered over my shoulder as I flipped through.

"Is this what you expected?" I said. I didn't mean the guest-book, but I might as well have. The last entry was from five months before, late January, and the entries from the last few years were sparse. Before that, the Descoteaux had had regular visitors. I even recognized a few names as those of tennis players famous a decade ago and a French soccer star from the good national teams at the end of the century.

"So this is a *bit* more bizarre than I was anticipating," Vicky said. She looked at me with one eye closed. "But I promise they're sweet." She kissed my cheek and then, unable to resist, took down a racket hanging with the coats to test its swing.

I looked over to see a small boy peeking at us around a corner. I grinned at him.

"Maman!" he shouted.

A moment later two slightly larger versions of the same boy appeared, and then Marion and an older woman.

"Ta gueule, Fabien," one of the older boys said.

The boys were all very handsome and might have been dressed for a photo shoot: white cotton tennis shorts, matching boat shoes, different colored but otherwise interchangeable Lacoste pullovers with little neck zippers.

"You shouldn't play with it in front of them," Marion told Vicky. "Léo has forbidden tennis and predictably they desire to do nothing else."

"Qu'est que t'a dit?" Fabien demanded, pulling his mother's skirt.

"Arrête," Marion said sharply. "The older two, Michel and An-toine, speak English, but Fabien is a beginner. N'est-ce pas, Fabien? Tu parles anglais ou quoi?"

"Oui," Fabien shouted. "Pussy!"

The older boys laughed and Marion slapped Fabien awfully hard on the back of the head. "Mais vraiment. They watch too many movies," she said.

Madame Lévesque appeared serenely oblivious to this exchange and herded the children out after we'd said our hellos.

"I can't find Léo," Marion said, "but c'mon, I'll show you your room."

•

By the time we settled in I'd lost any faith in my imaginary friendship with Léon Descoteaux and begun instead to imagine a prickly recluse liable to resent our being there. Marion and Vicky were off drinking wine and chatting on the garden terrace, and I had excused myself, setting up around back in a wooden chaise with my books and notepads. It was a brisk day. I was wearing a cable-knit sweater Marion had given me from Léo's dresser. I'd found coffee in the kitchen and was finally feeling like myself again, gazing out over the lush grounds behind the Descoteaux's house, which sloped down prettily to a pond and an orchard.

I had decided to read up on Rome. A year before, I'd written a long piece on Mexican wrestling and I'd found it easier to pick up assignments since then. This was my sixth year of freelance work, stringing together long-form nonfiction, travelogues, and the occasional trend piece. I was making just enough to get by, which meant dressing respectably, going out to dinner a few times a week, and paying nearly half the rent on our one-bedroom in Tribeca. Keeping up appearances, really. I had no savings and no prospect of any. And yet it was still a small thrill when I opened a newsstand issue to see my name in the table of contents, the words I had composed on my old battered laptop dignified by top-notch production. Friends and relatives sent notes when they'd read an article of mine, and it satisfied that old feeling, I suppose, that I was, in all my particularity, significant. I had no illusion at thirty-four that I *was* in fact, but I existed at the edge of the known world, and if I worried that I might get lost in my own head, which was always a fear, this public existence retrieved me, it located me on an objective terrain.

The anecdote with which I closed the wrestling piece came from an interview I'd conducted with an old wrestler, a man who agreed to talk to me only on terms of strict anonymity. He told me that when he gave up wrestling, he had thrown away his costume and never spoken again of his career. When I met him, he was a paunchy man in his fifties who chain-smoked and made a sibilant noise when he breathed. "The mask," he said, "is everything. Without the mask, you never leave the ring."

My Spanish was only conversational and the man had forbidden a translator, so I only realized what I had when I got back to New York and hired someone to translate the tapes. You can imagine my excitement. I remember a shiver running down my spine as I read the transcript. It was like hearing the echo of a thought I had never spoken aloud.

I was reading up on Rome and the Colosseum in the backyard when I saw a figure emerge from a patch of forest by the pond. It was a man, a bit above average height, wearing shorts and a cable-knit sweater like the one I had on. He had a beard and close-cropped hair, and he looked at the ground as he walked. I knew at once that it was Léon Descoteaux. His gait had the same overarticulated precision as his tennis game. I put down my book and stood.

He smiled when he got close. "You must be Daniel," he said, surprising me. "We have been looking forward to your visit. I am Léon Descoteaux, but please call me Léo."

We shook hands. "A pleasure to meet you," I said. "I was a big fan of yours on the court." He didn't respond, but I saw his jaw clench once and I followed his gaze to the pond and orchard, the hills behind them. "It's a magnificent place you have here."

"And we shall explore it," he said. "But now, come with me to the garden, please. I need to pick the lettuce and herbs for dinner."

Léo was on his hands and knees in the dirt when Vicky spotted us and came running over.

"Léo!" she said.

"Victoria." He rose and and kissed her cheeks. "We're delighted you came. You look even more beautiful than I remember."

"So you two have met," Vicky said, blushing.

"Daniel and I are in the early stages of a promising friendship." I gave Vicky a baffled look.

"I'm so glad," she said. Her cheeks were flushed and I guessed the women had opened a second bottle. "Marion told me not to bring up tennis, but I hope you'll at least hit around with us while we're here."

"No," Léo said pleasantly enough. "No, I won't." He smiled. "Smell these herbs. They're for our dinner."

First Vicky, then I, smelled the sharp, earthy thyme Léo had bunched in his hand.

●

I helped Léo with dinner while the women set the table. We roasted a chicken with potatoes and leeks. I assembled a salad from the garden foraging. Léo put on a Joaquín Rodrigo album and we busied ourselves in near silence. Occasionally he would ask a question or show me how he wanted something cut.

"Where were you born, Daniel?" he said at one point.

Kentucky, I told him.

"Ken*tucky*," he said and laughed. "This is a real place, where people come from?"

"A few," I said. "Not many." I told him about the rugged green country of eastern Kentucky, the low choppy mountains, the oak and hickory forests. I told him it was a bit like here.

"Like the Auvergne?" he said. "The Auvergne, you know, is a mystical place. Very strange. Full of old, secret societies." He cut into the chicken to see whether it was cooked through. "It was the center of the Resistance, did you know? They would hide in the mountains and hills."

I asked if that was why he'd chosen to live here.

"Of course," he said and winked.

That night Vicky and I turned in early after dinner. We had a second-floor bedroom that looked out on the tennis court and the moonlit hills beyond. Fresh wildflowers sprouted from a vase beside our bed.

"I'm worried about Marion," Vicky said. She lay looking up at the ceiling. I was reading next to her.

"In what sense?" I put my book down. "Your friends couldn't be more wonderful."

Vicky was quiet for a minute, then she said, "Marion told me some disturbing things. Léo refuses to touch her, she says. They haven't slept together in a year."

"That is disturbing," I said. "Marion's very attractive."

"Don't make a joke of it. She thinks Léo's turning into a . . . an ascetic or something." Vicky toyed with my arm hair, self-consciously, I thought, as though to confirm we still had this.

"That's not all," she said after a minute. Her voice had grown soft, so soft I could barely hear her. I leaned over and felt her damp breath in my ear. "Léo has a workshop he keeps locked, but Marion found the key when he was out on a walk . . ."

Vicky stopped speaking. The moon fell through the sky and through our window to pool on the tile below. I didn't want to betray my curiosity, but this excited me. My heart beat with a hollow, winey depth.

"And?" I whispered.

"There was a video camera on a tripod. A chair. A bunch of old-looking electronic equipment she doesn't understand. Maybe a VCR or something."

I laughed. "What does she think? He's some sort of abductor?"

"It's not funny," Vicky said. "She doesn't know what to think. She's afraid to ask him."

I told Vicky not to worry, but despite my jet lag and my fatigue I found it difficult to sleep. I had the impression of being awake the entire night, turning from side to side. I must have fallen asleep, though, because in the middle of the night I awoke to find Vicky gone from bed. I hadn't heard her stir, so I got up to check our little bathroom, which was empty. A sudden fear gripped me. I saw a grisly scene: Vicky tied to a chair, gagged, camera rolling. I was not in my right mind, struggling into a pair of shorts, when I glanced out the window and saw Vicky on the tennis court, hitting imaginary ground strokes by herself in the moonlight. She moved as I had seen her move on tennis courts for many years, with the litheness of a cat and a shot that snapped so hard it looked like it could dislocate her lovely shoulders.

My heart was heaving. First with fear, then with relief, then with a second fear that what I was witnessing was madness. I lay down for a minute to calm myself and awoke in the early morning with Vicky sleeping next to me. She was in a good mood when I nudged her awake and laughed when I told her what I'd seen.

"You must have dreamed it," she said and turned over to doze some more. But I hadn't dreamed it, I was sure I hadn't, and as Vicky fell back asleep I dressed and went out to look for scuff marks in the clay. I walked the lines of the court, but could scarcely find a stray crumble of brick. When I looked up, Léo was walking toward me with a pair of mugs.

"Tiens," he said, handing me a coffee. "I saw you out here, sniffing around the cage."

He stood at the gate. I sipped my coffee. "We say 'court' in English."

"Shall we go exploring?" he said. I thought he meant around the property and said sure, but Léo climbed into the Range Rover, coffee in hand, and motioned me up. We drove off without a word. The roads were empty in the early morning, the sun above us burning into a thin screen of cloud.

"I thought you'd like to see the Temple of Mercury," he said, "because of Rome."

I had mentioned the article at dinner and now said "Great," as though I had any clue what he was talking about. It turned out be a temple, dating back to Roman times, at the top of a dormant volcano called Puy de Dôme. The mountaintop had a distinctive hump shape which I found familiar, and I said as much.

"It is the end of a Tour de France stage," Léo said. "Maybe you have seen it on TV."

This seemed plausible, and I said—stupidly, I later thought—that it was always a bit uncanny to see in person things you have only ever seen on TV.

"Uncanny," Léo said. "This means what?"

"What does it mean?" I said. "Familiar—or almost familiar—but in an unsettling way."

"Ah," said Léo.

We were at the top of the mountain. The cool air whipped at the fabric of our shirts. The ruins of the temple lay before us, the long stone walls terracing the lava dome. Above the dark scattered rocks a broadcasting station with a tall antenna rose into the sky.

"This is maybe how it is when people look at me," Léo said. "Even Marion. Like instead of me she sees Léon Descoteaux. And who is that?"

We gazed out at the Chaîne des Puys, a string of ancient volcanoes leading off into the clouds that gathered above the mountains in the distance. It felt like a moment to say something generous and true and the story of watching Léo in the U.S. Open semifinal tumbled out of me before I could stop myself. I told him I felt I had seen something special that day, something personal, perhaps even *him*. I said it was like watching what beauty or grace could do against power, and it made me hopeful that beauty had a chance. I had a vague idea that you could talk to French people this way.

Léo frowned and gestured toward the temple. "You know, they used to think that Mercury, he carries the dreams from the god of dreams to the dreamer. I sometimes wonder if he ever switches the dreams along the way."

"Like a prank?"

"Maybe like a prank," Léo said. "Like say you're Oedipus and you're supposed to dream you fuck your mother and kill your father. But Mercury switches them and instead you kill your mother and fuck your father. Maybe you spend your life worrying you're gay."

"Or you're supposed to dream you're the journalist. I'm supposed to be the tennis star."

"Maybe you dream you're naked in front of the class," Léo said. "Except instead of being embarrassed, you like it."

We drove home through a small village and stopped at a market in the town square. Léo picked out supplies for lunch and asked me about Vicky, how long we had known each other, when we'd met, and so on. The story of our meeting, which I told him, was one I'd repeated so often it now had more to do with prior tellings than anything else. I'd worked for the paper in college and had been writing a piece on classmates of particular and narrow excellence when I met Vicky. I'd interviewed a cellist with perfect pitch, a math genius who wrote equations in the fog of bathroom mirrors, a poet anthologized in her teens. Vicky was my last interview. Compared with the others she was wonderfully grounded. To judge by the first three, superlative talent came with a form of insanity. They all admitted to me in one way or another that part of them hated the distorting influence of their abilities, part of them longed for normalcy, because what struck everyone else as incredible came to them so naturally it seemed unremarkable. Vicky said this herself.

"It doesn't feel to me like I'm great at tennis," she said. "It feels like I'm good, and like most of the time other people are worse. Sometimes I play someone and *I'm* worse, and I feel in awe of what they can do. But you rarely feel in awe of what you can do yourself." I asked whether this came as a disappointment. She thought about it and shrugged. "If I was someone who was going to feel awe all the time, I'd probably be going to div school, not playing tennis."

When I told people our meeting story, I would tell them it was this down-to-earth quality that drew me to Vicky, this mature wisdom about the limits of genius and her levelheaded rejection of the romanticism people tried to attach to her talent. But although this is what I told people and what I was telling Léo now, it wasn't true. I had already known Vicky when I interviewed her, not well but casually, and I had conceived the piece at least in part to get closer to her. I was attracted to her, and although I am ashamed to say it, I was attracted to her excellence.

I was rambling a bit by the time Léo turned up the drive. He stopped before we came in sight of the house and turned to me.

"What if I told you I slept with Victoria, years ago?"

I tensed and fingered the pebbled leather on the Rover's door. "Are you telling me that?"

Léo looked bored, or tired. "Maybe," he said. "If yes, what do you say?"

I tried to follow the eddy of my feelings, to still and look at them, but all I could see was Léo, handsome and lean, looking out through the windshield, awaiting my reply. We wore the same collared tennis shirt, mine white, his red, and it felt ridiculous, the two of us sitting there, discussing this like a hypothetical. And yet that was how it seemed—hypothetical—because I could sense a gulf between what I should feel and what I did. Because how could I begrudge Vicky this handsome man, his athlete's body, his perfect way of moving, all those years ago? Maybe she should have told me, but I couldn't be angry with her. What I honestly felt, when Léo smiled at me, was that this brought us closer, Léo and me.

"I don't care," I said. "I fucked Marion last night."

Léo looked at me. Then he laughed. Then we both laughed and drove the rest of the way to the house.

•

At lunch Fabien told an interminable story in French that I couldn't understand. No one translated. The air around the table was preoccupied. I was anxious to ask Vicky about her and Léo, so when lunch ended I insisted that we do the washing-up. Only then and gently, because I wasn't mad—I wasn't—did I ask why she hadn't told me about her and Léo.

"What about us?" she said, plopping a grape in her mouth.

"That you had a thing."

Vicky laughed and set down the dish she was drying. "Me and Léo? A thing?" Her mouth twisted in genuine amusement. "I think I'd know."

My relief was followed closely by annoyance and then, maybe, something like regret. I thought for a crazy moment of asking Vicky whether she would have, had Léo wanted to, but I could hardly ask her that. It wasn't jealousy I felt, after all, but the opposite. I felt—well, spurned.

Vicky and Marion went into the city that afternoon to play tennis at Marion's club, and I was once more left alone with my books and notepads on the back lawn. I tried to think about Rome, but all I could think about was Léo. What had happened to him? *Was* he crazy? Just as I was thinking, Screw Rome, this is what I should write about: the madness of Léon Descoteaux, his son Antoine appeared at my side. He announced his presence by putting his hand on my shoulder and looking down at my notes.

"Hello there," I said.

He breathed on my face for a few seconds before turning away from the papers. "You must think we're very strange," he said.

I looked at him appraisingly. He couldn't have been more than eleven.

"Everyone's strange," I said.

"Are people in America this strange?"

I laughed. Lots of them were, I told him. Lots even stranger. Antoine sighed. We looked off together at the hills.

"Nobody understands my father," he said, "but I do."

I asked what he understood and his voice grew soft. He moved his hand to my neck so he could whisper in my ear and I felt the clamminess of his fingers on my skin.

"He doesn't believe he exists," Antoine whispered.

"What do you mean?" I said.

He looked at me with wide, dramatic eyes. "How do you know *you* exist?"

I said I didn't really worry about it. He laughed. "Maybe you're crazy," he said.

"Do you think I'm crazy?"

He shrugged. "You're still here."

Léo emerged on the lawn not long after. He had a video camera on his right shoulder, the old boxy sort that a videocassette slides into, and a tennis racket in his left hand.

"I have figured out what we can do," he said.

"What we can do . . ." I frowned.

"C'mon." He beckoned me with his head and led me around to the tennis court, where, although it was only afternoon and still bright out, he flipped the breakers on the overhead lights. They glowed to life, bathing the already lit surface in a further saturation of light.

"Help me put up the net," he said. He hesitated at the gate, then strode purposefully onto the court. We strung and cranked the net until it was taut. Léo handed me the racket. He looked into the rubber viewfinder on the video camera.

"What am I doing?" I asked.

"Playing," he said. He had the camera pointed at me and was adjusting lens settings as he spoke.

"Against whom?"

"No one," he said. "We'll use our imaginations. I'll tell you what to do."

And he did. That was how it began, Léo calling out shots and movements. It seemed ages that we were on the court, Léo directing me—"To the centerline!" "Backpedal, four steps!" "Deuce court!" "Backhand slice!"—me floating across the surface, hitting imaginary shot after imaginary shot, sometimes missing too, heaving my body after a return with too much pace on it, a too-perfect location. My initial self-consciousness fell away as I played. The exertion thrilled me. My body moved naturally and fluidly, responding to Léo's instructions as its own. I served and drifted to the center of the baseline, found myself pulled left into the ad court, barely able to get the racket on a crosscourt forehand, lofting it for my opponent to put away with an overhead. At first Léo made me repeat strokes until I got them just so, but over time these repetitions became less frequent. I had to put more topspin on the ball than I was used to and Léo wanted a shorter service toss and a more open-faced stance. My body, surprising me, adjusted quickly, gave itself to him as a puppet, and when Léo called out an instruction I felt a thrill of sense pleasure run through me, like when a doctor puts a cool stethoscope to your chest.

The only times Léo stopped were to change batteries and VHS tapes. This alone marked the passage of time. My body had ceased to register it and I inhabited the moment in a way I never had before, as though a dancer in the pliant liquid of each second's unfolding. I felt alive. It is a silly phrase, we are always *alive*, but this is how I felt. It had to do with Léo's joy, I think, his excitement, his *watching*. I had never been watched like this and it was druglike, each movement attended so closely. I was bathed in sweat when I saw Marion's BMW kicking up dust in the driveway, and I felt purer and happier than I could ever remember having felt.

Marion parked and went quickly inside. Vicky approached the court with an odd look on her face.

"What are you doing?" she said.

"What *are* we doing?" I said to Léo, laughing. I felt grand. That was actually the word that came into my head.

"Making the level playing field," he said. "This is an expression in English, no?"

"Daniel, can you come in and talk to me a minute?" Vicky said.

I looked at Léo and we shrugged at each other. He handed me a white towel and I wiped my face and arms and handed it back to him. I gave him the racket and went in with Vicky.

"What is it?" I said when we were in our room. I peeled off my shirt and caught a glimpse of myself in the mirror, strong and lean, glistening. I had the urge to throw Vicky down on the bed and fuck her.

"We have to leave," she said. "Marion broke down on the drive back. She pulled off the road and almost crashed us. She said she's going crazy. She couldn't tell if she was crazy, or Léo, or both of them." Vicky jittered and I held her with reluctant tenderness. "And then I saw you doing"—she fluttered her hands in incomprehension—"whatever the fuck you were doing when we got home."

"We were just horsing around," I said.

She didn't seem to hear me. "Marion was so normal before. It's Léo that made her like this. This place. It's haunted or something. Please, we need to go."

"Léo?" I said. "He's eccentric, sure, but he's harmless, he's sweet. Isn't Marion maybe exaggerating a little?" I didn't know what I believed. The truth was I didn't care. I hoped Léo and I might continue our filming the next day and I wanted to stay on, no matter the cost. "I think Léo feels like Marion never really tried to know him."

Vicky looked at me strangely. "What do you know about it?" I was on the verge of saying I thought I understood Léo on a pretty deep level when Vicky added, "You know what Marion told me? She said she doesn't even know if she *exists* anymore. She's losing her mind."

I couldn't help smiling. A whisper of excitement tickled my throat and without quite meaning to I said, "How do you know *you* exist?" I said it softly. Vicky lurched in my arms, looking up at me with revulsion.

"What do you mean? I exist because I exist. Because I'm here, having this conversation with you. What the fuck are you talking about? Oh, fuck. Oh, fuck."

"Easy," I said. "I didn't mean anything. It was a bad joke is all."

But who was I, and who was Vicky, and if I could go back to that moment and do it all again, knowing what I do now, would I? Would I really?

Léo didn't come to dinner that night. He had locked himself in his workshop, Michel reported. Antoine grinned at me. Marion and Vicky drank wine and pushed the dinner around on their plates. No one besides me seemed to have much appetite.

I wish I could say that I gave in to Vicky and agreed to leave early the next morning, but I badgered her into staying on another day, as we'd planned. Vicky wouldn't turn toward me in bed that night, and when I woke up we were both outside on the tennis court, under the burning metal halide lights, rallying back and forth. There was no ball between us, but I was keeping up with Vicky, which was how I knew it wasn't real, and at one point I called out to her, "You look so happy!" and she said, "*You* look so happy!" and we laughed at ourselves and played on ecstatically to the flash of cameras, which caught the spindrifts of clay our feet sent up, the beads of sweat we let go in the air.

Everything was a little better in the morning. Marion was up before us and seemed fine, although Léo had yet to emerge from the workshop. The three of us, Vicky, Marion, and I, went on a drive by ourselves. Marion took us to a small restaurant in the hills, where we sat on a terrace shaded by apple trees that looked out on the rolling country. We ate lunch and drank too much wine, and Vicky and Marion told stories from the tour. I listened, vaguely. The stories all had a similar cast. A wild point in some ancient match. Drunk evenings lost to a glittering world. How dim and dickish world-class athletes could be. Mostly the last, how complacent, how spiritually lazy, you became under the habitual glare of the world's attention. I said as much and Marion said, "Ah, but sometimes don't I wish I was more like that."

"I don't," Vicky said, and I squeezed her arm.

When we got back in the early evening Léo had already started on dinner. He kissed Marion when she came in, and Vicky and I raised our eyebrows at each other. Marion blushed and played affectionately with his hair. The look in her eyes however is not one I have forgotten. It was the look you might give the ghost of a child you knew to be dead.

"I have watched your tape," Léo told me when Vicky and Marion had left us to the dishes. He dried his hands on a dishrag and hugged me. He gave me a kiss on each cheek. "It was beautiful," he said. He seemed for a second about to go on. But he didn't.

•

When we awoke the next morning Vicky and I were surprised to hear the sounds of heavy machinery in the yard. It was early, and we looked out the window to see a construction crew dismantling the Descoteaux's tennis court. Marion was in the kitchen preparing breakfast and humming brightly to herself. "I can't take you to the airport," she said, "but we have it all arranged, a car service. Oh, and they called to say they have your bags, finally."

We ate. We said our goodbyes, to the children, to Madame Lévesque, to Marion, to Léo. No one mentioned the demolition, which crashed on all around us. As we went out the door Léo handed me a padded envelope with something rattly inside.

"For you," he said. "A surprise."

I took it but didn't open it until Vicky and I were in the hired car on the way to the airport. Inside was an unlabeled black videocassette.

"What is it?" Vicky asked.

"I don't know," I said.

But I did know! I *did*.

After a while Vicky turned to me and said quietly, "You have to do something for me. You have to throw away that tape without watching it. I promise you'll be happier if you do."

I didn't say anything. We arrived in Rome. I began my explorations, my sightseeing, my note taking. Vicky came with me some days and went off on her own others. I moved around the city. I moved this way and that. I felt my legs move, my arms swing through the Roman air. I ran my fingers along the stones. No one saw any of it. Did I exist?

Even in those days it was hard to track down a VHS player, but I finally found an outfit that transferred video to DVD and I gave the proprietor my credit card to leave me alone in the room with his equipment. When I got back to the hotel I threw myself on Vicky and we had torrid sex. I couldn't remember the last time we'd fucked like that and I half expected her to look at me with gratitude when we were done, but she wouldn't meet my eye.

"What?" I said.

"You watched it," she said.

"So?"

I couldn't lie. I could still see myself in triumph, walking onto the court, clapping my racket with my hand, getting down in a crouch, waiting for the first serve. I only thought later how remarkable that Léon Descoteaux, after all those years, had remembered every shot, every twist and lurch, with such precision. His memory of the match was perfect. By the time I thought this Vicky had flown home and our relationship had begun the rapid crumbling that would leave it scattered at our feet. I would like to say I didn't watch the video again, or many times after. That others didn't have to intervene. That I didn't have to burn the damn thing and spend years finding different ways of describing what it meant to feel "hollowed out." I *wasn't* hollowed out, was the thing. I was brimming to the exclusion of all else with this sickly joy. And even then, when I'd burned the tape and moved on—even now—I wake up at night with the image of camera flashes hot on my retina, the tidal roar of the crowd in my ear, shifting weight lightly from side to side, gazing placidly into the eyes of my tall opponent, listening for the chair umpire to come through on the speakers high above.

That's how it begins.

Epithalamium

Hara had to think there were better ways to say fuck you, although it did take a certain ballsiness, what he had done, in the middle of their divorce no less, and she could see, in fact she couldn't *not* see, that the flip side of this prickishness was the quality she loved in Zeke, loved best in him perhaps, when she did love him, and she did love him—she still did—she just hated him now too. Yes, she would probably laugh about it when she stopped being angry. She was always smiling inconveniently in the throes of anger, like the very notion of fury in lives such as theirs dragged a subterranean absurdity up into daylight. But first she would milk her valid rage for the drops of acid in it, the drops with which it had become her job to dissolve Zeke's teasing, so that she could have her part in the cruelty, so that they could pretend they were hurting each other and were equal in this.

Of course she was *glad* for the company, which made it all a bit awkward. It was rather fun having a companion, another presence to leaven the melancholy of cold gray days. On the hardwood of the living room, below lights dimmed to embers, Hara and Lyric moved through their vinyasa poses. The day at that morning hour was often no more than a charcoal disclosure, the islands rough-hewn ribbons in the fog. On mild afternoons they kayaked out to the smaller islands or explored the rock and shell coves into which the ocean ran. From the beaches they took smooth stones, worn colored glass, and the green and ashen domes of sea urchins, laying them on shelves and window transoms. Lyric did the shopping, for which Hara gave her money. When Lyric returned one day with a jigsaw puzzle, they set it up on a painted table looking out to sea. Then in the evening they would spend an hour or two coaxing forest from piecemeal green, a frame for the puzzle's meadow, so that finally the wolves had something to run across.

Lyric made Hara feel girlish. It had surprised her how much she liked the girl. Hara even felt at times that she were the younger of the two, for while it was true what Lyric had said of herself— that she didn't *know* anything—the faultless quality of her spirit made Hara feel petty and irascible and about nine years old. And of course what you assumed people traded for such uncomplicated happiness were lives of a certain ambition and regard, but it was Hara, wasn't it, who was forty-two, childless, performing a job she liked about as much as washing semen from underwear, and getting divorced?

Maybe she had made an error long ago. Maybe she had profoundly mistaken the terms of the exchange she was making. It wasn't envy Lyric brought out in her, no. It was more that Hara had stumbled on a kind of *play*, as if they were sisters left alone by their parents for the first time to explore the different ways a day could be deconstructed. She had never had that with Daeva, of course. The one time she recalled being left under her sister's capricious administration Daeva had spent the entire weekend shouting at her. Well, God bless her, Daeva now lived half a world away. They hadn't spoken in nearly a year, not since Daeva had called—*typical*—to enlist Hara's help in shipping a metal sculpture to India.

"It's very heavy *and* very fragile," Daeva had said, as though it took a superior mind to envision such a thing.

"Imagine this," said Hara. "I'm very busy *and* I don't give a fuck."

Daeva had called her a cunt and suggested that she wasn't even a very grateful cunt. Grateful for *what*? Hara wanted to know. For having a sister who had made her tough, presumably, who made her give off the impression. She didn't ask.

Theirs had never been a family for emotional pleasantries. "Think of it this way, Hara, darling," her father had said years ago, at the family home in Haryana after they returned from the States for her final year before college. "If you let on too readily how you feel, people will have that over you. They'll know how to make you feel this way or that." Well, Hara didn't agree—not once she got old enough to have her own opinions and hate her father's, she didn't. A lousy servant-class idea, she thought, dressing up powerlessness as strength. But parents' notions got in deeper than you realized and resurfaced when you least expected, least expected to learn you were *like* them, so that you could feel your bleeding heart spilling across the linen tablecloth at dinner only to hear your husband say how *fucking sick* he was of this dignified and embittered reserve. Couldn't you just lose it? Not this stylized sniping anger, but truly undress yourself before him? But if you lived inside me, Hara had wanted to say, you would see I lose it all the time. You make me lose it. You excel at *nothing* so much as making me feel small. And although she hadn't said it then, she had remarked to herself how strange were the invitations of dignity and restraint, how when you pretended something didn't hurt it only encouraged people to push the blade in deeper.

But so with Lyric: a plausible paradise. The day disassembled into simple tasks, an intimacy that demanded nothing. Hara even felt foolish about how she had acted on first arriving. Well, it had been startling—a shock—to find someone in the house. She had come to get away, after all. Two weeks of peace, of distance from the divorce, the endless briefs to compile at work, her martinet trainer and the sympathy dinners, the endless *dinners*, and that new awful flat she was renting in Rose Hill. All up the coast she had felt a current of freedom flowing in from the night, a sweet tidal loneliness indistinct from the ocean brine that hung in the air around her as heavy as cloth.

But if she had gotten away, made her escape, why then were the lights on in the cottage? Whence this brash, happy music stirring up the millpond of her pacific gloom? Through the window Hara saw a mostly naked stranger perched on a ribbon of tightrope strung between interior posts.

"Excuse me," she said, trundling her luggage in behind her. "Hi, hello. Who are you?"

The girl dropped lightly to the floor and turned down—well, apparently the soundtrack to some poor toy factory's demolition.

"Sorry?"

"No, nothing," Hara said. "Just, oh, out of curiosity, what on earth are you doing in my house?"

The girl smiled—as if this were *funny*, as if she were often surprised, in no more than panties, in the midst of some aerial trespass.

"So . . . my parents have this place for the week."

"Have this place . . ." Hara tested the phrase. "Hmm, see the thing is I *own* this place, and I'm not in the habit of letting it to the parents of circus performers." The brightness in the girl's eyes made Hara sleepy. "Don't tell me they know Zeke."

"Zeke . . ." The girl shook her head. "Something about a charity auction?"

Hara found she was staring at the girl's nipples, tiny shallow cones nearly the color of her skin. She had tattoos running across her body too, garish colorful things that were actually rather pretty. She might have been sixteen or twenty-five. Hara hadn't the slightest idea how old young people were.

"I'd love it if you put a shirt on," she said.

In the study, waiting for Zeke to pick up, she looked out at the ocean. In the dark it was no more than a suggestive absence, an un-broken pane of black beginning where the dock frame showed in a glimmer of light from the house. Of course Zeke would find a way to spoil even this for her.

"Zeke, how *are* you," she said when she heard his voice. "So, funny thing—you'll like this—there's a girl in my house."

She heard shuffling, a word spoken to someone, then Zeke came back on. "Who *is* this?"

"Zeke."

"There's a girl . . . in your house. Well, these things happen, don't they. Did you invite her, by chance?"

"As a matter of fact, no. You've hit on just the crux of the thing."

"Ah, I see. You mean there's a girl in the cottage, *our* cottage, the one we both own. Well, look, it was whoever won the auction. I didn't know it would be a girl."

"Oh fuck you, that's not the point. You know that's not the point."

"It was for a good cause, if that helps. Children with rabies or something."

"You are such an exceptional asshole, do you know?"

"Just think, think of all the little kiddies who won't be running around, foaming at their tiny mouths . . ."

Hara closed her eyes. She wanted to laugh; she wanted to pound Zeke's face until she heard bone crack. It was simply maddening how since going ahead with the divorce they had been getting on so well, the way they had at first, years before. They went to coffee and sometimes even an early dinner after meeting with the lawyers, like perennial rivals putting a hard-fought match behind them. And that's what it was, a game, a farce. Everything with Zeke turned into a sort of game. Hara didn't even *want* his shit, very little of it anyhow. But she wanted the cottage, there was that.

"I can see everyone thinks this is a riot," she said, "but I'd re-mind you I'm a licensed attorney. I have no problem evicting Joan Baez."

"Joan Baez? Hara, you lost me. But look, there's paperwork, I'll have Cliff send it up tomorrow. And in the meantime you have a new friend, who sounds fun."

But by the time the papers arrived the next day (lupus, of all things, Hara knew Zeke did not give two *shits* about lupus) she had decided that maybe she liked the sylphlike girl with her ridiculous name. Maybe she liked having someone around. She always ended up glad for company, even when she felt herself most eager to be alone. And Lyric had a serenity about her that was, well, lovely. An irrational part of Hara entertained the notion that Zeke might have done this *for* and *to* her. It didn't really matter. She kept from probing the arrangement. Happiness was fragile. You named a happiness to doom it. So she bit her tongue, glancing only obliquely to confirm it was there, still there, and still the next day and the next . . . and so on and perhaps forever if not for Robert.

•

The day Lyric returned from town with the news she'd met someone, Hara had been busy watching leaves knock about and fall off the trees.

"It was so funny," Lyric said. "I asked this guy at the market where I could find something and he didn't hear me. So I said, 'Hey, hello, can you understand me?' and he turned around real casually and just goes, 'Probably not.'" She followed Hara's gaze up into the trees. "Isn't that funny?"

"Funny," Hara said experimentally.

"Oh, and I invited him to dinner. I hope that's all right."

What was Hara going to say? *No?* She leaned back in her chair and watched Lyric carry the groceries into the house. "Crazy girl," she murmured, feeling just a pang of envy for the girl's perfect ease, her way of making herself at home wherever she was.

What granted a person that capacity? Yes, Lyric's childhood had been a bohemian mess of, well, *money*, it seemed, and a kind of inspired heedlessness to round things out. To hear her describe the years she and her siblings had spent under the care of their erratic mother you might think most children moved between communes and expatriate villas, rubbing shoulders with artists and the occasional criminal element, that a certain brand of chic international vagrancy were available to anyone. Hara could all but feel what Lyric left out, the rain-soaked nothing afternoons, the endless downtime of childhood, homework, the necessity of eating, and so on, and still, told in this manner, as outlandish trivia decontextualized for the sake of wonder, the girl's life seemed otherworldly, as though for her very ingenuousness the treasures of strange accident she blithely enumerated could only flash in the light of your own astonishment.

What a funny thing talking to this girl! Hara worked a puzzle piece into the border and a tree, given a trunk, came to life. She had her stories too, of course. Maybe less incredible than Lyric's, but she could tell them how she liked. In the kayaks paddling out to the islands Hara told Lyric how when she and Zeke camped there, summers, they played a game called "sex tag," stripping to boots and chasing each other across the rocky forested terrain. She felt aroused just recalling it, the peculiar sexiness of nudity above boots; Zeke's cock flopping about as he ran, like a bodily afterthought; how, caught, she might feel the soft, rough birch bark against her cheek, holding a tree to steady herself, or how she might squat over Zeke in the moss and feel the floral life in the air on every inch of her. And then naked and lit in the alpenglow of fucking, as they waved to passing sailboats from the rock beach, how sure Hara had been that of the lives of women and men hers was among the free.

But anything could be a prison, it turned out, perhaps most of all the notion that you were free. And once you started to believe in the *idea* of your life, well, the filaments of a cage had already begun to lattice themselves about you, hadn't they?

"But what do you believe?" she asked Lyric.

"Hmm? What do I believe about what?"

Their kayaks were close and Lyric dipped her oar gently in the water as the brightening day carried skeins of mist up from the ocean.

"Do you see your life as a project?"

Lyric laughed. "God, wouldn't I be in trouble if I did?"

"But what then?" Hara persisted. "Atomic chaos?"

The girl shrugged. "I don't know. This, for now?" She gestured with her paddle. The water was vitreous before them in the stillness, as though setting back into a pale solid—nacre, white opal, shell.

At the island they pulled their kayaks onto the pebble beach.

"But you're rather a free spirit, aren't you?" Hara said.

"Why am I the weird thing?" Lyric said. "What are other people? *Un*free?"

"Yes. As a matter of course." The haze was clearing. The silver sleeve of ocean ran from the fringes of brindled rock to the distant line where it vanished.

"Then I think everyone should be a free spirit," Lyric said.

Hara laughed. "That does sound nice. When you're older, though, it seems more like a question of having or not having insurance."

"You're not so old."

"Oh, wow. Thanks."

And Hara was about to say yes, but not all moments were like this, not seizures of the day's latent glory but the dull, poor labor we did to permit moments of grace, though maybe that was a tired point, wasn't it, and arguing with Lyric was to pretend she had access to some higher knowledge, which of course she didn't. But Lyric was undressing, Hara saw, her jacket and sweatshirt, her pants, her undershirt, her bra. She slipped off her underwear and stepped back into her boots, and there she was—not an object of desire so much as a torrential immediacy, shallow nipples, pale skin, fawn ravel at her crotch. The wind caught her hair and blew it as thin as silken wheat. She gave Hara a smirk, her flamelike body reveled in tattoos flickering in the wind, and she was off into the woods.

•

It was that night Robert came to dinner. He arrived, rudely, on time, just a few minutes after seven and before Hara even had a chance to finish her first drink. He had his dog, Banjo, with him and a bag of clams.

"Thank you," Hara said. "Am I supposed to know what to do with these?"

He gave her a look she had encountered before in the town. The look, perhaps, of boys dead set on being men. He hung up his coat, took the clams from her, and put them in the sink to wash. Lyric had flitted off somewhere of course—Hara could have *strangled* her—and now Banjo, after sniffing around the edge for a minute, was attempting to choke down the tasseling on the living room rug.

"I hate to be a bother, Robert, but I'm sort of fond of that very expensive rug your dog is mauling."

"Banjo." Robert spoke sharply to the dog. He finished rinsing the clams and shook the water from his hands, drying them on a dishcloth Hara gave him. "You've got a nice house."

"Do you like it? I like it too."

"I've been here before," he said. "Not inside. I helped Gerry clear the yard this past spring."

"Ah, you know Gerry."

He nodded. "Lot of downed branches after the storms. We cleared the field and the beech grove you got."

"Yes, Gerry said. You did a bang-up job. It looked lovely when I got up this summer."

Hara saw Robert glance past her and felt Lyric there in his look.

"So you work with Gerry? Look after houses?" she said.

"Some. Work where I can. Preston's in the off season"—he pointed his chin at Lyric—"where I met this one. Clam, lobster. Odd repair job . . . Steamer?"

"Oh, someplace." Hara opened the nearest cabinet and closed it. "My husband was the chef, see. Or when it suited him."

Robert looked at his palm. "The director."

"Producer," Hara said, "which can only be worse." She held up a flopping armature she imagined to be a steamer. What pretentious nonsense cooking had become! "So you're quite a jack of trades then?"

Lyric tongued an olive from its pit in her mouth. "Robert's in a band," she said.

"Ah, right. So day jobs to support the artistic habit."

"Don't know about that," he said.

"Well, I think it's perfect," Hara said. "Lyric here wanders the earth like—like—some sublime *nomad* and stumbles on, oh, I don't know, a Yankee handyman or some such. 'The Townie Dreamer and the Vagrant Muse.'" She cleared a space in the air for the title. "It's like a fable."

Lyric didn't look up from the joint she was rolling. She licked and sealed the paper and tapped it on the table. She lit up. Hara finished the vodka nestled among the ice shards in her glass.

"Don't mind me," she said. "I'm going through a divorce that has turned me into an absolute monster."

"One thing for that," said Lyric. She handed Hara the joint and Hara dragged on it twice before passing it to Robert, thinking how tiresome the courtships of young people were.

At dinner they were good and stoned. They left the dishes when they were finished and took a bottle of whiskey down to the shore. Hara and Zeke had done this when they had guests up, gathering driftwood for a bonfire and sitting up late into the night drinking and smoking. The groups were always the same, people Zeke knew from the industry and a few old friends, putative adults who because they ate mushrooms once in a while and bore the tattoos of some lapsed rebellion thought they deserved medals of non-conformity or abiding hipness. Well, Hara got it. It was a pleasing notion to entertain and simple enough to encourage when you were drunk and high, tuned in, or so it seemed, to the deeper channel of communication that bound your life to the mantling commerce of heaven and earth. Possible, for instance, to see the sparks the drift-wood sent up answering a call, passing up, up, and out of sight to cool and settle as the irony points high above. Possible, if you cared to, to see yourself outlined in their grid. Really though, no one was passing out medals in the end. People knew this, didn't they?

"So who gets the house?" Robert said.

Hara laughed. "Robert," she said, a hand to her chest. "My!" Not that she of all people minded a little bluntness. "Oh, who knows. I hope I do. My husband's such a shit." She took a sip from the bottle and passed it along. "I feel like some shrill hausfrau complaining, but you know the *distance* you travel—I mean, mentally—it just kind of shocks you. You spend so long assuming it will all just fall into place, successful doting husband, kids, the whole *tableau*." She gazed out at the sea, the furnace of the sky taupe and livid with moon. "And when it doesn't just happen you start to compromise—a little here, a little there—and slowly, bit by bit, any sense you had of what was supposed to happen falls away, just slides off into the ocean, until there you are, alone, on the tiny island called your life."

They stared at the fire for a minute, then Robert knocked his head back toward the cottage. "Nice island."

Right, Hara was spoiled, dreadfully spoiled, not that it made a bit of difference.

"It's like the frog," Lyric said. "You know, put it in boiling water and it jumps out. But heat the water *ever so slowly* . . ."

"Yes, people are always saying that," Hara said. "But how do they *know*? Who has all these frogs and pots and no lids and, like, this pressing need to boil frogs alive?"

"I guess I've known some people," Robert said.

"Perhaps you have met my husband," Hara said.

Banjo barked to be petted and Hara saw Robert catch Lyric's eye. She should leave them, she knew, that was the decent thing to do. Only she didn't *want* to. She didn't want to go to bed and wake up and have it be tomorrow, and then the next day. She didn't want to go inside and be alone. If she ever had to be alone again she thought she might disembowel herself with a reciprocating saw. When had she become like this? Or, that was euphemistic, wasn't it? The question was when had she *become* this? It was very easy to blame Zeke or the divorce, but hers was a condition, was it not? This desperate need for people, all of whom she loathed. Even the ones she *liked* she loathed. And that was the maddening thing about people. Yes, she had her friends from college, a few, and her law school friends, four or five women spread around the country and globe, busy with their jobs and children, and yes, they could speak to one another like sentient creatures and every so often wash up together for an hour on the shores of lucidity. But only a lunatic would call that *companionship*. Or the fifty-minute phone sessions with her therapist, because Lord knew she was too busy to physically *go* there, and drinks with colleagues that ended at 6:45 after chattering on with the absentmindedness of watering a garden, waiting your turn to offer some idiotic little discourse on the numbing fiction of your public life. *Marc and I just started kitesurfing. Oh, you don't say. Yes, we picked it up in Mauritius over the holidays. How remarkable—I can't think of a single thing I give less of a fuck about!* And Zeke or the equivalent threading some conversational déjà vu with that rote inattentive teasing, his mind clearly elsewhere, until you managed to get upset enough to exact maybe twenty minutes' careful listening to expressions of *how things make you feel* and apologies roughly as nourishing as swine flu, and those twenty minutes, it turned out, for a surprisingly long time, were just enough to build back the hollowed little Jenga tower of your collapsing marriage.

No thank you, really. Hara would do without if it came to that. She was proud enough to prefer suffering to fooling herself, which was only a less dignified form of suffering in the end. The phone in the house, on some perverse cue, rose shrilly above the quiet, startling her. Zeke, no doubt. Well, she needed to excuse herself.

"All right, you've got me. What is it you want?"

There was a pause. "Is Boris, I call from Russia."

"Zeke."

"Boris," Zeke said. "Anyway, there you are. I left you a thousand messages."

"The thousandth must have done the trick." She picked up a framed picture from the desk. She and Zeke at a wedding on Skiathos. They looked, well—formidable.

"You're not back in New York."

"Oh my God, what a master sleuth you've become!"

"Hara."

"Are you having me followed? Is there a man with binoculars in the hedges?"

"I wanted to see how you were, make sure you weren't hacked to bits by your houseguest or whatever." Hara was silent. "Okay, it was stupid prank, I know. You don't have to say it. But she's gone now anyway."

"Actually, no."

"Really."

Oh, how she *hated* that crystallizing attention in Zeke's voice, the typical distraction it laid bare.

"It's been more than a week," he said.

"Oh, has it been? Oops, silly me. I'll go kick Lyric out right now." She glanced at herself in the glass of a framed movie poster. It acted as a mirror in the dim light.

"Lyric?"

"You were right," she said. She felt she were speaking in a dream. "I made a new friend. She's fun."

"You sound odd, Hara."

"Well, I'm drunk. And stoned. And I'm hosting *two* young people tonight, if you must know, and I need to hang up in a minute so we can all go make love in front of the fire."

"Hara."

"Hmm? Or does that sound like you, Zeke? Now really, don't you have some cardboard Tanya to escort around Bel Air or what are we talking about?"

She felt her mood strobe gently within her, but with the act of speaking, stringing these words together and feeling them hum in her chest, she found herself brought into momentary focus. How strange it was to be talking just like this, the two of them, alive in each other's ears, invisible pinpoints in the black immensity of night. Zeke was here in the phone. But he was also out there somewhere, in some city, in some unknowable room. It was absurd. It was a cruel joke.

"I don't know when you're being serious anymore," he said.

"That's funny," Hara said, "because now I'm racking my brain for when you were *ever* serious."

"I'm worried about you. Should I be worried?"

"The thing is"—her voice had fallen, the spite deserting her that quickly—"you don't have to be worried about me anymore. More to the point, I'm not sure you *get* to be." How tired she was. "Don't call unless it's important, 'kay? I'm hanging up now."

She lay on the window seat and closed her eyes, careering for a minute on the tide of intoxication that bore her. She was further gone than she'd realized, good and stewed, but what use was that when no one would rise to her bait? Why were people so horribly decent only just after they had knifed you in the Theatre of Pompey? I come to praise Hara, not to marry her! And what had she been thinking, really, when Zeke *had* come to marry her? Well, it wasn't hard to remember, just hard now to account for the feeling of possibility that crept in to scatter her prudent doubts. She would blame it on the beauty of that wind-bitten day, the fragrant hills above Sorrento, the high clouds trailing out to sea. The sort of day that for its very clarity startled you into an unarmored sense of your own vital heart. She had known so clearly in that moment that life gave its fruit to the bold, the unhesitant. And beneath her apprehension, her judicious dread, her understanding that toughness was no more than the scarring on sites of a more vulnerable and immediate contact, beneath it all her heart beat its silly hollow yeses. It made her want to throw up, it did *now*, for if the reasonableness of her objections would be borne out—that Zeke was not a person who came to rest and perhaps neither was she—all she could think just then was that it was happening to her, the thing you wait for, telling yourself you aren't waiting, sure someday it will come, and sure just the same it won't, that you will be the one passed over while all the repellent millions walk hand in hand into the insipid lava of a setting sun. But she would be one of them, she saw. She felt the dull embrace of that contentment tumble about her like curtains from the wings. And as she adjusted to the weight of the ring on her finger over the next few days, she marveled that without this anchor, for so many years, she hadn't floated up, up, and out of sight, to that point far above where the things you could once see right in front of you disappear.

•

When Hara woke it was morning. Out the windows in the study a gray sky lingered at the treetops. She had a blanket around her she didn't recall getting.

Lyric was in the living room reading when she emerged. "Morning," the girl said, her voice as sweet and languorous as honey. "We thought we'd let you sleep."

"Oh. Is Robert—"

"No, but he says thanks."

Hara doubted that very much, but the room *was* neat, the trace remains of a fire in the fireplace.

"He seems nice," Hara said, lying on the sofa, watching as Lyric rose to fetch her water. "A little surly, maybe, the strong, silent type, but to each her own."

They worked diligently on the puzzle that week. The evidence of their progress, so slow in the moment, was undeniable in sum. The field had begun to form in emerald swatches floating within the forest. The wolves galloped at the center, shabby specters unmoored. What heart Hara once had taken in the irremediable mess began to desert her as order emerged.

"What if you stayed on?" she asked Lyric. "When I go back, I mean. You could look after the house. You'd be near Robert." Lyric had taken to visiting Robert in the evenings, asking whether Hara minded if she used the car—as though Hara might suddenly have made plans and neglected to tell her! "I'd see you when I came up," she said. "I'd pay you, of course."

Lyric demurred, rolling a papier-mâché pomegranate across the table so Hara had to catch it before it pattered lightly over the edge.

When Lyric left her, nights, Hara would retrieve a bottle of Zeke's expensive wine from the cellar and scatter the family photos she kept in shoeboxes on the living room rug. It was not clear to her if a clean line could be drawn from the hipshot young girl in a bathing suit on the beach in Goa to the self-pitying wretch she saw gazing back at her in the glass of the French doors. Rather a lot had intervened, and yet certain patterns and casts of mind endured. If Hara wanted Lyric to stay, and she did, there were complexities within the impulse that did not submit to easy or entirely comforting explanation. The presentiment of abandonment, for instance, an understanding that the girl *would* leave, that Hara had nothing to make her stay, and a dread of this prospect that so upstaged the matter's why as to eclipse it. As in, *why* was Hara so anxious that Lyric stay? In the way of one disinclined to look square at a thing, Hara nonetheless *sensed* the connection between her fury and her hurt, her feelings toward Lyric, toward Robert, and then of course toward Zeke; or, further still, saw the netting of connection cast out to embrace that girl on the beach in Goa, out alone at night, with her parents sleeping and Daeva holed up in their room calling some boy, that girl wandering the white bow of sand where diminutive waves fizzed through the night and the sounds from bars garlanded in lights were lush and ugly with the mysteries of adult happiness. And as she drifted in the furling breeze, even then she had tended the implausible hope that someone might know to come out and find her and lead her inside, not to a bar, not to any one room, but to the sanctum of shared reality where a mind took its form in another.

When Lyric had gone to Robert's, Hara removed pieces from the puzzle. Not so many the girl would notice, but a few here and there. On the nights Lyric stayed in, they might replace exactly these. Sometimes Hara would trace the composition of the girl's tattoos. She knew them by now, the sinewy thicket of green tangles on the girl's shoulder, bursting here and there in a red corolla, the ox-eyed nymph washing fruit in a brook; the brook that flowed beneath the flowers, ran out into a river and shimmering ocean, crossed Lyric's back and washed up below a fishing village, an outpost of sand and stilted huts. Above the village a city rose into the ocher sky, sunlight spilling onto the clouds, where a pair of naked angels embraced and an amazon warrior with one breast and a sword occupied a throne. Then on the girl's neck errant rays of sunshine fed a painted vasculature, turned from gold to red, merging back into the flowers and carrying crimson blood along green stems to the calyxes where the roses bloomed.

Sometimes it seemed to Hara that if she looked hard enough she might find herself there, a timeless fixture in the fretwork prophecy, and then she would know that this life was all a joke, subject to an extraneous order, and that her suffering and happiness, by implication, had meaning. Other times she thought, Enough of that. You could measure the line between craziness and isolation on a day's shed eyelashes. The flakes of an early snow fell softly on the ocean, dissolving into it, and Hara thought, Maybe I can live here and dissolve into the ocean myself.

"You feel like real life is going on somewhere else," she told Lyric. "You're young. You think if you keep looking you'll find the place you're meant to be."

"I *don't* think that," Lyric said. "I've been to Morocco."

Oh, sometimes Hara wished Lyric *would* leave. The girl's presence, having become the very augury of its absence, could seem at times the worse of the two. It wasn't only the pleasure you took in a person's company that made you covet it, Hara knew. Just as often it was the compulsion to ensnare something elusive, fleeting, the urge to establish a state of permanence, if not of happiness, and then too the fear of what solitude permitted, the flights and phantasms of inner life, of unuttered thought, and the terrifying possibility, absent the correlative of another person, that you were not at all the composite of your past, but merely the confused nerves of the present, ever-supplanting moment.

And it was this fear, this possibility, when you got down to it, that Lyric did without.

•

Hara begged off the night of Robert's party. She begged off, and she implored Lyric to stay in with her, a demand as reckless, it seemed, as a straight last-dollar bet on a roulette game, and she might have bared her soul, she thought, if she knew how to do that and where a person began. The party sounded ghastly, though. The idea of hearing Robert's band play made her expectantly ill. And she had less than zero desire, really, to rummage around for fellow feeling with locals, mutual curiosities, feeling old while Lyric made friends easily.

They drank in joyless fashion, sorting puzzle pieces, until Hara asked Lyric whether she hadn't given it more thought.

"Given what more thought?"

"The Church's views on women," Hara said. "What do you think? About staying on."

Was it possible Lyric was pouting? Hara wouldn't have believed it, but she had never seen this reticence in the girl, her lower lip thrust ostentatiously forward. It was hard to remember sometimes that the girl was just that, a child, subject to emotions all her own and yet emotions she could not have lived with long enough to understand in all their unoriginality and predictable rhythm, their mendacity, their worthless force.

"What about Robert?" Hara said, hating herself a little as she said it.

"Robert and I are *friends*," Lyric said. "I've told you that."

"Okay, God. Did you ever hear about the lady who protested too much? But let's go to the party if it's going to be like this."

"Don't you think it's strange," Lyric said, "you've had the house, what, six years and you don't know anyone who lives here?"

"I know Gerry. Now I know Robert," Hara said. "I know people who come here in the summer."

"That's not what I mean."

"I'm not an adorable sprite like you. I don't like people nearly so much. What do you want from me?"

"A minute ago you didn't want to go to the party because you said someone named Dwayne was going to sneeze type-two herpes in your cornea."

"I don't think I said that, and anyway," said Hara, "I can't be held responsible for every dreadful remark that escapes my mouth." She affixed a puzzle piece and sensed a bit of humor stealing back into the girl. "Look, I'll take the risk."

"It's late," Lyric said.

"Oh, it's barely ten. I'll bet we're just in time for some chip detritus or whatever they eat."

"They?"

"I'm *joking.* The Morlocks."

Perhaps Hara had misunderstood. Perhaps Lyric merely wanted to bring her two worlds together. Perhaps she wanted to help Hara make friends. She seemed to have enough of them, Lyric did. And the girl was right, the party *was* outside, although why Hara had disbelieved her she couldn't quite say. It was next to the site of a new house going up. There was a fire at least, a faint hint of rippling heat coming from the crowd dancing at the foot of a platform on which a few underdressed young men were trying to damage some instruments. Hara shivered and pulled her jacket around her.

"I told you," Lyric said.

"All right, you don't have to gloat." Hara took a shot of bourbon, then filled her plastic cup. "What? Oh Lord." She drifted away from Lyric, toward the fire, catching in its sweet odor a second scent, bodily and intimate. A man pressed a small pipe to his lips.

"Excuse me," Hara said with her most obliging look. "Hi, would it be a terrible bother . . ."

"Be my guest," the man said through a held breath.

He was a few years older than her, she guessed, his face leathered and ruddy. She took the pipe from him and sucked the flame over the embers while he gazed off at the stage.

"Shit that passes for music these days," he said.

"They said the same thing about Schoenberg, though, didn't they?" said Hara.

What on earth was she talking about? How old did this man think she *was*? She was, come to think of it, exactly the age Zeke had been when they married. She tried to hold the thought still, to explore it for the deeper meaning it seemed to promise, but her attention was turning molten. The lights around her, blazing at points along their catenaries, edged into a sharper dazzle.

"Don't believe I know you," the man said.

"No, it's unlikely," Hara agreed. His hand in her smaller, softer hand felt like clay, the hand of a golem. "Where, um— Do we pee in the bushes then?"

He laughed. "Probably your best bet. There's a porta-potty down the road. Plumbing won't go in for another month or two."

"Oh, is it your house?" Of course it wasn't.

"No, no. House like this? Summer folk, you know. All the new construction, really."

It was Hara's turn to laugh. "An invasion then! How terrible! No doubt you just want to be left in peace to pursue your venerable folkways."

He looked at her, his mouth seeming to flicker between uncertainty and something else, but he left whatever it was unsaid.

Of course. She was hated. They all were, seasonal invaders, self-important snobs from their effete enclaves, bringing the entire *economy* with them but full of prissy needs and ideas, their impossible diets, their fussy attachments to foreign wine and East Asian calisthenics. So peculiar and helpless, weren't they, babes in the woods when it came to anything practical, but not above affecting a chummy tone and shedding grammar to mingle with the brutes who cleared their lawns and fixed their toilets. Well, Hara would love to see them try the contract law on a corporate merger. Ha! Or— She tripped on a root and righted herself, just.

"Easy," Lyric said. "You okay?"

"I am, thank you," said Hara. "And I don't need to be babysat." The girl was silent.

And how Hara *loathed* her just then, loathed all of it—her simplicity and openness, the opacity of her openness, the light, flitting quality of her affection, her quiet restraint.

"You think it's so easy," she said, "traipsing about without a plan or care in the world, with no job or money. But not to worry! Just throw yourself on the mercy of fate! How magical life is—fa la la!"

Lyric toed a twig. "I never said it was easy."

"No. But you don't buy the groceries, do you? Or the gas for the car that takes you to and from what's-his-name's house? Or the heat that keeps us from freezing? Or the electricity, et cetera, et cetera."

"So?" Lyric said. She said it as an actual question and so simply that Hara lost her point. What was her point? Something stupid, clearly.

"Right. *So.* So what? So *what?* Let's just wear flannel and mosh to Nirvana and say 'So what?' when life gets, like, totally annoying."

Lyric laughed. "What are you talking about?"

"I don't know," Hara said. "I don't know, and now I have to pee. So excuse me."

She pushed past Lyric down a path in the woods. When she had finished, she followed the path the rest of the way to the water, to the shoreline strip of dark rocks where a downed tree shone a ghostly color in the moonlight. She sat and lit a cigarette.

"You missed us play."

Hara started but didn't turn.

"Alas, alas," she said. The feel of his presence behind her set a tingle at the base of her neck. When he didn't respond she said, "I heard a different band play. If you sounded anything like them, never might be too soon."

He snorted. She looked up to see him shaking his head, lighting his own cigarette, face yellowed in the flame.

"Strange thing, you and Lyric," he said.

"Yes. Well. My husband's a twat." She could just make out the islands in the distance. She should have built the house there, hidden in the woods, with embrasures to fire arrows through. "It worked out well enough though."

He nodded in a ruminative way. "Maybe, maybe."

"Or, strange that I let her stay, do you mean? Strange that we got on so well?"

His laugh rang false in Hara's ear. "Do you know anything about her?"

She stood and stretched. She hugged herself. "Oh, enlighten me, Robert. What is it you're just dying to tell me."

"Jesus," he said. It thrilled Hara to hear even the faint note of exasperation in his voice. "The way you treat people—"

"People, Robert, let themselves be treated this way or that. Or did they not teach you that in clam school?" A warmth was passing through her, a taste as charged as blood. He looked her in the eye and she wanted to laugh. "Are we fighting, Robert? Over Lyric or what exactly?" Her expression was all concerned incomprehension and nothing else.

He dragged on his cigarette until he had the tempo back. "Her parents didn't win any charity auction, you know."

Her lip twitched. "Well, somebody did."

"Yeah, I guess she overheard—"

"Are you her savior, I don't understand? Do you imagine you're protecting her from me, her knight in armor, that little trip?"

They were standing rather close.

"You never owe anyone anything, huh?"

"*Owe?* I think you have economics there backwards, Robert."

"People like you . . ." He flicked his cigarette away.

"Yes, people like me. Go on."

"You—" Oh, he did seem childish, didn't he, struggling to find his words? "People aren't there for your amusement."

Hara laughed and clapped her hands. "Oh, very good, Robert. *Thank you*. Thanks for letting me *know*. Is it quite disorienting to get a woman of my age and not a mother's selfless charity in the bargain? Not that you'll ever know, but that is what the world seems to expect." She had closed the remaining ground between them, a glorious ringing pressure in her head. "But, ah, is it that you feel *you're* owed something? For your honesty, perhaps? Your masculinity? Your stern good looks? Does the world owe you something because you're awfully handsome?" She felt the destructive element swim into the night, as beautiful and wild as the surf below. "Or for the clams, how could I forget? And clearing the yard, and stacking fruit in the market, there's that . . ." She thought he was looking at her like a windup toy whose program had simply to be endured. She forced her voice to a hush and straightened a lock of hair on his forehead. "Does it take an awful lot of restraint? And now you have to listen to some spoiled bitch. Because that's what I am, isn't it? Some spoiled bitch tossing about handfuls of glitter, expecting everyone to be grateful. But you have to clean it up, don't you? That's your job. Sweeping up all the glitter spoiled bitches leave around." She looked at him with sympathy. She felt herself partway enwrapped in her own words, the tightening ligature of silk, but she was tempted to laugh at herself in the same instant, her ridiculousness, the ongoing and self-regarding performance of her desperation. It was his look that stopped her. Her hand had found its way to his cheek. And now she saw uncertainty there on his face, the utter absence of the irony that opened channels in one's own seriousness, and this absence seemed to her, in précis, the very gross vulnerability of youth. Children, always thrilling to an adult business with no ability to follow through. Flinching at the moment of consequence because they had gotten only as far as its pantomime. It was uncertainty, hesitance, that was ugly. And youth thought beauty was a matter of looks! She shivered and turned in to him against the cold. "Oh, Robert," she said consolingly, and it might have been no more than instinct that made him hold her, instinct, habit, or the confusion of seeing tenderness offer to replace contempt, attention lavished in hatred suddenly as a permutation of ardor. "Brr," she murmured, no longer cold but simply intent on the tide of uncertainty in him, on not letting it settle, the warring impulses that cleft men, so eager to possess, to protect, and to get away. Her cheek brushed his. When she turned her eyes to him, open wide and faintly imploring, she might have set a clock, she thought, by how long it took their lips to touch.

In the fantasy she would play out for herself Lyric found them like this. Or better still, found Robert fucking her with her dress hiked up on the log. And Lyric watched, dismayed, entranced, relieved in some way perhaps, or just submissive to the actuality before her, the new order spread as creaselessly as linens on the sovereign bed. She would go down on Robert, yes, with Zeke watching—that was good—and her father, their precious *flower*, defiling herself and for nothing, for no more than the monstrousness of their own vanity, the wild-burning ego that had to vindicate itself in the ashes of all it laid to waste. She, the daughter of a goddamn Indian ambassador, wed so regally and for all to see, front and center in the *Times* notices, like a fucking princess! Look, Daddy! Look, Zeke! *Look* . . . But even as she entertained the wish, she felt the gap between the fantasy and reality like a plummet in the mist, a fall awaiting her, a dizziness, a despair. She would come back to herself, she and the dream would fall apart. And there she would simply be, bereft of even shame and anger, bereft with only her life before her, all the things that made it up, her job and few friends, the rental, the cottage, the knowledge that it would all be there waiting for her tomorrow and the next day, and through all the days ahead. Days demanding to be filled, because even if you got rid of the *stuff* there would still be days. Time had to be filled, one way or another. And what an obligation it was! There had once been places for people like her, hadn't there been, walled off in the countryside or mountains, where you were spoken to in a soft voice and spent your days beneath arbors, wandering garden paths, stilled in the lovely sedation of pills from tiny plastic cups? Yes, that sounded right. And Daeva would come visit once a year, citing concern but really there to gloat, to delight in her sister's ruination. "If only you'd been less sure you were special," she would say. "Less certain that the world *cared*. But you were always very self-involved, weren't you?" And Hara would smile and nod agreeably, lost to the wondrous indifference—that's how it would feel—the delicious peace of no longer having a life to fight for, an identity to pretend was hers.

•

Hara did not remember getting home. She remembered very little, in fact, when she heard Lyric speak and felt the project of locating herself in space and time crash in on her with such violence it seemed she might never pull clear.

"Hey, are you all right?"

She was in the living room, her own living room, that seemed true. Yes, on the sofa; she could feel it now as more than a cloud holding her aloft. Was it daytime? It was. Lyric sat facing her, a magazine open on her thigh.

"I think . . . I'm alive," Hara said. "You look like a friend of mine, but of course the devil takes many forms." She tried to catch Lyric's eye. "Joking."

"I'm leaving soon."

"To town, or . . ." Lyric was silent. In the stillness Hara saw something flash at the periphery of her consciousness, something awful. She squinted. She couldn't quite make it out, darting and flitting among the trees. Another flash. It nearly gave itself up, dodged away, dashed this way and that, almost at hand.

Then she saw it.

"Ah," she said. She hoisted herself up—it took some effort—and went to the kitchen to make coffee.

"Where will you go?" she said. "Do you know?"

The girl shrugged.

Hara shook her head. "Just friends," she said under her breath, too softly, she thought, for Lyric to hear.

But the girl said yes and laughed once. *"Just."*

It was Robert's car Lyric piled her stuff into. Well, that figured. Hara couldn't see into the driver's seat and she didn't go out. She stood in the doorway with her coffee and watched Lyric carry out her bags.

"Well," Lyric said when she was done. "Bye."

"Bye," Hara said, feeling that crippling dignity hold her in the doorframe and seal her lips.

But the things she could have done, the things she could have said!

She watched the car drive away and listened until the sound of the tires faded on the drive. Then she took her coffee to an armchair. She didn't move until the sun began to dip in the sky.

By evening she felt better. She got up and wandered around the house. How big it was! How quiet. Had it always been so big or was it bigger in the silence? The lights were off and shadows lengthened across the room. The early evening had turned a golden color outside; the light seemed to burn as it fell, catching on the lawn, scattering on the ocean. There was the puzzle. Her hand had fallen on it without her realizing. God, she had been truly crazy to think Lyric wouldn't leave until it was done. She touched it tenderly for a moment, the stiff-edged cardboard, the soft joints where the pieces met. Then on an impulse she swept it to the floor. The sun pulsed. Good riddance, she thought. The sun pushed into the clouds, *good riddance*, pushed through the clouds, and she saw them, the wolves. Out in the meadow the pack was running. The sun caught their backs as they tore across the grass. They reminded her just then of the golden jackals she had heard calling from the grassland in her youth. On the darkening porch she heard the jackals calling and her mother calling—"Haaaaaaara"—summoning her to another of their prim, stately dinners. She strained for a moment to hear the jackals. She wanted to join them, as if such a thing were possible! They were deniable, she supposed, the wolves. But then who was to say? Who was there to contradict her now? The trees around the yard were so much fiber and pith. Milkweed and primrose flowered here in spring. The moon was rock, Hara thought. The ocean so many particles of water. And people—what did they say?—minerals and proteins, was it? Minerals and proteins who ate to persist. Who slept to persist. Who fucked to persist. At some point the stories had to stop. At some point the wolves died, the people died. The alarm clock went off. The particles did what they did and at times, out of chaos, suggested order. And at times, out of chaos, dashed order. And at times, who knew? The facts were stubborn. They were also stories. Quite a lot, in other words, was left to interpretation. But moments continued to come, this one on the last one's heels. And a new one. And a new one. And a new one.

Dynamics in the Storm

The storm was coming. The storm was coming. For days that's all we heard. How big it would be. How the colliding systems might encounter each other. How long power could be out. Towers would come down and houses too. Lives would be lost (about that we heard less). About how to protect ourselves we heard a *lot*. Residents stockpiled candles, batteries, and canned food, cleaning out stores. Critical patients were flown to hospitals inland. Those who could, left. Most stayed. They had nowhere to go. And could they leave every time, could they make it a habit? Train and bus stations were mob scenes. Flights were canceled en masse. Grounded fliers camped out in airports, amateur survivalists. We saw them on TV. Going nowhere in an airport was now news. I was still brash and foolish enough to wait for the day of the storm to drive south. I had a car, the storm wasn't due until evening, and I had no interest in cutting my visit short. It wasn't often I saw my old friend Mark and his wife, who had once almost been my wife long ago.

So, brash and foolish, yes, but not quite young. Nor was I well-off. I was okay, I was doing okay. I taught filmmaking and video art at the college in the small southern city where I lived. I had two kids, three and five, and a wife I loved who no longer loved me. I drove an old Nissan Pathfinder that was, like the rest of us, doing okay. It had four-wheel drive and I thought it could handle the trip even if things got wet. That was how, Monday morning, I found myself walking the thirty or so blocks north from Mark and Celeste's to the cheap lot near Penn Station where I'd left the car. The sky that morning was clear and pretty, a violent, indecisive wind the only sign of the storm to come.

It was on my way to the lot that I saw Susan. The streets were a mess but I picked her out at once, and then, because it was so improbable to see her, I convinced myself it *wasn't* her, couldn't be, watched for another minute wondering whether she hadn't said something about a conference, ducking and pushing through the crowd to catch her face (she was in front of me), only to realize, unbelievable as it was, that it *was* her, and I called out, half in jest, I suppose, "Dr. Duranti," and when she didn't respond to that and yelling "Dr. Duranti" sounded ridiculous, I called out "Susan," which she responded to at once, turning and seeing me, and then we had to acknowledge each other's existence as people outside the rarefied context in which we habitually encountered each other.

"Ben," she said, a bit the way you say hello to an ex you've run into on a date. At times she seemed tense around me, I thought, as though worried I might bind her to my distress, but Susan was a therapist and you would have been forgiven for thinking she was prepared for this.

"Of all the places," I said.

"Yeah, this is funny," she said, like it was maybe the least funny thing ever.

"You told me you were out of town, I forgot. What was it?"

"Conference," she said. "APA, or last week. I saw my sister over the weekend." People streamed by us, an island with our luggage in the middle of the sidewalk. "Actually, I was supposed to head back yesterday. My flight got canceled."

It came back to me then, a conversation the week before, the schedule juggling. I was teaching three classes and trying to keep a few of my own projects afloat. I was preoccupied. Maybe I preoccupied myself to keep from being alone with my thoughts. Susan's eyes were red, I saw. Her hair unwashed. She looked like she hadn't slept.

"So what's the plan?"

"I don't know, I don't think I can get anything," she said. She took a deep breath. "I've been bouncing between Penn Station and Port Authority all morning. It's a nightmare. People are paying five hundred dollars for bus tickets. Five hundred dollars! I can't even withdraw more cash from the ATM. I'm just really—"

She stopped herself. I was so used to telling her things while she listened quietly that this speech surprised me. I couldn't remember the last time I'd heard her string as many sentences together.

"Well," I said, knowing it would make her uncomfortable, but still myself, a person who doesn't believe in rules or in standing on ceremony, life's too strange, "I'm just on my way to the car. I'm driving back now."

We had moved onto Thirty-Fourth Street to stand aside the flow of pedestrians. Susan's bag kept slipping from her shoulder. She looked small next to the rolling suitcase in her hand.

"I don't know, Ben. It's what, an eleven-hour drive? Do you think that's such a good idea?"

"These are pretty exceptional circumstances," I said. "I think we need to triage the bad ideas."

I wouldn't go so far as say I was *invested* in her coming with me, but I thought it would be silly of her not to. And I liked her, I liked her company. I thought it would be fun.

"It's the kids, though," she said. "They're at Karen's, and I told her I'd be back last night. I told *them* I'd be back. They were upset on the phone . . ." She wasn't saying it to me. "It's all such a disaster."

"Literally," I said. "Look, this is stupid. I'm driving back right now. We can listen to music the whole way if you like."

"Okay," she said. "Okay." She smiled, but her smile seemed mostly to convey that she was too tired to say no.

We got the car. We braved Hell's Kitchen and the Lincoln Tunnel, which was clogged many blocks back. At last we dipped beneath the river, lurching forward and stopping, watching the tail-lights of cars paint crimson streams on the white tile. For a time it seemed that the rest of our lives would take place in that tunnel, but finally we emerged. It took maybe two hours to reach 95, and 95 was a mess too. By then the clouds had begun gathering. A breath of luminosity lit them, but you could tell the thickening would continue, that the sky would turn brown-gray, then gray and darker, that the rain would come. And still it felt okay in the Pathfinder, which was warm and dry, it felt okay to be driving into the storm.

We were in stop-and-go traffic among the oil refineries of northern New Jersey when I said, "You mentioned that the kids were unhappy on the phone last night?"

"Yes, well, they're young—what do you expect? They've been at a friend's place for five days."

"I'm just asking."

"Sorry," she said. She seemed to mean it. She had two kids, a boy and a girl. Alice, the younger, didn't talk much, which worried her. Like certain other people I know, I thought, realizing how easy it had been at points to take Susan's inscrutable silence as tacit approval of me, of my life and my decisions, and how in many ways this assumption was the basis of our relationship.

"Is your husband worried?" I said.

She looked at me. I thought she almost rolled her eyes. "You'd have to ask him."

In the river of cars ahead an ignition of brake lights rolled back to us like a wave. I told her it wasn't really fair, how I told her such intimate things and she conceded so little. I hardly knew what was fair game to ask.

Our eyes met and she gave that look I knew so well, which said that just because I had stopped talking didn't mean she was obliged to speak.

"What's fair game?" I said.

"Ask," she said, a hitch of exasperation in her voice. "I can tell you if I don't feel like discussing something."

"Okay, your childhood then. Tell me about your childhood."

She laughed. "Now you're just fucking with me." It was playful the way she said it, playful and warm, and with this lightness the drive seemed to open out before us as faceted and lovely as a long descent into a twinkling valley. Was Susan pretty? Sort of. Not extravagantly, not at first. But she grew on you. Maybe anyone who listens to you attentively for seven years will.

"Start at the beginning," I said. She played along. "This is where I come from," she said and spread her hands to include the scene before us.

"You were born in an oil refinery. Continue."

"Don't be *crude*," she said, and when I didn't respond she said, "Oh, that was bad, wasn't it?"

"Pretty bad," I said. But it made me happy—the silliness, the lapse.

"No, a little farther down the turnpike and to the west. One of those nice suburbs without any 'urb' to really do the whole sub-dom thing with."

"That was a little better."

"I guess I've said that before."

I switched lanes and the lane I'd abandoned, of course, pulled forward. "Shit," I said.

"Do you really want me to do this?" she asked.

I said I did. She was my age or thereabouts. It had been a long time since I'd really investigated my choice in her, but her being my age and a woman surely mattered. I didn't need someone who would explain me to myself. I wasn't in the market for psychological insight, really. I may have wanted a little mothering. A sense of stability, attention, a place to be heard. I am not too old as a man approaching forty to admit it. I wanted the warmth and understanding a mother teaches you, wrongly, to expect.

"I come from a big family," Susan said. "There are four of us kids, I'm the oldest and—let's see—my mother's kind of this all-American mom. Soccer practice, dinner on the table at seven. Dad's a real guy's guy, owns a drilling company. Wells, abandonment, pumps, irrigation . . . I guess he's doing exploration for gas companies now too, the whole fracking thing."

"I saw that family in a truck commercial."

"It *was* a little like that." She smiled at the memory. "When we were little, Dad used to say he could drill through anything—rock, metal, you name it. We'd ask him if he could drill to the center of the earth and he'd say, 'With enough pipe, sure.' Silly." She shook her head. "He was Jersey Italian, you know. I told someone at school once that he worked for the mob. Maybe he did."

I couldn't recall the last time I'd seen Susan this way, light-hearted, gushing a little. It gave me a warm feeling even if her father's machismo got on my nerves. I seemed to remember having once read about a Soviet attempt to see how deep they could drill into the earth, how around seven or eight miles down the pressure, or maybe the heat, had become too great to continue, but that nonetheless it had confirmed how little we know about what lies even a short way underfoot.

"We were a close family," Susan went on. "We did everything together, as this big family unit. Our house had this huge communal room and meanwhile our bedrooms were like closets. Our parents wanted to *see* us, you know?"

I said that it must have been hard—omertà, the lack of privacy. I was joking, but Susan didn't laugh.

"We liked it," she said. She looked out the window, retreating, I felt, a small way into herself. The traffic had eased a little, the clouds growing thicker, the sky darker. The car listed in the wind.

"Well, I come from a *traditional* American family," I said. "Broken." She knew this, of course, but I was trying to make amends. "We children of divorce, we're used to thinking there's something creepy about marriages that last, a Mayberry fanaticism or something. Probably we've just confused creepy with healthy."

"I don't know," she said. "Sometimes it's healthy to split up, right? *Healthy.*" She shook her head. "God, what do we even mean?"

And who are we talking about now? I thought, but I held my tongue. I said the no-privacy thing must have given her a terrible time with boys.

"Oh, boys! I had to wait until college, really. Dad was Catholic, you know, and owned guns."

"Fathers with guns," I said and hypothesized that we'd never get around to fixing the gun problem in this country with so much teenage pussy to protect. I wasn't really thinking when I said it, but Susan laughed, a real laugh, not the polite one she used in our talks to let me know she understood I'd made a joke. "I guess so," she said after a minute. But as the laughter faded we found ourselves left with the idea, and behind the idea the image—of Susan's teenage pussy—and I scrambled to move us along so that we wouldn't have to consider the other considering Susan's teenage pussy and the awkwardness of our shared understanding of what we were both simultaneously considering.

"I don't think I ever had a gun in one of my films," I said. What a stupid thing to say. "Are you hungry?" I said, because what I'd said before had been so stupid.

"Actually, I'm starving."

The traffic wasn't too bad and it seemed like a decent time to get off the highway, fuel up, and eat. It wasn't yet noon but I was hungry too, looking forward to the junk you permit yourself on the road, when the trial of the day overtakes and obscures any thought of the future. I was worried Susan would want to find a Starbucks and I'd be stuck with a cheese plate with like two red grapes, but when we pulled off into the clutter of roadside chains there wasn't a Starbucks in sight, and Susan suggested Denny's, which made me want to kiss her, and so Denny's it was.

Over breakfast Susan asked about my current projects and I told her. One involved filming violent criminals remembering happy moments from their childhoods. For another I was following around a trucker I'd met who liked to dress in drag. Susan asked what interested me about these projects and I said it was difficult to talk about them that way; it was the fact that you couldn't summarize them that made them art and to try to capture their effect in words would only lead to my sounding pretentious and evasive. She said that all sounded pretty pretentious and evasive so why didn't I just try, and I said, Fine. I was interested in our response to seeing people in situations that seemed to run directly counter to their public identities. Imagine a group of Fortune 500 CEOs at a petting zoo, I said. Imagine leaving them there too long. If I could get Fortune 500 CEOs to give me an afternoon, that's what I'd have them do.

"Interesting."

"Do you think so? When people say 'interesting' they usually mean '*not* interesting' or 'I'd like to stop talking about this immediately.'"

"No, it is interesting," she said. "Just, how do you make sure it's not gimmicky?"

I told her this was always the worry. It was why these projects took so long. You had to film for a long time before people got so used to the scrutiny that they stopped playing to the camera, before authentic moments of self-discovery could occur. "You can always tell an authentic moment," I said. "I don't know how, but at some point you can see that a person has stopped trying to manage your perception of them. The true self peeks through."

"I wonder if I believe in such a thing," she said.

"Well, forget the word 'true,' if that seems problematic. I mean the self that's not an actor. The self we are in private and with our best friends, our spouses. The effortless self, let's call it."

She looked at me, but past me, to the point in space where the truth of words is judged against reality. She was quiet. The look on her face, as she gazed off, passed from caught-up to sad and then, I thought, to something like a premonitory glimpse of the possibilities and limits of a life. It was brief, this terror—if that's what it was— and I longed and dreaded to know what she was thinking. In another second, though, she had returned to the moment and to picking the crusts of her chicken sandwich, which I had found and continued to find a strange order.

It was raining when we left the restaurant, light, sparse drops shuttled about by the wind, a pleasant rain that seemed to be cleaning you rather than getting you wet. The lights of restaurants and gas stations shone wetly all around, and it was lovely, in the rain, at a Denny's, in New Jersey.

"You don't have to like my films," I said when we were back in the car.

"It's not that . . ." I could feel her on the edge of an admission, having second thoughts but caught in her point's momentum. "It's . . . just my boyfriend in college, he was a filmmaker. He was always telling me about his projects. At first I liked it, I thought he was brave. But the intensity, you know, it kind of wore me down. I think I'm not smart or edgy enough for experimental film."

I didn't say anything. I stared straight ahead. I wanted to give Susan the impression that she had hurt me, which she had a little, but that I was going to ride the hurt out stoically. It wasn't that I needed Susan to like my work, although for what if not pockets of intensity were we in the business of living? But I was jealous of that young man, a man who now of course would be my age, but who in memory preserved something of what is lost to time. What had he done to capture her affection that I could not? And what had Susan been like all those years ago, before intensity came to seem a burden and discretion led her to hide away the treasure of herself, discovered and buried some day long ago under a soil of rotting youth? I wanted, pointlessly, to return to college, to *that* Susan, excitable and unformed, spilling slightly beyond herself as people when they are most beautiful do.

"I'm sorry," she said after a minute. "I'm distracted. The storm, the kids . . . I know your films are very good. You've had a lot of success, right? They matter to people."

"Why did you become a therapist?" I said, ignoring the dubious logic of her last remark. I remembered sitting in therapy with her, week after week, wondering if she always believed the things she said, the terse, careful words she committed to, waiting for what I thought of as her true self to peek through.

"I guess the idea just grew on me," she said. "I like listening to people, hearing their stories. I wanted to do something that helped people. I believe in the therapeutic space."

"But how do you know you are? Helping people, I mean."

She did that thing again of retreating a degree or two into herself. "I don't," she said. "I do my best. I trust the process." I may have snorted. "What happened to listening to music?" she said.

It was really raining now. I had the wipers on their continuous setting, not the really fast one, which by the time it's raining hard enough for you to need is kind of impotent anyway. The clouds had charcoaled and thickened so that, although it was early afternoon, it was as dark as evening. The weather felt obscurely punitive, and though I knew the storm would cause extraordinary damage and harm many people, part of me longed for it to come, for it to get worse, for it to be as bad, or worse, than they said. I wanted to see it curdling the ocean and bringing waves and wind over the coast, over cities and towns, ripping up sidewalks and porches, downing power lines, traffic lights, trees. I wanted the chaos, to feel the power of something powerful, and then the still aftermath of chaos in which we get to be our better selves and rebuild. In which the challenges are simple and communal and vast. I thought somewhere in this mess of longings and contradictory impulses was a film, and then I knew why I'd taken 95 instead of heading inland to 81. I wanted to encounter the storm. I wanted to film it.

"It's really coming down," Susan said. "Oh, there's my exit!"

"Your exit . . ."

"If we were going to my house, I mean. Where I grew up."

"Ah, the panopticon."

"You're making too much of this."

"No," I said. "Let me see if I understand." A tangle of lightning flashed on the retina of the sky. "There's no outward privacy in the panopticon—everything can be seen, right?—but inward privacy exists too, the privacy of the mind. All you really need for inward privacy is to keep quiet, to shut up. So you learn to keep quiet, keep your thoughts to yourself, not betray your emotions. That seems safe. And by the same token the idea of being open, really open, with another person seems terrifying. Yes? Tell me if I'm missing anything."

We didn't speak for a while after this. I knew I had gone too far, as no doubt I had at other times when I thought I saw the shadow of an emotion cross her face. I had the unpleasant feeling of seeing myself act in a way I didn't approve of and would reproach myself for later. But it was a hard moment for me. Cracks shivered out through my marriage, threatening at any moment its collapse. And had I married my wife out of much more, really, than my own aggrieved inner plea for stability? When I thought about her, a woman I had dated in college and parted ways with only to meet again seven years ago, I supposed I had married her because I was tired of thinking about that side of life, because she was smart and self-sufficient and maternal, in her way, and because I *did* love her. I loved her honestly, in a reasonable way, a way in touch with her flaws, and so sober and quiet, this love, that it seemed far truer than the fevered infatuations I'd been used to as a younger man. But I also think I had the idea that we would grow together over time, that our differences would soften, and that we would erosively remake each other in the gentle spaces of domesticity and parenthood. And so I was haunted, when this didn't happen, to see, and even more to feel, that there were parts of her I still had never gained access to and probably, therefore, never would. I wondered achingly what these parts were, because I never doubted that she was honest with me, and she could be warm too. It was not so much *information* that lay beyond my reach, I felt, as a sort of presence, of shared and consummate open-ness, a kind of psychic nudity.

And then Celeste, this past weekend, my friend Mark's wife, whom I had dated for two years before Mark and had almost asked to marry me but instead dumped—because we were young and I thought we should part to reconnect later (maybe), because I had my first solo show (at twenty-six!) and felt powerful and important and suddenly bored with Celeste. We live with our mistakes. We regret them, we move away from them in time, and later we tell ourselves that they were necessary to create the person we have become. In time we grow to love our mistakes because we are inseparable from them and they comprise our belief in ourselves as people with access to wisdom. But all this retrospection never confronts the counterfac-tual mood, which of course it is beyond us to confront, though still, at times, there are mistakes that so resist our revisionary impulse that we are left wondering, When this path branched, what really *did* I decide? And Celeste is such a mistake for me.

An example. This past weekend Mark was called into the office on Sunday and Celeste and I went out to walk the High Line. It was cold and we cupped espresso drinks in our hands. Celeste's cheeks burned with a rosy blush. She'd cut her hair short and it was tousled prettily. I was telling her about my problems at home, that although I dreaded the ending, dreaded admitting defeat and losing my wife, there were days when part of me longed for it to happen, longed at least to have it out, because I was sure my wife and I were both, in private, looking at the same decaying structure, and I no longer knew which was worse, the collapse of our marriage or the tacit consensus in our silence.

"I know what you mean, Ben." She had taken my arm and turned to me. "I have days too when I look at my life, at Mark, the kids, and think, What the hell? When did *this* happen? And it feels almost like panic. Like, how did I get in this deep? And I want it all to disappear. I have this fantasy where I just walk off into another life and nobody comes looking. How terrible is that?"

"It isn't terrible," I said. "But what do we do with that feeling?"

"I don't know," she said. "Be open to it. Feel it. Let that openness wash over you. Refuse to be ashamed of the things we feel."

The buildings ensconced us, the hotel above, the path below with its brown vegetation and little branchings. The wind ran against us like metal, and in that moment, feeling understood, feeling her response against me like the naked flesh of a sibling soul, I had the urge to take Celeste's hand and lead her away into that other life, to start over, the two of us. And just as I thought this, at that moment, we ran into someone I knew, a gallery owner in Chelsea who wanted to know all about my recent work and what I thought of Rist's and what was I *up* to, and it was so nice to meet Celeste, she said, although she mostly ignored Celeste, and by the time she left I had more or less transformed back into the Ben who is a little crasser and more abrasive than he feels, because you have to talk to these art world assholes like you give even less of a fuck than they do, and I don't mean to say I'm not one of these art world assholes myself, just that I left New York and decided to teach because I wanted to rope off a few spaces in my life where I could be genuine, or what I felt to be genuine, and where I could give a fuck.

And Celeste is one of those spaces. And I'd let her marry Mark, who is a wonderful man and surely a steadier soul than I. I no longer remember why I let Celeste go, except that I probably thought we understood each other too easily and would therefore exhaust each other quickly, whereas my wife kept me at a remove from the central space that I believed constituted her her-ness, which for no clear reason I believed *existed*, and which I longed to get to the way you only long for things you can't possess.

"We have kids, though," Celeste said. "That helps a little. Our lives aren't just our own."

"Yes," I said, "except I took them to be the cement of our family, my marriage, and they turn out to be kids and not building materials."

"You're a wonderful father, Ben."

I could, and perhaps should, have stopped to wonder what

evidence she was drawing on, but I didn't. I could have lain down and made a bed in no more than the tone of her voice. She said it so warmly that I felt the prelude to tears gather at my eyes and wished briefly that she were the mother of my kids. We sat by the Hudson and watched evening come over it, lurid and grandiose in the fall cold, then we walked back to Mark and Celeste's to relieve the sitter. Soon Mark came home. And there I watched Celeste as she melted back into her family and away from me, watched her laugh with love at the not-funny jokes of her small children and put a hand on Mark's shoulder, until she was gone from me, back into her real life, where I didn't exist.

That was all the day before.

The rain was heavy now, heavy enough that I was having trouble seeing in front of us. I had slowed to 45 and was hunched over partway, as if my posture could affect the visibility.

"I was playing basketball the other day," I said. We had been driving in silence for maybe half an hour. "There were these kids in the park with me, high school kids, I think. Kind of the weirdos, the freaks. It was just me and them." I was shooting by myself, I told Susan, and they were being loud, joking around a little crudely, and at first I was annoyed. But this one kid kept looking over. A big kid, awkward, with shaggy hair and a black leather trench coat. "At first I thought maybe he was gay and that was why he was looking over. He kept stealing glances, giving me this shy smile. But no, I realized, no, that wasn't it. He was trying to find his *place*. Do you know what I mean?" I looked at Susan. "He was trying to find his place in the world, and this wasn't it. This was the best he could do just now, but it wasn't it. And it made me feel tenderly toward him. He looked at me and thought I was at home in the world because I'm grown, because I can shoot baskets by myself and don't really get embarrassed by things anymore. He thought I was at home in the world, and I'm not. Do you see? I felt protective of him but also nauseated—by his mistake, by the innocence of his mistake—and part of me wanted to step into his life and make it better, and part of me felt helpless and sick because I couldn't, because you can never do that for someone. You only have time to live your own life, and mine was falling apart."

"You're a caretaker, Ben," Susan said.

"You say that—" I wiped the windshield with the back of my hand. I didn't mean to sound so bitter. "But tell me, am I really grieving other people's loneliness and suffering, or my own?"

"Are you lonely? Are you suffering?"

Don't you *know*? I wanted to say, but it seemed indulgent of me to insist. I am, after all, a white American man with a toehold in the upper middle class, with a good job, a wife, and two kids—someone the world has licensed to express himself. A heartbeat of hope raps within my suffering, and while I am thankful for this, truly thankful, I have had to wonder at points whether the hope and the suffering were really two different things.

"What about you?" I said. "Are you so happy? Are you never lonely?"

"I don't know." Susan ran her fingers through the condensation on her window. "Maybe I don't expect to be unlonely."

I pulled to the side of the road, unable, in any case, to see. The clouds had opened up, the rain no longer seeming to fall so much as to *be*, there, beyond us, everywhere—a matrix suffusing the air. All we could see through the windows was a wild silver tide dashing itself on the glass.

"That boy in college," I said, "the filmmaker. It sounds like he wanted to be unlonely with you."

Even in the half-light I could see that Susan's face had paled. She had a way of looking stricken and distant, wounded but unwilling to name the hurt, to let you in to soothe it. The shadows of raindrops ran down her face.

"I couldn't be close in that way."

"Because of your family."

"Yes. Maybe. I don't know."

"Your whole family?"

"What's the use, Ben?"

"Let me guess," I said. I was being cruel, and I'm not proud of it, I'm rarely cruel, but I was being cruel, and I'm sorry, Susan, darling, I am. "It was your father, wasn't it? The guy's guy. You were his favorite. There was a sense, in this family that was so close, that things were maybe a little *too* close."

"Stop."

"So you turned inward. Closed yourself off."

"Ben."

"That poor boy in college."

Susan was quiet. The rain tapered abruptly, bronze light cutting through the clouds. Drops still fell, more the afterthought of rain than rain itself, glistening in the ocher ashes of the sky. How was your mood to keep up with a day like this?

"I'm sorry," I said.

"It's all right." She had composed herself and it terrified me, her ability to compose herself like this. "It's not that simple, Ben."

"No, of course. It's just your job, right? Inventing these plausible little stories. Anyway, you're too strong for me. I keep trying to break through, but I should probably just accept that you're too tough."

She smiled. It was not a smile of compassion or tenderness, I saw, but a broad smile of unfeigned delight. She beamed and I thought— it came to me powerfully, dizzyingly—my God, this woman is a *child*. She wants to be *praised*. Well, goddamn it, I can praise her if that's what she wants.

The light painted her face gold, her hair, her eyes. The sky parted in flaxen sheaves, and I began with the ridiculous story, the one we have all, with each year, loosened our grip on a little more, about how we came to our parents in woven baskets, gifted from the second world, the world behind this one: how we are all sacred children.

"Ben," she murmured. "Please. I'm just a flawed, selfish person, like everyone."

But do you really think that? I wanted to say. Does anyone—but especially you? Her eyes were closed. Are we not all born with wings we take out only in private? Except the beauty scared you, Susan. She was still smiling. She had laid a hand in mine, those delicate fingers, leaned into me, breathing slowly. We are all failed imagoes, earthbound under each other's weight. I could hear the doves in the dripping trees. We are all scared, Susan, I told her. All scared no one else will find them as beautiful.

She kissed me so I had to stop talking, a kiss at first contained, but that gave in to itself until our mouths pressed together, made a seal, and our tongues sought out the depths or sought to show themselves in pursuit of the depths. We can argue forever about the meaning of a kiss. After a minute she pulled back, a hand on my chest. We looked into each other's eyes. I wanted to see longing in hers, sorrow, any sign that she needed me, or anything, but she looked only happy, held once again gently within herself, brimming with the seraphic light of some perverse joy.

"I fell in love with you once," she said. "You must have known."

"I did," I said. "It was a dirty trick. It made me love you, and now I'm stuck loving you and you've moved on."

She stopped smiling and the sun passed behind a cloud. It was cold in the car. I started the ignition and pulled us back onto the highway. In no time at all warm air flooded the cabin. And it seemed almost sad to me, that warm air could flood in just like that.

On the radio we heard reports of the storm. It was flirting with a Category 4 off Delaware, gale-force winds with flooding deep into the coast. Millions of people were without power now, states of emergency had been declared everywhere, National Guards called up. The coast guard had suspended rescue operations north of Point Pleasant. A Fujiwara interaction was possible. In my mind I saw the rainbands of the storm, the falcate concentric arms, reach out across a thousand miles to embrace the coast.

The rain had picked up again, a hard, steady downfall. The wind too. On the side of the road it forced the trees together like lousy drunks. I suggested we get gas—although the tank was more than half full—and load up on provisions in case we passed through a large area without power.

"Do you think that's a worry?" Susan asked.

I said I didn't know, but not knowing meant it was possible and if it was possible it was a worry. Susan said she meant *likely* and I said that's what I didn't know when I said I didn't know. We were near Philadelphia. We had missed the 295 bypass in the rain, but when we took the next exit the world we pulled off into was deserted and it was impossible to imagine a city anywhere nearby. The lights were off at the first gas station and the whole strip had an unearthly feel. The gallon prices on the sign were out of date, as though the station had been closed for months, maybe years.

"Maybe we should get back on the highway," Susan said.

I said let's go a little farther, how far could a gas station be? The road was empty, narrow, and surveyor-straight, with no more than a bleak-looking house every mile or so. The vegetation had a stunted, marshy look, like we were near brackish water, and then, out of nowhere, we were climbing a bridge, a vast suspension bridge rising up over a river—the Delaware, surely—an immense gray bridge lit at intervals along its cables and frame, where a bright fizz seemed to clothe the steel. The air was alive with water. So much water! Tons no doubt, *millions* of tons. The forms things take amaze me. Water in the river as waves, in the air as moisture, falling as rain; in my blood, against my skin, dissolving and colluding with salt shorn of rocks, catching light from glowing wires and breaking it into strands and shards of colored light, collecting as clouds above us blotting out the sun; water in the milk my children drank from my wife's breasts, in the cooling systems of reactors, the turbines of dams, and the forensic patterns of rock on Mars, the afterthought of water, stagnant pools in the waning moon, and then all around us, everywhere, except the bubble of our car. We were the only car on the bridge. At the high point of its arcing roadway I pulled us over and put on the hazard lights.

"What are you doing?" Susan said. I was rummaging around

in back for my camera and its waterproof case. "Really, Ben, I'm not sure this is the best idea."

But I was out of the car as she said it, out and filming into the raging storm. The river rolled heavily below, seething with a whitish foam in which new life, for all I knew, was in the process of constituting itself.

She came out and stood beside me.

"It's beautiful, isn't it?" I said.

She stared out into the storm. "It's strange," she said, "how terrible things are beautiful when you're safe from them."

"Safety first."

"Ben." I could hear in her tone that she was tired of this, tired of these conversations. "There's a pitch you live at, Ben. It's not a pitch I can live at all the time."

I can come down! I wanted to shout. I can come down, just *ask*. But it was a little late in the day for that. And what was I proving out here, chasing the storm, but the opposite? And yet who knows his own capacity to change, her own, or the capacity of two people to change together? Who can ever say where the line falls between I *can't* and I *won't*?

We saw headlights in the distance coming our way. I turned the camera from the river to Susan.

"I was wrong before, so tell me," I said. "Why couldn't you be close?"

I filmed her in profile, watching the car approach over the long, straight road. "There aren't easy answers, Ben." She looked so beautiful with the rain streaking her face and hair. "Sometimes you have to grow tough or never leave. Sometimes comfort and independence seem to be at odds. Or maybe you get scared of your own desire to fall in too deep, what would happen if you gave in to it."

I put the camera down. I couldn't look at her. "What a stupid way to live," I said. The car, highway patrol, flashed its lights and pulled up behind us. A trooper got out.

"Sir, ma'am. What's the trouble?"

I told the officer everything was fine, that we'd been on the bridge and decided to get out for a second to look at the storm.

"I saw the hazards," she said, not entirely convinced.

"Sorry to inconvenience you," I said. "We'll be on our way."

"All right." She had her hat off, hair pulled back like wet reeds, a plain face. She considered the storm with us for a minute. "Some people, you know, drive into the storm," she said. "Thrill seekers. Stubborn folks. Puts us in a bad spot because we're on the hook for getting them out."

I said it was selfish and the trooper nodded. "No great mystery what's there—more storm. Some folks don't know what's best for them."

"But people need to be free, don't they," Susan said, "even to make terrible mistakes?"

The officer looked at Susan. I did too. "I guess so," she said and laughed. "I guess so." She shook her head.

And I could have kissed them both just then. I could have taken their hands and jumped with them into the frothing river, I thought—would have done so happily and lived my life forever in the swollen moments of that mistake.

We waved to the officer as she pulled away and then got back in our car. I kept on to the end of the bridge. I could feel Susan waiting for me to turn around, I could hear it in the language of her body, tensing, but I refused to turn.

We heard further reports on the radio: sea levels, wind speeds, guesses at the damage wrought. In coastal North Carolina, southern Virginia, on the Eastern Shore, along the Delaware coast. Towns had been washed away. *Towns.* Barrier splits dissolved, swallowed by the sea. Power was out everywhere, lines and towers down. Water ran through city streets, turning streets to rivers. People kayaked through downtowns, waited out the storm on rafts. Water touched everything there was to touch.

"I don't like this anymore," Susan said. I said nothing. She had taught me the power of keeping silent, of giving the other person no shared reality to build off of, no ground on which to begin working around to a compromise. If you want to have your way, Susan had taught me, shut up.

We passed by a town, an intersection with a dark gas station, a small retail bank. There were a few other cars, old ghostly Buicks and Lincolns. They drifted by us, pale headlights dying short, swathed in the cerements of rain.

We would get to the coast, as near as possible, I had decided. Let Susan fight me, let her strike out from the bunker of her frightful composure. In this one way I was too strong for her, within the logic of the storm. I was taking charge. I could continue—continue driving, continue loving her—and she couldn't stop me. Because I wanted her there with me at the ocean, watching its power, watching it surge. I wanted to film it, to capture it so I could say, Look, Susan, the unstoppable ocean!, so that she would have to see it and to stop pretending the ocean didn't exist.

"Our poor kids," she said.

We were past the town, in flat farmland. Silos stood by barns, wood fences squaring off fields. The water before us was no longer rainfall, I saw, but standing water. The far point of its incursion. A new beginning to the sea.

"Why did you fall in love with me," I said, "way back when?" We had been watching occasional cars pass the other way. I kept having the sensation of seeing people from our past in them, our parents and friends, old childhood friends we'd introduced each other to, grandparents who'd been dead for years, cousins we hadn't seen since the wedding, old teachers and former lovers, all glancing at us with worry but glancing away quickly too, old enough to have learned that you never talk people out of their mistakes.

People are bullets, fired.

"I wanted to be the sort of person who could love you."

"But you are," I said, seizing on the logic like it would matter, like I could twist her words into a prophecy against her. "Because you have."

"Ben, you think because you're loving that you can't be dangerous."

Perhaps she didn't mean dangerous, but something more elusive. Or perhaps she did.

"Some women like danger," I said. I was being funny.

I looked at her. She smiled—in spite of herself, I thought. I smiled too. Our smiles grew as we looked at each other and then we were laughing. The wind rattled the car and something—a branch? a rock?—hit the window and sent a web of shattering through it; and as this happened the air shifted, a sudden brightening in the sky, and I felt the wind grow confused, like the tide does when it changes, bucking. And then stillness, perfect stillness. Sunlight. The eye.

I pulled us to the side of the road. It wasn't a road any longer but a tiny river, eight inches deep. The land stretched before us— submerged, sodden, jeweled everywhere with light.

The skin of the earth, I thought. We are still just only on the skin.

The air right then was soft and moist. The sun burned on the fringes of far-off clouds, at its evening cant, glancing in. Oh, those evenings! I thought, like the first hot evenings of spring, when the air is satin and as warm as your body, as though you have descended from an airplane into some warmer place, L.A. or Tucson, say, and the breeze feels like an uncomplicated lover, and the air, that air! so full of plant life and dirt, as full of these things as the ground. That is what I smelled just then, the smell of life, the vaporous smell of life. And I had a memory of Susan, when I knew her in college, of bicycling on a night like this and watching her put her hand out by her hip to feel the breeze collect in it. And another time, of watering the lawn one evening and seeing a figure at the end of the street jogging, and knowing for no more than her awkward, determined stride that it was her, my wife. Or when I lifted her up on the kitchen

counter three weeks ago, late one afternoon, and she yelped in surprise and gave me a look of lovely and time-softened lust—because
time softens things, it does. If she felt I was dangerous, was it any
more than this, that I threatened to pull us under in moments as
small as these?

She was standing next to me. We leaned against the front of
the car, smiling into the sun, letting the light explore our faces. The
water ankleted our calves. Susan took my hand, took it with a kind
of purpose I recognized that said, C'mon, we're getting out of here.
We're going home.

The air was crazy and beautiful with life. The sun, the hills, the
water at our feet. Do you remember what it's like to go home with
the person you love? Do you? Don't say yes. Remember. Stay there
with me, linger. Then make me laugh while we drive home.

Amy's Conversions

A (Reluctant) Melodrama

(I)

It is in certain moods that I take it upon myself to tell the story of me and Amy, the years we have known each other, our friendship, and my love for her. They are moods of course that tend to the self-serious, when the inner decoration of life seems very rich and heavy in color and to call such and such simply purple or red would be a crime of inattention or laziness, a failure of patience or nerve. When you want someone to see just *exactly* what you are seeing and already pretty much hate everyone for not being able to get there. Not having the stubbornness or the perversity it takes.

I am a painter. You must forgive me my cynicism about the sensitivity people bring to the act.

But first, years before I work up the nerve to say, I am *this*, I am *that*, I run into Amy in the bookstore. It's the one out on the northbound highway due to metamorphose into a candle shop, a discount shoe store, and finally an unrentable gap tooth in that sad strip. Amy and I trade a sly smile that says, Yes, of course we are the only ones in our town who would come here to escape the heat, and it is then, as we are talking, that she tells me she's left the church.

My God, I say.

Well, she says—gallows humor—not *mine* anymore.

We are home from college that day. It is June, and we are
twenty. To the west somewhere a storm remakes the sky to suit its
wild fancy, and if I could do the same maybe it would be *Women in
Love* in Amy's hands, though life is rarely like that, is it? *Fitting*.

On the mission trips we took as high school students, back
when we were devout—Amy and I and pretty much everyone we
knew—we used to lie in ministry basements far from home, whis-
pering things too hopeful and foolish for the light of day. Amy
would say how when He came, we would live a thousand years of
peace and happiness on earth. Can you imagine, she said, the hungry fed? The sick cured? The needs of the world met? A breeze
might bring the thick, exotic leaves scratching against the low windows. We talked of mundane things too, school-year gossip and em-
barrassments, who was *gorgeous* or getting hotter, teachers we liked
and those we found ridiculous. I remember those nights, but nothing of the countries. An image here or there: bright colors, dirt
roads. I do remember thinking, Amy, will you shut the fuck up and
listen to yourself? Do you really think it's possible to meet *all* the
needs of the world—everyone's—at the same time? But I also thought
that in a perfect world my love for Amy would find its proper form,
so I could be stupid too.

What did it? I ask.

I just couldn't take the hypocrisy, she says.

Which?

Do I have to pick?

And because we are young and this has the cadence of a joke,
we laugh. But of course she has to pick. Who doesn't have to pick?

Amy was a pastor's kid, see. Her father, Pastor Bob, was our
family's pastor, a man I found fatuous and condescending at the
time but who in retrospect probably deserved better. Amy loved
him, of course, and took his faith as her own. So there must be
more. I press Amy, and she tells me—about the varieties of life and
belief she's encountered away from home and can't believe lead
briskly to hell. I bite down the irony, the irony *of* me. I know I

should have given Amy more grief, then and all along, but we grow into our toughness like snakes, molting hope. And before you judge me, understand: Amy and I are different; we are the only ones who would come here to avoid the heat; the only ones who look at these fine pages of violent dreaming and think how delicate and timid a lunge at optimism should be. We spent our childhoods under the same southern sun, where possibilities grew and budded or withered silently within us, and we had only each other to look at for confirmation or its opposite. No one parted Amy's legs when they were as young and faultless as they are that day in the bookstore. Someone should have. Youth should be used. It should be ruined and swallowed. We all know this. What else is youth for?

Amy blushes the way she does. Less from embarrassment, I think, than from the surprise of continuing to encounter herself, the white stone of her own stubbornness, beneath everything. I know the look from the days in high school when she would pass me in the hall and whisper, Hey, we're going out to . . . , thumb and forefinger pinched to her lips. And then in the catalpa grove, among the hackberries, with the floral musk of spring in the air like sex, we passed the joint around, our little group. We stole for a time too. Bras and soda, eyeliner, chewing gum. Anything you could slip into a pocket or purse. We were devout, we weren't prudes. And what I saw at last was that Amy would have found it easier *not* to steal, and so she stole.

This petty theft ended the day the cops were called. A crowd gathered on the curb to watch as they handcuffed Amy and put her in the car. She was weeping. She kept asking the cops whether it wasn't all part of God's plan. Doesn't everything happen for a reason? she said again and again. Don't you think everything happens for a reason?

And I am sure this is what we all would like to know, but really, what reason would you devise for a scene like this? Tell me, because I'll take a good lie over a pitiless truth. Did I expect the wind to rise up and free Amy? No, I can't believe I did. We had been taught from a young age to put great faith in the unseen drama of our lives, but even as a kid I think I had a good sense of where the literal and figurative began and ended. Pastor Bob liked to rest a hand on the church wall and say, *This* is not the church. Then he would point to all of us and say, *This* is the church. But the building had been a department store not long before, and we could all remember the rows of perfume and sandals, the fishing tackle and cotton dresses, lining these same floors. Pastor Bob must have known as well as I did that he was correcting a mistake none of us had made. And the question begged: What then *as* the church did we make up? What did our privacies sum to?

The hopeless things we want to know. I try again in the bookstore. I ask Amy, Why now? as though she can tell me something meaningful about where, in the fluid process, sentiment hardens into conviction, decision into action, or molten spirit into the rock of belief.

It wasn't like that, she says. It was like . . . You know when you're on the phone with someone you're into, and you don't even realize you're speaking in this weird, airy voice? It was like that. Like realizing I was speaking in a weird voice and stopping. Returning to my normal voice.

She looks at the open book in her lap. There is a little universe inside it, wonderfully still.

But how do you know? I say. How do you know which is which?

She considers this. I guess you don't, she says. One just feels more natural. Other answers begin to make more sense.

Uh-huh, I say. Uh-huh. And only now do I wonder: What is an answer? What satisfies us?

How did her parents take it, I ask. Dad threw up, she says. She stares straight ahead. But you know, we took the boat out the other night, just the two of us. We'd been fighting for days and we went out on the lake at dusk. We didn't say anything, just held hands. And I kept thinking, In a way I should be dead to him. If I'm serious, I should be a little dead. But we just sat there watching the mist rise off the lake.

I don't know what I saw then. What I see now is the twilit lake, soot clouds in the distance, sky that faint humid orange blur it could be some summer nights, a burning calico, heat rising from the water like the ghost life within it. I see Amy staring out into the dim luster at the edges of enveloping shadow, like out there somewhere are the small girls we once were, without a hard decision to our name, tottering happily after a mindless joy, and I think, Those poor, unready girls!

Are we ever prepared for the things we find ourselves incapable of agreeing to or helpless to pursue? Our twelfth-grade English teacher, Mr. Gerard, liked to say that you hate what reveals the part of you you hope to hide and love what reveals the heroic part of you looking for its cause. And who would say that, say a thing like that to teenagers, already riven with the bladelike purity of our desires? But we loved him for it, for telling us what we already believed.

Hey, guess what? I say. I stopped spelling my name with the *i*. You stopped . . . Amy looks at me, perplexed, her confusion melting slowly into a concerned and even delicate understanding. And as I watch it settle over her, I am brought back to the last Y.G. trip we took as seniors, when hiking in the Ozarks that hot, bright day, in the sunshine and scented air, I sensed my feelings for Amy slip into a higher register, on the order of righteousness or selfless virtue, when even the need of them, crippling and illicit—illicit in God's eyes— seemed to me as natural as the day itself, the trees and scattered light, the birds in the wind-shaken trees, when high in the mountains where the breeze swept the humidity from the air I confessed myself to Amy.

I love you too, Jessie, she said—that same look.

But no, no, you have come too far to be misunderstood. No, Amy, you say, and you explain.

And she listens, with patience and sympathy, so much it makes you *sick*. Because even then you know where these things stand next to lust.

(II)

A few years later I am moving to Baltimore—

No. Let's try something different. Step back, get outside my head. If Amy's reinventions make a mess of the perspective, shivering it glasslike in a cheap cubism, can we say that my constancy deserves no less? Can we grant that if there is no clean angle in on my friend, there isn't one in on me either? Yes? From the top then.

A few years later *Jesse* is moving to Baltimore.

How's that?

A short young woman stands in a hallway. She has just arrived. She wears her hair shorn close, a faint rip-curl at the front, a black tank top, shorts. Dirtied brass numbers call out the apartments, the corridor steeped in a residuum of cigarettes and takeout. It is summer, hot. She shrugs under the weight of her bags. Sweat blossoms on her body in the stillness. The woman who finally opens the door is Dot, she explains, Amy's roommate and a fellow student in the literature program. Amy will be back in a little bit. Jesse sets her stuff down, the duffel bag, the painting she made Amy as a gift. It is of a naked woman in the woods, wearing the bloodied head of a slaughtered stag. This is Jesse's idea of a joke.

Or no. She may not intend it as a joke. She may intend it as a provocation. She may intend it as a Serious Work of Art. We just can't say. These are the things the facts omit, the things you can't know from the outside.

Jesse and Amy last saw each other when Amy came home for Easter. That's a certifiable fact. They met for coffee and strolled through Retford until the rain came up and forced them under the gazebo on the green. It was very pretty there, the leaves of cloud admitting a flush of light into the rain.

Are you sure you want to be here? Amy said. Retford, I mean.

No, Jesse said. She told people she was there for her mother now that her father had left, but all she said to Amy was, No, I'm sure I don't.

I don't miss it, Amy said. I keep thinking I should, but I don't feel like myself here anymore. She watched Jesse light a cigarette. You're going to leave then?

The rain tapered, the sound of it hitting a bulkhead coming slower, heavier. A breeze picked up. Drops trembled everywhere in the wind. Jesse tapped the ash on the railing and shrugged. How's grad school?

Amazing, Amy said. No, really. It's like whole *worlds* have opened up.

You like it in Baltimore?

I do. Amy seemed to place the words at careful intervals on the air. She smiled. I like never having to explain myself.

It was after Amy left the church that Jesse returned to college and began tearing the last remnants of pretense from her life. At times she felt she had seen the tape of her childhood run backwards, until there the two of them were, frozen where they had begun. And if you ran the tape now would things unfold as they had before? You could lose a lot of time wondering. Better to leave it alone. Did people really change or were parts of them suppressed while other parts were allowed to grow? Jesse decided she didn't care—couldn't care. Fuck identity, fuck self-expression. Live, look, listen, be. Don't apologize. That most of all. This is what she tells Dot and Amy that first night in the Hampden dive.

It reminds me of this D. Z. Phillips thing, Dot says. How we need to move from a hermeneutics of suspicion to a hermeneutics of contemplation.

Uh-huh. And what on earth does that mean? says Jesse.

Dot blinks at her. He's talking about what it means to understand something, Amy says. Different modes of inquiry.

Modes of inquiry, Jesse says.

Yes, Amy says. How do we understand something? By picking it apart or considering it altogether? For example.

I don't understand anything, Jesse says. Starting with this conversation.

Yes, you do, says Amy.

Jesse smiles. No, I don't. It's nice of you to say, but I don't. Because where do you begin and end, right? There's that rubber spider above the bar. Okay. What's it doing there? You could say a lot of things. You could say they put it up for Halloween and kept it. You could say a child glued it together in Malaysia or wherever and it was shipped here to be sold in drugstores. You could say we find spiders creepy because they bite us, or look weird, I don't know, or that we think it's hip to put things where they don't belong for whatever reason. Or— You get the point.

But there you go, says Dot.

Where? says Jesse. I don't want to go anywhere. I'm tired.

Dot smiles. She'd do well in grad school.

No, sorry, Jesse says. No. I could never spend all that time worrying about what mode of inquiry I was using.

Don't you though already? says Amy. She stares into the Christmas lights that hang from the wall. I mean, I think about why I'm in grad school. I think, Here we are brought up being told all truth and meaning can be found in one book. What if I've just added lots of other books?

That's a bit glib, though, isn't it? says Dot.

Is it? I didn't mean it be.

Dot turns to Jesse. You were brought up religious too then?

Jesse finishes her beer. I think of it as a very narrow literary education, she says.

And they laugh—they laugh!—and Jesse would cast the world in bronze right then to keep it still.

Smoking outside she makes eyes with a tall woman. The woman has dark hair and broad pale cheeks. She holds Jesse's look a beat past comfort, turns, spits.

You don't do that so good, Jesse says, hacking up phlegm and spitting herself. The woman looks on behind impassive eyes. Boredom hungering after unlikely surprise. This is what Jesse sees dancing in the dark light of her pupil.

But I can spit farther, the woman says.

I'd like to see that.

They take turns spitting and spit until their mouths are dry. Tell me your name and I'll buy you a drink, Jesse says.

I'm not telling you my name.

I'll call you Randi then.

Fuck off, the woman says, smiling.

Jesse flicks her cigarette. Bye forever . . . Randi.

We were just saying how it's like that whole 'religion without God' thing, Dot says when Jesse sits back down. You know, what's-his-name's?

No.

Oh, never mind.

Sorry, I don't mean to be an asshole. It just feels like intellectual masturbation to me.

So?

So I guess I never came jacking off that way.

Dot looks right at her. Oh yes, you have.

It is a flash like the unbending of time's clenched fist in which Jesse sees it, the hours laid out before her, half lost to the shadows of drink, some zealous making out in a doorframe, arms lifted to ease a passage of shirts, the emigration of clothes from body to floor, new skin—all that is waiting for them back home in a chapter of the night breached by visions. Cigarette smoke drifts in tendrils to the streetlamps. Midges play in the hot dirty air. And how many nights like this must a life contain, spent half waiting to be caught up in urgencies we can't invent?

But of course waking in Dot's bed the next morning, it is Amy Jesse imagines beside her, among the tangles of thrown sheet. If she could stop right then and disinvest Amy of demure mystery, the innuendo of beatitude, this would be a different story. A happier one perhaps, if she could rebuff the small imaginary production in which she rolls over to Amy—Amy asleep, with her head cradled in her arms, kinked hair falling at her shoulders, heavy, graceful curve of her ass to the ceiling—and kisses her shoulders, telling her she's sorry as she comes awake.

About what?

I acted like I didn't understand you last night when I did. I don't know why I did that.

And what had Amy said? There's a bit of cruelty in every judgment, don't you think? Don't you think every judgment enacts a kind of violence on the world?

Enacts violence on the world . . . Jesse had said, like she were confused, which she doesn't understand because of course she *knew*, of course she *thought*. When were we not violence to one another? Her father's ungiving silence, Amy's unreachable heart. Marissa in college, who after months of ardent fucking introduced Jesse to her parents as a friend. Jesse's mother, lit on wine, so *sad*, so *scared* Jesse would have no one to protect her and would never know the joy of having a family of her own. *This* sort of joy, Ma? Her mother was not a stupid or an ignorant woman. From within the grip of what elect delusion did she speak? Through the kaleidoscope of what half-turn disarrangement of truth?

But Jesse had pretended Amy had lost her.

How's your sex life? she'd said.

Ha, what sex life, Amy said.

And how funny now to think back to a night like that and remember that they had no idea what came next, that they sat in the bar happy enough to let the blank nothing of the future open out before them like a landscape in the process of being drawn. That in that moment, before the night collapsed into nothingness, into three still images perhaps, into itself and other nights just like it, they let themselves believe that for its very vividness, for its *particularity*, it might never end. But there was so much still to happen. This was before Amy had been touched or loved. Before her family shook apart after her father's affair with an elder's wife—an unconsummated intimacy, not unlike prayer—and he was driven from the church he'd built. Before Jesse's mother got cancer (breast, she is fine). Before Amy dropped out of school and disappeared into the revolutionary politics that would consume the rest of her youth and Jesse took the job as office manager at the start-up clothing company in Baltimore, painting in what free time she had left. She had a dog, Peter, and a girlfriend, Sally. On good days it seemed she had grown old enough to feel at home in her skin. She considered her friend sometimes and wondered how much thought one ought to give to the way one lived. Then she thought that only Amy knew.

I was a child raised by wolves, she tells Sally one nothing October day. They are on a beach in Delaware, the ocean wrought and glinting. In grays and browns the day presents as grades of rupture, bands of oblivion unfolding outward—the sky, the water, the sand, the sedge. The thought settles over Jesse in the absence of other thoughts: there is nowhere else she needs to be.

Later she will think how foolish our dreams of arrival are. How many times must we say to ourselves, Maybe this is it, maybe the struggle is over, when we are only on the vast crescent of an expansive boredom, some beach in Delaware with our back to the sea?

Peter runs after a flight of sandpipers that rise into the air like spangled filaments after light.

Everyone thinks they were raised by wolves, Sally says.

(III)

You are twenty-nine. You are going home. This is happening. Kick and scream if you will. Carp all the way to the airport. Complain to your friends, to Anita. Such a *drag*. A duty, really, and joyless. No, you *love* your mother, she's just impossible, deluded. The way parents are. Such lame-o's, irredentists lost to an irrecoverable past. You look a bit bedraggled, you must admit. A bit showily causal in your knockabout jeans and Keds. No sense getting dressed up for your mother, but it's like you're trying to prove you've left. Prove you don't belong. And yes, you've been away too long, it's true. A year, can it be? And yes, everyone else in what was once your family now has a different family of his own. Meanwhile your mother's life has shrunk to the space of three stories she tells herself not exactly riveted to the truth: that she and your father continue to enjoy a spiritual bond since the split; that she is happy, all things considered; that you and she are a pair, alike in loneliness, although you often have girlfriends whom she continues to conceive of as very close women friends.

It rains your first days home. You sit with your mother in the back room and she says she's been feeling close to God lately. We talk, she tells you and says He put her on her own to know Him better. Water runs down the frosted glass. You should have more conversations with real people, you say. You know the sort: flesh-and-blood, *visible*, prone to unfortunate differences of opinion. I never knew what profound companionship I could find in God, she says. And what you want to say is that a person can't find companionship in an echo, that she is listening to her echo and the thing about an echo is it will never surprise you. But you say nothing. You can rip the bandages off everyone else's private wounds, not hers.

Your father and me, Jesse, we just wanted different things.

Anita told me to tell you to date more.

It's nice you have such nice friends, she says.

The rain taps out your silence. On your third day home you escape Ma.

The weather has broken and hot sun floods the shadeless downtown. The heat culls moisture from the hollows. You pause at the old department store. Through the windows you can see the dais and pulpit where Amy's father used to preach. People you don't know are gathered at a card table with coffees and notepads—congregants, strangers, new stewards of what was once yours—and you have the brief urge to go in and tell them to stop, that you and Amy have explored this blind alley and can tell them the dimensions if they like. It is a kind of vertigo you feel, a queasy lurch at the precipice of collapsed time, seeing those things continue on from which your own life has diverged. And it reminds you of watching the high school girls play soccer on a visit home years ago, the sudden truth in your stomach, as they ran in their red pinnies through the quickening dusk, that new bodies would keep coming to fill those jerseys year after year, shouting in a joy that was itself the very act of forgetting—forgetting those who had come before, forgetting how they would disappear themselves.

At the new coffee shop a barista pulls the lever on the espresso machine like she isn't sure what will happen. A finger taps your shoulder. Oh, goodness, you say, and you and Amy's mom are hugging. She's grown bigger over the years, cut her hair short, let it gray. How is she? Just lovely, she says. She's remarried. Yes, you heard. A younger man, a naval engineer, the stuff of light gossip. Larry, she says. You look so great! Well, thank you, she says—but she does. And how beautiful are women of a certain age, when they stop obsessing over weight and clothes and come to inhabit the world without pretense.

I'm doing yoga, she tells you.

My girlfriend likes that, you say. She smiles, says nothing. And what do you hear from Amy? you ask.

A shadow passes over her face. Do you know, Jesse, I haven't heard from her in *months*? I hardly recognized her the last time she was here. She got involved in, what do you call it, helping the janitors at her school get a decent wage? And she was in those protests up in New York. Helping folks after the storms hit. I said, Amy, we got storms down here, honey. People in need down here. That's what the church teaches, after all. And you know what she said to me, she says, What *about* the church, Ma? Do you have any idea what goes on in this country while we talk about Jesus this, Jesus that? Well, I said, you can't save everyone, sweetheart, try as you might. And she says, Talk to me when you've tried. But I think she felt bad because she said, We could all be trying a little harder. My own daughter! But you know, I was proud of her too, Jesse, because I could hear God's love in what she said.

If God loves one person, it's Amy, you tell her.

What a sweet thing to say, she says. But you know, she kept saying how revolution was the only hope. I mean, *revolution*—in this day and age?

Amy's very pure hearted, you say. When she thinks something, she's got to believe it all the way down, as deep as it goes.

But Amy's mom is staring out the window. She kept saying how all the problems were structural. Everything was *structural*. I don't pretend to know what that means.

You say you guess it means we're all caught up doing one another little harms we don't even notice. You touch her shoulder. You and Amy are still young, you remind her.

But you don't feel particularly young. In fact you feel older than just about everyone on earth. And how did mothers get so innocent as they aged? How, instead of revealing itself to them, did the world grow ever stranger and more worrying, as though you formed a system with them and moving in one direction caused them to move in the other, unseen cables in the dialogue of souls?

So you're still up north, Jesse, she says. You like it up there? You'll let me know if you hear from Amy, won't you? She always admired you so much.

Oh, well, did she now. *Really?* You'll take it. But parents say shit like that all the time and who knows, who really knows? Who can say the filters of necessary illusion the lives of children pass through on their way to settling in parents' minds? What did your own parents think all those years as your hair grew shorter, when you gave up makeup, dresses, and the posture of an apology? No doubt they had their own confusions to approach in glancing and unpracticed dives. No doubt they would hold whatever they could still in their shifting world, even you. You would hold them still. You would sit like dolls at the kitchen table. What noise? you would say. What rumbling?

In the days after, your thoughts run to Amy and the trip you took as high school seniors. A storm had torn up the coast where a friend of Pastor Bob's, another DTS alum, had his congregation, and it fell to you and Amy to drive down the van with all the clothes and food, the tools and blankets, your church was donating. Our very own angels of mercy, Pastor Bob said. And how exciting it had been! The open road, the two of you, set free in service to a simple good. South and east you drove, on country roads that cut through spectral cotton fields and shuttered towns, places boarded up but for old gas pumps and Chinese takeouts. Embry's. Golden Chopsticks. You ate lunch at a rest stop, sitting next to Amy by a bushy swale that smelled of moist decay and life, and you thought, *This*. Right *here*. I will live forever in states of exception, like today.

Since her arrest the year before, Amy had been more devout than ever, but you had become interested in painting—and what did she make, you wanted to know, of art that flirted with sacrilege, beauty assembled from the raw material of sin?

But that's what's so exciting, Amy says. Looking for God— *finding* God—where you least expect to.

In your memory the sun is spilling through a crack in the afternoon. Pale gold sluicing the tidal gray. Washed-out starlight above a Chevron station. And what will you think looking back? That in your rush to know your friend you forgot how statements are postures, not truths, and most people mysteries even to themselves?

How we are all waiting to be stripped down to our least garment and known when we can't even manage it ourselves, from the inside out?

Years later you paint a series of scenes from your arrival in town. The vantage point hovers in midair, several feet above the eyes of a standing observer. It is evening. The houses have a posed beauty in the glowing light, splintered, hushed, spilling forth clothing and furniture, curtains, toys, downed gutters. People on lawns carry panels of siding and plywood in their hands. They move, as you remember, in something thicker than air. The breeze through the van window is as warm as skin, alive with salt. You sleep in a stranger's living room that night. Candlelight laps at the ceiling. And you wonder what resolve leads people to go on living in the path of storms, only to remember, slipping among indistinct strata of consciousness, that the people here don't believe things happen by accident.

And where would they go? Amy says the next day in the car. Their lives are there. Their families and friends. Their job, their church.

And what's the difference, does she think, between a thousand acts of charity done in faith and the same one thousand acts done without it?

Well, Amy says, but falls silent. The farmland rolls on beside you, tracts of cash crops growing hay colored in the autumn sun.

The difference, I think, she says at last, is that the person without faith might think a thousand acts were enough.

And you remember this much later, like a last remark at the crossroads where you and Amy part. How otherworldly she seemed just then. How awesome and unreasonable. You felt you were walking down into the valley while Amy, growing tiny above, climbed the steep and narrow path to a distant temple. And you felt so *happy* all of a sudden, so inferior to Amy and so *happy* to be.

But that wouldn't be her last incarnation, not by a long shot. And how does the force of belief not diminish as one conviction supplants the last? Where does Amy go to reemerge, to break apart and come back whole? Where is she now? Where are you, Amy? you whisper. Where do you go?

And then you see her. It's back in Baltimore, at some pop-up dance event Anita's dragged you to. You step outside to smoke and there's Amy, looking off at the dock lights in the distance, the harbor beyond her, the low buildings and piers like a crust along the shore.

Amy, hey!

You might be a ghost to judge by her look. No one else in her group turns.

Jesse, she says. My God.

What are you doing here?

What do you mean? She smiles. Same as you.

That's not true, you say. I came to dance.

She tilts her head toward the group. *Anarchists*, she mouths— like that explains anything.

So, what? Anarchists don't dance? I'd have thought that was about all they could get together on.

She laughs. It's good to see you. She shakes her head. Boy, a little strange. But good.

It's been forever. Hey, I saw your mom.

Her smile fades and she shakes her head. I just can't talk to them anymore, she says. And while you know she means her parents, with her words it is your town that lurches into the night, your childhood behind it, as fake as a soap you watched too many seasons of long ago, a fairy tale wound in gauze, *that* false, *that* rich in dream life, in the shabby promise of days bandaged in their amazing heat, ropes of water turning coruscant in the sun, parents—yours, Amy's— congregants, group prayer, praying next to Amy praying, the endless pretense of shared dreaming, of so many privacies obscured below the canopy of that easy discarnate happiness, as if the thing billowing in the laundered shirts that blew from clotheslines, fanning streamers on your bike, and glinting in the eye of the horse across the street who ate apples from your hand were *one* thing and you it. And later if you snort coke in a club bathroom? And later if you run your tongue in Anita's cunt? Will home know anything of this? Will this know anything of home? And if we say no, how is it then that the woman before you in black clothes, with a streak of pink in her hair, was once the girl reminding you to take out your contacts before a crawfish boil, before your fingers grew sharp with spices, raffia dishes of potato and Jell-O salad appeared to anchor blown linen, before children's cries filled the air and fireflies emerged to sear the ripening canvas of twilight? How is it some people listen to the wind blowing through the vacancies of their hearts and hear a voice urging them on in flight, and some don't hear it at all?

And Amy must feel it too because you ask her, So babe, when's the revolution?

And she says, You know the funny thing about that word, Jesse, is where you wind up at the end of a revolution.

(IV)

Honesty is a lie, a more arduous self-deceit, like a white light that approached and seen up close decomposes into every color but itself. So begin the problems with ideas, with chitchat, with nuance. Nuance is a terror, a widow turned courtesan. Pillow talk in a bed that collects everything and nothing. It is a nice bed, of course. Certainty is no better.

On the day I think this—something of the sort—I am sitting in BWI waiting for a plane that will take me to another plane and so on in this manner to Berlin. It is a year and a few months since Anita left. She left just after my thirty-fifth birthday, the night she said, I'll do anything you want, just ask, and I took it as a provocation, the way it made itself out to be a present when it was really the request for a gift. There was a time it might have thrilled me, of course, the submissive possibility of it, but by then I didn't care. It rang only with Anita's desperation and her desperation with the pain I would cause her, which made me want to get out, leave at any cost, made *me* desperate and ready to punish her in advance for the pain she would make me feel in making me hurt her.

And still, we make messes at night to have something to do with the day.

Here is what I want, I said, meting out tequila in two glasses. I might have been a child holding a glass statuette—knowing not to drop it, knowing I would to watch it break. You're not going to like it though, I said. And that's how the role-play comes about. We curl Anita's hair with an old iron; it's darker than Amy's and her skin darker too. Outside, the whistling black winter is a banshee train caroming through the streets. The loft's light is bleak against the dark, the room as empty as a stoned mood. Anita sits at the paint-stripped vanity we found on Keswick one afternoon, the two of us out exploring the city in the idle improvisation of early love. We apply makeup, a little to lighten her complexion and return a hint of dewy youth—not that Amy ever wore much. We give her black jeans, a loose sleeveless top, a bra to hold her tits. She looks, when we've finished, like neither Amy nor herself, but maybe a monster's dream of human beauty, a child's crayon drawing of lurid glamour.

I don't know why you're doing this, she says. There's nothing in the rocks glass when she sets it down.

I don't know. It's exciting to me.

To pretend your girlfriend's someone else.

Christ—she's right of course, *I* am the monster—but *Christ*, aren't we past that? I say. Those ridiculous little stories about identity? I've got *mine*, and you've got *yours* . . . It's all such nonsense. What's the point of role-playing anyway?

To play a role, Anita says. Not someone else. When I don't respond she says, Look, just tell me how this isn't demeaning, okay? Just walk me through it.

It's my fucked-upness, isn't it? My perversion? If it's demeaning to anyone, it's demeaning to me.

You are such a fucking sophist, she says and laughs bitterly.

I clear her hair from her face. I'm sorry. Forget it. Forget Amy, I say. Be my high school crush from Bible study, that's all I wanted. And maybe it is, and maybe it isn't, but it would be too much to say it is exactly *Amy* I want when I sit Anita down at the desk with the Bible between us, caressing her as she reads, words from a book that says love does not dishonor others, is not self-seeking, and keeps no record of wrongs. That says so many ridiculous things it is hard to know what is contradiction and what is just violent longing for a world not our own. With my lips at her shoulders and the floral sweat of her hot skin in my nostrils, I say, Let's study something else. Okay, she says, what? God's image, I say and laugh. We were made in God's image, right?

She lets me lead her to the bed and lay her down. She lies there tremulous, rigid, wide-eyed in the role. And how do you enact the fallen moment? Sneak a finger up her pant leg and under the elastic of a sock. Pull it down. One, then the other. Touch her thigh. Feel her flinch. The waist of her jeans, the button at the fly. Undo, unzip. Take the jeans down around her ass so they come inside out. The skin below crimping to gooseflesh. Hairs rising together and flesh cold where her thighs bulge. Watch a tremor pass through her. Circle her and ease the shirt up over her body. Let your hands brush her sides. Her breathing is an audible wind. Pinch the bra clasp, let it go—let the fabric calve from her, nipples alive, tight. Circle each with a finger. Let her shudder . . . Underpants last. Take them down so slowly they grip and release each tangle of hair.

She breathes in.

And I stop.

I can't go on.

Something is off.

Or no, that's not right. Something is *gone*. But who can say, really, what founders on the dull thingness of a body? Who has ever been able to say? It is not what Anita says later, that I am in love with Amy and stopped when I saw it wasn't her. That keeps things legible, so that's where Anita goes. But it isn't so simple, not when desire turns in on itself, switches back, burrowing like roots into the hollow cavities of what inside us is hardest to fill. May never be filled. May never *want* to be filled. Or perhaps we make peace with those pockets of wind. Or perhaps we keep costuming strangers in our vain hopes. But either way, right? *Either way.*

Or let us go deeper for a moment because this is a religious story—that is one way to understand it—and every religious story is a love story, and every love story a story about childhood. For how are we to know if the noise we strike on after is more than the echo of our footfalls? Would it be too fanciful to say we are pearl divers in despoiled harbors? Blind archers among wet trees, forever hunting the phantom quarry of our perverse compulsions? The blackbird sits in the cedar-limbs, the arrows in our ribs. I have been single since she left.

This is not a *decision*, exactly, but perhaps the repetition of a choice. I paint. I clock in, out. Walk Peter, paint some more. Sometimes I call my mother, who tells me God is keeping her cancer-free. It's nice he's come around, I say. She is quiet on the other end—the beauty of inflection, or just after.

Hey, do you ever talk to him about me?

Sometimes, she says.

And what does he say?

He says you're stubborn.

Ha. You say that too.

We both know you very well.

Okay, it's not wrong. God is stubborn too. In our battle of wills we at least respect each other. He and I, She and I—whatever. Sometimes it's a blessing, sometimes a curse, this ability to keep to myself, to brook unhappiness before compromise. I don't miss Anita. I wish I missed her and I don't. I miss *missing*, if anything, the belief in the nonabsurdity of your life that seems to be a precondition for valid longing. I spend hours in the studio, watching time spill through the paint-flecked windows. Peter dozes in the geometries of puddled sunlight. And although I spend morning and evening here, those hours when the day reconstitutes itself most radically, not even this secondhand sense of movement can push forward my stone-bound spirit. I drink wine from a water glass, stop leaving the bottle in the kitchen. This is my hermitage, I think, my chrysalis, my penitence.

One day I decide to take a trip. It is a day quite a while later and it happens to be spring. Rather, it is spring the way it is sometimes spring, without warning and just everywhere, mild air charged with that unmistakable damp estrus. The breeze is fragrant against my skin, the day heavy with the prurient scent of flowering trees. Chalkboards line the sidewalks in front of cafés. People shout to one another across the street, flirting. And I feel something steal over me, a happiness so tepid it might be the smell of cut grass. A spiderweb falling across your face. The sense of someone's hand just above your spine. I will visit Berlin. I've always wanted to and now I will. I ask for the time off work, book a ticket, get a friend to watch Peter. And of all the people, on all the days, who do I run into at the airport, but Amy.

No fucking way.

Jesse.

She smiles, startled.

And then we hug. And then we say the things you do. *How crazy is this? How are you? What are you doing here?* She's on a layover, she says, heading home. Nothing serious, I hope. No, no, just a visit, she says. I have an hour. Get a drink? She hesitates, glances at her watch. What the hell. And as we walk to the bar and sit down, it might be that we are stepping out of the river of our lives, out of time itself, to watch it flow on without us from the banks.

That's how it feels. Amy pokes the olives in her drink with the little spear. It's so strange going home, she says. Everything's so different. Every*one*. How is her family? They're good, she says. Her sister had a baby. Her mom started a small business arranging flowers. Her father's teaching Greek and Hebrew at the college, if I can believe it.

Well, yes, I can, even if it is nonetheless strange to consider the accidents of history that lead to a man like Pastor Bob, in a town like ours, running his hands daily through the sands of those ancient worlds. But it is really the absence of strangeness in people's lives that with each passing year I have come to suspect. And accident must only be the wide-angle view besides, because here is Amy, and here am I, and it is so easy to pick up after all these years that we cannot be accidents or self-creations, the people we are. For an instant I feel the plunging acceptance of having been there from the beginning, witness to the earnest stupidity of every mistake, of being able to travel back along the violent current of life to the days when as small girls our bare feet slapped the lush, moist earth, when the sound of choirs were ribbons plaiting the air, and on damp tended lawns the voices of adults carried over, the very timbre of what was knowable and known. We remember things differently according to our purposes, of course. When my mother reminded me how as a child I liked to undress and break apart my dolls, she said it like it explained something primal and forbidding in my nature.

It's why I'm a serial killer, Ma.

I could have been more maternal, she says.

Amy wears pearl earrings, wool pants, a cream halter under a black cardigan. Her hair has lost its oxbow curls. Lord knows what she does to stay so thin. But it is less these things, I see, than that she appears to belong here now, flying off on a Tuesday with these businessmen and businesswomen. She *is* in business, she tells me. She works for a textbook publisher and lives in New York. With her partner of two years. She is happy. Life is quiet, manageable.

I thought you were a revolutionary, I say.

She sips her drink. Well, I still think we're fucked if that's what you mean.

No, it isn't.

What then do I want her to say? What happened, I suppose. I want her to tell me what happened.

Life, she says. Exhaustion. I don't know.

Not good enough.

Love?

Please.

I wanted to be happy, Jesse. Isn't that awful? Isn't that just awful? I wanted my *little* happiness, like everyone, and Sundays to read.

But it isn't happiness for which she needs to apologize. It isn't even an apology she's on the hook for. The mood comes to me un-bidden, the resurrection of old roles. I've had enough, it seems—two bourbons on an empty stomach—not to care much what I say. That sunburnt feeling is moving inside of me, like light breaking in double time over the crops.

So you're happy, I say. And less tired. And in love.

Yes, she says. I am exactly those things.

And what I would ask her, if I could say it in a way that made any sense, is whether this is one more costume in the pageant or if it's *her*.

In the stillness the airport noises rise up. Shoes ring against the polished floor. Outside, a plane takes off as soft and heavy as a dan-delion's seed head. Bye forever.

Amy has collected herself and changes tones. Did you tell me you were going to Germany? she's saying. That sounds *amazing*. It's going to be so fun. A lot better than going home. Ugh. I'm going for a while, actually, did I say? I got promoted and while we're tran-sitioning anyway I thought I'd take a little break. Three weeks. I mean, I won't be home the whole time, but still— She pauses. Isn't it strange how we do that? How we call it home after all these years?

But I'm only half listening. I'm thinking that were I to paint her in this moment I would have her in three-quarter view, looking down, wearing a look that shields her from me, a posture uneasy with the viewer's gaze. That gestures at the things we can't know from the outside, different angles on the impenetrable mapping its armor, nothing more. An écorché would be no help, of course, it is not a matter of anything material can touch. We must let the strange gods come and go. That light in Amy's eyes. Faint doublings in lacquer and liquid. The black rimming shadows of a day that seems already the intimate of its own regrets. And it is not so simple anymore to say who is purer or more stubborn, but what I understand just then is that Amy is *not* happy, and has never been. She is fighting a battle. I am fighting it too.

Tanner's Sisters

It had been two years since I'd last seen Tanner, when he called out of the blue to say he was back in town and wanted to get together. I was busy at the time. I'd just been made editor at the publishing house where I worked, and my girlfriend, Tess, and I had moved in together. It was a pleasant one-bedroom with a cutaway view of the river, and with everything going on I fancied myself in what we term, with equal parts self-satisfaction and error, a period of *growth*. Was it more than acquiescence, really? Gracious defeat? A sort of buying in or selling out? This line of thinking no doubt typifies someone with a child's idea of purity, and maybe I am such a person, but at the time of Tanner's return I was enjoying with some complacent satisfaction how my life looked to adult eyes. I did not want Tanner disrupting things, that is. We had never been such close friends, besides. But he was insistent and didn't even sound put off when I suggested an evening two weeks later. That was when we met, in the early spring at an outdoor café, and that was when Tanner told me this remarkable story.

I had first come to know him because we had the same thera-pist, Dr. Kirithra, a moonfaced Jungian with a sad smile who worked out of a church in the East Seventies. Tanner was leaving one day just as I was ducking in, or perhaps the other way around, and we said the awkward hello you do at the shrink's. It turned out later that he knew Travis and Clea, and my old friend Marilena—that Tanner knew *everyone*—and we met again at a dinner party and made a big joke of the whole thing at our expense. How typical, how neurotic, how *this city*. Tanner, loud, witty, and personable, struck me as exactly the sort of person who doesn't need a shrink but gets one anyway, because he can, because it seems like what an interesting, theoretically tormented person does. He had a job at a reputable bank and he came from money too. He spent lavishly and indifferently. Everything he did had an air of worldly apathy about it, the sort that shelters under a melancholic idea of itself, and I mistrusted the seriousness of people like this and so kept Tanner at arm's length.

But this is not to say he was without earnestness or charm. Tanner referred to his firm as "the well-represented conspiracy" and once memorably described their business model as "light-footprint imperialism." He wasn't dumb, he liked to talk this way, and if he didn't quit his job for whatever truth lay behind his words he owned up to his complicity grandly. In the evening, after hours, when work got out and the long city night buzzed to life, you would find Tanner at gallery openings and literary events, dressed in the hip tatters of the set, trying to work Agamben and Deleuze into his small talk. I joked that he only slept at night secure in the notion that he was deepening the contradictions of capitalism, but what was truer, no doubt, was that it took a certain and ironic consequence before anyone much cared what you had to say about *homo sacer* or your own moral implication. Such are the true contradictions we drown in, like grapplers in the ocean at each other's throats. Then, maybe a year after I met him, Tanner left his job to enroll in film school, and while I would hardly have called this a *risky* departure for Tanner, it did seem to validate some of the dreaminess and fitful integrity that had always appeared in him to swim just beneath the surface, fighting up for air.

Knowing Tanner as I had, then, when I saw him that night, sitting outside in the sweater weather of early April, it took me by surprise to find him looking a bit unkempt. His blond hair had grown out and darkened, a greasy mess atop hollow features. He seemed thin, his clothes hardly fit him. And although I had gotten to the café early, he was there when I arrived, fiddling with the silverware. I watched him for a minute before he spotted me. "Jonah," he said when he had. He smiled, rising, extending a hand, and then in a rush of unexpected warmth he pulled me in for one of those one-armed hugs that pass for affection among men my age.

"Tanner," I said, more stiffly than I meant to. His appearance set off a faint alarm in me. A subtle impression, I don't mean to overstate it. He seemed distracted, unmoored. And yet if I am being fully honest, alongside this apprehension I felt the opposite, a quiet triumph at seeing Tanner like this, for he had always struck me as a person destined for a luck he hadn't earned, the sort of person who inhabits the world so effortlessly that good fortune can't help but attach to him, and because of this I had at times taken his life as a measuring stick against my own, which was by comparison the life of an outsider, someone without Tanner's social grace or ease, without his ability to fold seamlessly into the currents around him. I felt vindicated seeing Tanner like this, even if knowing what I do now, having heard his story, it is a feeling I would rather disown. I am ashamed of it, and still, undeniably, it is what I felt.

"So," I said, breaking under his gaze, "long time. I heard you'd left the country."

"I did, I did," he agreed. "I only just got back."

"When was that?" I motioned to the waiter, who ignored us with a kind of élan.

"Oh, two or three weeks ago." He waved away precision with a hand, as though weeks were hardly a thing to keep track of. "Look—" He smiled, suddenly self-conscious. "I hope this isn't odd, my calling you, asking you to see me. It's been forever, I know. My sense of what's odd and normal is a bit off these days . . . But see, the thing is, you were my first thought when I got back. I thought, If anyone will understand what I've been through, it's Jonah. I can't say why. An intuition, I guess."

Privately, at this point, I was thinking something along the lines of "Oh, great." I am a person who has been taught to listen, to ask questions, and to respond appropriately. It is amazing how few people do any of these things, and I often feel, as a consequence, that my attention is taken advantage of. I didn't think of Tanner as a particularly bad offender, but I assumed this was what he meant: that I of all people would sit there and listen to him.

Our waiter had finally come and taken our order with—what else to call it?—stoic disgust. I asked for a Carménère and Tanner said, "Make it a bottle," waving away my objection and assuring me that he was buying. "Thank you," I said, meaning surely something closer to the opposite and wondering a bit vertiginously what we had to discuss that would take us an entire bottle.

"Well, here I am," I said. "You've got me."

"Got you . . . ," Tanner said vaguely, but it appeared to be the prompting he needed, because he asked me then whether I was reasonably *au fait* with his time in film school—his phrase—and I said yes, I supposed I was. "Well," he said, "it turned out I was too restless to make films. You remember how I was, hardly able to sit still. I *liked* films. I had *ideas*. Who doesn't, right? But you get the stray idea and think, Fuck, what an idea! I'm going to *do* this. And then you get down to it and it's a shit-ton of work. And you're on to the next idea before you've even roughed out the first. And pretty soon it dawns on you that *everyone* has ideas, and we're all just jerking off, mourning the falsehoods of youth or whatever. Because we've all been taught, right, every last one of us, that we have some unique *something* to offer up to the world. But c'mon. Let's be real."

His eyes brightened as he spoke, the gleam, I thought, of restless people who find refuge in the moment, the exigency of its impermanence, if I can say that. And while I noted the dirt under his

fingernails and the grease at his temples, building a case for my initial impression, in his words the old Tanner showed through, a person
whose wry and crude honesty, I had always thought, betrayed a
longing for things a bit nobler or more serious than he permitted
himself.

Our wine had come, but Tanner seemed not to have noticed.
"So what was I doing in film school?" he was saying. "I've asked myself quite a few times. Some people aren't searching for anything, I
think, but for the rest there's an emptiness, isn't there, and we're all
looking for things with that particular shape to fill it. Before I met
Rhea I'm not sure I even recognized any—what do I mean to say?—
lacuna. I thought I had things in hand, more or less. I thought a
certain brand of, I don't know, urbanity would see me through."

I felt then, drinking my wine too quickly, a brief stab of recognition in my gut, the way you do on hearing someone begin a sentence and knowing instantly what he will say. I do not mean I
anticipated Tanner's words or point, exactly, but I could see certain
lines of inquiry begin to braid, I felt an intimacy in the pattern, I
understood, however reluctantly, why Tanner had sought me out—
because without our quite saying it we do somehow communicate a
receptivity, or else impatience, when it comes to matters of the spirit.
Questions of the heart in crisis, dark nights of the soul—that sort of
thing. I remembered at an exhibition once seeing Tanner turn from
Bacon's *Pope Innocent X* with a strange, faraway look in his eye. I
had taken it for preoccupation at the time, but I wondered now
whether I might not have had the true pretense in Tanner, the pri-
ority of his allegiance, backward from the beginning.

"Rhea?" I said, perhaps a bit weakly.

"Oh, yeah, right. Rhea. Rhea Magnusson. This girl in film
school with me," Tanner explained. "I didn't know her at first. I'd
seen her around and hadn't paid her much mind. I didn't find her
pretty and she had this revolutionary-garb thing going that put
me off. You know, patriarchy *this*, hegemony *that*. How utterly

compromised we all are by Western culture. Not that it's wrong, you know, just so fucking humorless, so exhausting. All those little right sentiments to offer up in worthless atonement for our dreary privilege . . . That's the vibe I got anyway, and I kept my distance. Then we were assigned this project together—we had to make a short. Well, we met for coffee, and coffee turned into a walk, and the walk into dinner. I was spellbound. It wasn't so much Rhea as the manner of our conversation. Its honesty. Its sweetness, even. I had her pegged all wrong. She had this quality—I'd never met someone quite like her before—it was like she'd never been exposed to a single idea. Not that she was stupid, not at all. But like every idea we stumbled on had the force of revelation, a kind of *joy* almost. I mean, can you imagine, coming from the world we do, what a— you know—*baptism* it is to be treated as a source of mystery and insight? I didn't care if it was all a complicit delusion. Let's pretend we're special and all that. I didn't care! By the end of the night Rhea had come to seem beautiful to me. And I don't mean her soul was beautiful or some crap like that."

They made the short, Tanner told me. It was Rhea's story. She had it all worked out the next time they met: script, actors, shooting locations. The plot was incoherent—this was my impression— something tiresome and postmodern about an architect who designs the world's most beautiful skyscraper, or so some magazine calls it, finds he can't handle the success, and begins wandering the city at night. Later he's unable to locate his apartment building, or finds it's been destroyed—this isn't clear—and he winds up at the harbor, where a ship is waiting for him. He boards the ship, which soon departs for lands unknown. Tanner described the final shot in unnecessary detail (I'm skipping over a great deal) and said "To black" loudly, chopping a hand down to end the scene. He took a sip of wine, his first, and I said something uninspired about exile and anonymity.

"No, no." He waved me off. "Don't get the impression I think this is some great film. It's just . . . *Rhea*. She had an actor ready to play the architect, a ship lined up for us to film on. We got the project on, like, a Tuesday and by Thursday she was ready to shoot. You can't believe what an amazing person she is. I was just starting to realize it myself. She knew people everywhere, had friends all over town. People willing, *eager*, to do her favors. I thought it was a put-on, this—what do I mean?—*innocence*, this blithe . . . *capability*. So I introduced her to a few friends, Reece and Scooby, you know, people so oppressively hip there are about four square blocks in the world where they can exist, and she just melted them." He shook his head. "You had to see it."

This predictably annoyed me. So Tanner had a new girlfriend. *Great.* He would have a different one next week. And I was disposed against the curatorial approach to human beings, besides, strewing them about your life like oddments or knickknacks. This was Tanner's bag if it was anyone's, and people are not jokes or curiosities, not in my view anyway, although I don't mean to say we are ever very good at investing ourselves in another person's reality. That might be why, after all, I hadn't realized that this was a different Tanner, why I still felt the need to bring him down a notch when I said, "Well, how did this Rhea wind up in film school? Where did she come from? Who was paying the bills?"

I sounded peevish to myself, I admit, brimming with the sort of pedantry I loathe at least as much as our mythologizing impulse. Tess has said that if we didn't snag on ourselves from time to time she has no idea what a self really is, and I grant this notion a certain truth. It takes on a *mise-en-abyme* quality if you look at it too long, but yes, maybe there are times to forgive ourselves our inveterate pettinesses, those dead limbs of personality we're always hoisting about into their awkward, casual poses.

"Oh, didn't I say?" Tanner grinned. "But you're the storyteller, after all."

I wasn't, I hadn't been for many years, but Tanner had a charming faith, I think, that underneath everything we were all artists manqués. And maybe he was right, maybe the soil below the placid lawns of everyday life was always rich and black, rife with a chaos of growth and rot that called out for acknowledgment or cultivation. Nonetheless, I had done what I could to let the question alone, to tend the lawn, see the books bound, and gaze out from the safe distance of the museum floor. And now I could feel Tanner dragging me gently but insistently from the safety of this firm shore. I wasn't even sure he knew.

"Rhea was Danish, see, or half Danish. Their mother was Chilean," he said. "Rhea and her sister were born in Demark, then moved here as girls. Their father got some big fucking appointment. The Neue Galerie, I'm pretty sure it was. Arts administration. You should have seen their place: just off Lex, modern, minimalist, all white impenetrable surfaces, you know, but then Groszes and Kirchners on the wall. They had a Schiele too, I think.

"I first saw it when Rhea brought me by one afternoon. We were wandering around town and she needed to change. We were in her room. She didn't send me out or ask if I minded, just started changing—her pants, her shirt—and almost out of habit, I guess, I went over and kissed her. She didn't move away. She seemed to go along with the kiss, but when I pulled back, her look was ambiguous, something between surprise and amusement, like she didn't know what I was doing or else knew so well that it amused her. The predictability of it maybe. But then I'm not sure Rhea expected or anticipated a single thing in her life. That was her charm. She took things as they were, without apparent judgment, so much so that it didn't seem strange when we had sex right then and there. Or if anything was strange it was only the look of baffled amusement on her face, like I was taking her on a long detour and hadn't told her the reason. Well, we finished, and I got dressed, and she got dressed, and as I left the room I turned to say something and almost walked right into a young woman sort of loitering where the hall turned.

"I collected myself enough to say hello. I'd thought we were alone, I don't know why, and in any case the look the woman was giving me was—I don't know. Horror? Disgust? Rhea came around from behind me, smiling.

" 'Elena,' she said. 'Tanner, this is my sister, Elena. Elena, Tanner.'

" 'Pleased to meet you,' I said, putting out a hand which she regarded briefly as if I'd offered her a piece of rotting fruit.

"Elena turned to Rhea. 'I have to run down to the pharmacy.'

" 'Do you want Tanner to take you?' Rhea asked.

"She looked me up and down with a more moderated disgust. 'Fine,' she said.

"Well, sometimes you don't ask questions, you know. You want to think of yourself as someone who can say yes without asking why, who can take a break from living under the sovereignty of clear intentions, and this must have been one of those times because soon we were riding the elevator down together in silence. I was wondering how two sisters managed to look so unalike, Rhea with her sunken, strung-out mien, her messy gold hair, and Elena, very fresh looking, with drum-tight skin over wide, gently tented features, her jet-black hair cut short.

"I was on the verge of saying something dull to make conversation when Elena asked whether Rhea had told me about the time they ran away as girls. I said she hadn't, no. 'Well, we weren't girls exactly,' Elena said. 'Teenagers, I suppose, or I was on the cusp. We used to summer way out on Long Island. "Land of the insufferables," Rhea called it. It really was awful. Papa used to make us wear these little dresses and stand around at cocktail parties listening to adults act like the most *enormous* children. God, we hated it, smiling at these little factoids about ourselves that weren't even true—"Elena just *loves* Satie!"—while old men sort of pawed at us. It gives me chills just . . . But anyway, this particular summer Rhea had befriended a fisherman she thought would ferry us to Block Island in the middle of the night.

" 'A ridiculous plan, but very Rhea if you know her. She's been my sister my entire life and I don't begin to, but she's also the most amazing person I've ever met. Well, the day came. We packed a small duffel and struck out in the dead of night. Two small girls in flip-flops and shorts that didn't reach mid-thigh. Can you imagine! It was a steamy night. We walked along Umbrella Beach, watching the waves roll in under the moon. Leave it to Rhea to read the lunar calendar and leave the rest to fate. Of course her friend never came. After waiting ages, we finally trekked back to town, where we found the streets covered in mist.

"'I was so expecting it to happen, I saw later, expecting it while also not entertaining the possibility, that when the truck pulled over in front of us my first thought was that I was in a dream. Only a dream could so perfectly bring forth the object of an unconscious fear. But what I think now is that dreams may simply be preparation for those moments we have to float away from ourselves. A man got out of the truck, a thin man, not quite old, unshaven. *Greasy.* I remember him glistening in the faint light. He smiled at us, a sneering smile, and I glanced at Rhea, expecting to see my own dread mirrored on her face. I was shocked instead to find her smiling, a smile that today I would call coy but that then I experienced as a kind of annihilation. It's difficult to explain . . . There was no *place* for me in that smile. "John," she said. "Hello there, girlie," the man said. He grinned and reached out his hand for Rhea's, which she gave him, and he helped her up into the truck. He turned to me. "We want company?" he asked, at which point Rhea, in really the most bored voice you can imagine, said, "C'mon, I'm thirsty. Let's go."

"'The man gave me a last look, laughed, and turned to leave. It was only once the truck had pulled away that I realized I'd peed myself—just everywhere, pee soaking my shorts, running down my leg . . . The night had turned cold and I was shivering as I started to walk, stumbling along. I felt, not terror, but something beyond terror, a numbness or stiffness—that even if the kindest stranger stopped I would be unable to speak. I had the sudden strange jealous thought, which I've never understood, that trucks would always stop for Rhea and never for me. I wanted—it's an ugly feeling, but true—I wanted to be at one of Papa's cocktail parties, to stand around and smile and have nothing to *do*. I thought this the whole way home, shivering. I will wear the prissy dresses, I thought. Anything you ask me to.

"'I have never known how to *act*, you see. I lack the gift of pretense and am incapable of lying, even those little half-truths with which we affix a story to our lives. Papa says I can be literal-minded to the point of idiocy, and the next morning when they asked me where Rhea was I said I didn't know. Which was *true*, but hardly comprehensive. I was terribly sick. God, was I sick. For *weeks*. I soaked through the bedding constantly. I had visions of my mother singing to me, stroking my hair. Only very gradually did I get better.

"'One day, quite a while after, Rhea came into my room. I hadn't seen her since the night we'd run away and I was surprised to find her looking so happy and well. She had a nasty-looking scar on her arm—quite long, perhaps you've seen it. I ran my finger over it, but I didn't ask. Later she said to me, or maybe she said it in a dream, or who knows, but I've always connected the two things, she said, "Someone is always afraid. So just make sure it's never you." Honestly, there are days when I think an alien ship must have come down and put Rhea in Mother's belly because any other explanation seems less likely.'

"We were in Duane Reade by then, paying for what Elena called 'Mother's pills.' I walked her home and when we got there she said, 'Here,' took out a notecard and pen, and wrote her name and phone number against the wall of the building. 'I don't get out much,' she said, 'but you can call me.'

"Well, the weeks went by. I had coursework to do, but I couldn't be bothered. I was following Rhea around. She was always heading off to neighborhoods I'd never been to, reading books to old women, running intake at free clinics, helping set up stalls for street fairs. I hung around like some mooning poet on the foreshore. I had no clue what I was doing. I just knew there was something essential here, something I had to keep exploring. Rhea and I were sleeping together, but it wasn't love. No. I kept sleeping with her, I think, to reassure myself that I still could. I feared terribly that one day she would say we had to stop or say something crushingly banal like Where is this going? or Would you say we're a couple now? but she never did.

"So I felt stable—*just*—felt perversely that this held me together when the rest of my life was fraying at the seams. A ludicrous feeling, this security, and if I'd known then who Rhea was I wouldn't have managed it. Because of course I still believed, on some shadow level, that sex was a ritual of possession, a covenant, as insane as that is . . . And why Rhea? Your guess is as good as mine. I had never felt this compulsion about anything. I had been a person drifting across the surface of life without realizing that at some point you fall in. And Rhea was my plunge, I suppose. Maybe because she was my opposite—someone who didn't believe life had *any* surface, for whom each person and every moment was an alluring depth. I don't know. All I can say is that in her ingenuousness I saw, I *felt* I saw, that everything I had been before had been some fraction of a lie.

"Not long after, Rhea told me Elena was hurt that I never called. So I did. She had her own line and picked up every time at the end of the second ring. 'Hello?' she'd say, like it might be anyone calling. And she was never busy, never had to do something or get off the phone. She told me stories about her family, mostly, vaguely fantastical things set in Denmark, which I came to imagine full of bright painted buildings by the water, caught in the low, slanted light of suns that took all day to set.

"'Mother and Papa should never have happened,' she said. 'They were like ridiculous proud beasts who encounter each other on a path: each is still waiting, I think, for the other to step aside. But then it's also true that it was Papa's foundation that brought Mother over from Chile. She was an artist, see—a good one, I don't know. Papa says she hasn't worked in all the time he's known her, and what she did during her fellowship is a mystery to all. She stayed on in Copenhagen afterward, that we know.

"'Papa would see her around, sitting in parks, staring out to sea. One day he went up to her and asked how she was and where she was staying. She shrugged, and to make himself clear, because they had only broken English in common, he said, "Where do you go at night?" She shook her head in incomprehension. "Where do you go?" she said.

"'When he realized what she was saying he decided to take her in. I doubt he could have said why. Frankly, the idea of my parents even speaking to each other is beyond me, but somehow, over the weeks, a romance developed. They really couldn't have been less alike. Papa was always ambitious, successful. Mother is like a lost creature from the spirit world. Nevertheless, in two months' time, Papa had stopped showing up to work, quit his job, and the two moved to a cottage in the north overlooking the sea. To hear Papa tell it he spent the years up there writing poems. That's where they had Rhea and me.

"'Who can say what finally made Mother go crazy. Maybe she was always crazy, or maybe crazy is just the simplest word for something else. We moved back to Copenhagen when we were young. Papa returned to work and Mother went away for a time, then came back to us very different. She had her own room, which she never left, and after dinner Rhea and I would play there for an hour or so, on a thick rug with gold tasseling, while she sang to us. Chilean folk songs or so I've had to assume. Neither of us speaks the language.

"'Our parents' relationship remained a mystery. Papa ignored Mother so completely that I sometimes thought only Rhea and I could see her. Then one night we mysteriously awoke together with the same premonition to creep through the apartment to Mother's room. The door was ajar when we got there, and I'll never forget what I saw. Papa was crying in Mother's lap. She had his head on her knees and was stroking his hair, humming something soothing, staring out the window at the moon. We watched for a while, transfixed, before finally tiptoeing back to our room. In the morning it was as if none of it had happened. Papa continued to ignore Mother and to tease the help in his airy, caustic way. We moved to the States not long after.'

"The stories came out over many weeks of talking. I would sleep with Rhea, wake to find her gone, and call Elena from Rhea's room. Elena was just down the hall, but it never occurred to us to talk in person. One evening, eating dinner with their father, it came to me that I no longer remembered the last time I had left the apartment. It was a big place by this city's standards, and it struck me that there was no longer anything outside that required my attention. No friends to meet up with. No courses to attend. My parents had written me off long ago, I figured. My life, it seemed, had shrunk down to the dimensions of this place, this family, these strange sisters.

"We were eating a butterflied lamb prepared by the Magnussons' cook, Margarite. Their father, who always showed up to dinner very soigné, in a tailored suit, his tie knot undone just so, ate in a brisk, formal manner and seemed to accept me at the table without surprise. 'Tanner,' he might say, 'tell me. Are you a man of the world or a poet?' I probably told him I didn't know, that I had always wondered and often felt myself in a sort of purgatory between the two, because he said, 'Ah, yes. There is a fifth column inside us all, *nicht wahr*?'

"I didn't know what he meant, but I asked, if such neat divisions could be made, what he considered himself.

"'I am a man of the world, Tanner. For now at least,' he said. 'I must believe in all of its *things* . . . Broccolini. Bushwick. Bikram yoga. And that's just the *b*s. It's breathtaking, really, the things one is expected to take seriously these days.'

"I must have ventured that he felt inauthentic, because without hesitation he added, 'Yes, yes, I am a fraud through and through. I don't deny it, I celebrate it! A buggy-whip maker in the age of SUV limousines. What is one to do, what *can* one do, but embrace the gross anachronistic fiction of one's own existence? Smile in public, put on a good show. Fine and good. But at the end of the day a gentleman is not a hero to his valet, isn't it so, Tanner?'

"I wanted him to say more, but just then Margarite came in to ask how we were enjoying the meal.

"'What shall I tell you, my dear,' he said. 'You surpass yourself. You are the progeny of gods—and no minor divinity but the sort that springs fully formed from the skulls of monsters! What is left to say? What are words next to the unknowable thing itself? Oh, they will sing songs of you when you are dead.'

"'I know what I'll do when you're dead,' Margarite said under her breath.

"'Very good.' He laughed. 'Very good.' When she had gone he turned back to me. 'And so, Tanner,' he said, 'you enjoy the company of my daughters, do you?'

"'I do,' I said. 'They're remarkable.'

"'Ha, yes. "Remarkable," was it?' He dabbed his mouth with his napkin and sat back in thought. 'Well, you have my blessing,' he said, 'but I will not do you the generosity of my warning.' He checked his watch, a practiced move to free it from his sleeve, out of no more than habit perhaps, a certain rhythm of preoccupation. He smiled and said, 'Margarite really *did* outdo herself tonight, don't you think?'

"That was the first night that Rhea did not return. I lay on her bed, ill at ease. Feeling restless, at last I got up to walk around. The apartment was more expansive than I had realized. Tight staircases I hadn't known were there, doors opening onto skinny branching halls. I was absently inspecting little *objets*, decorative curios on the shelves and coffee tables, when at the end of a desk I came across a manuscript, neatly stacked and bound in string. It must have been hundreds of pages in all, although it wasn't numbered. I undid the string and settled down at the foot of a recamier to read. This is how it began: 'Imagine you speak to fallen angels in a dead language invented by living statues. You are an adding machine woven from blades of grass; this explains your friendlessness, and your comfort with high-caliber handguns. If I told you the dimensions of our lives were one greater or one fewer than you suppose, would you cancel your package vacation to the Dutch Antilles? Would it matter that I lived in bogus clouds of cast-off aerosols, teaching birds to dismantle power lines?'

"It went on like this for pages, mesmerizing, impenetrable. At some point I must have fallen asleep because the next thing I knew Elena was standing over me. She took the pages from my lap, set them aside, and undressed in the deliberate way of someone alone, folding her clothes as she took them off. I hadn't seen her since that first day. Maybe I had forgotten her sad beauty, or maybe our conversations had led me to invest greater allure and poignancy in her body, the thin swayback figure, its marble skin untouched by sun. She hadn't a hint of muscle, the breasts of a boy, a fatiguing melancholy in her sloe-eyed gaze, but she was beautiful, I thought, and we made love, or whatever you care to call it, right there on the carpet, in that corner of the apartment I'd never seen.

"Rhea woke me with a finger over her lips a few hours later. I was at first confused to see Elena dozing next to me, then I remembered what had happened and searched Rhea's face for any clue to her state of mind. It was its typical mask of amusement. She seemed herself but just to be sure, thinking, you know, *I could interpret between you and your love if I could see the puppets dallying*, I asked if she wasn't upset.

"'About what?' she said. Only then did I notice she had a heavy jacket on and a duffel bag over her shoulder.

"'Quo vadis?'

"She laughed. 'Denmark?' She said it like we'd discussed it all before.

"I was stunned. 'When did that happen? Does anyone know?'

"'Of course,' she said and looked at me sweetly. 'Take care of Elena, won't you? She's a little directionless at the moment.'

"Time began passing more quickly after that. Elena stayed

indoors all day, but I began to venture out through the city. I walked the same streets I had since childhood and hardly recognized them. I didn't know what was happening to me. I've spent my entire life here and, as you no doubt know, this place teaches you nothing if not a profound blindness to the strangeness and horror of people's lives. We live to validate for one another the insane pretext that this is normal and right, and what are we all searching for but some moment when the world's gaze falls on our gross, petty lives and says, How *special*. How *hiply* thrown together. How baroquely *casual*. I don't know ... I felt crushed, just crushed, by the profligacy of a single block, the effort of it, the florid misfortune and exhausting Kabuki of other people's lives. I could scarcely pass someone on the street—young, old, men, women—without falling neck-deep into the idea that at that very moment, like me, they were taking some internal stock of their frustration and misery, of where they stood next to their most extravagant and private dreams. And what were their dreams? Or the trials of their daily lives? Was it presumptuous and condescending to think myself happier than them? But I didn't. I *didn't*. I was *not* happy. I was just young, vital, credentialed, moneyed ... I am not the first person to think these things, clearly, but if it's patronizing to pretend to understand the trials and miseries of other people's lives, it is no doubt worse to use this as an excuse never to try. And the greater misery seemed, suddenly, the soulless disregard of people like me—anyone really—and not for other people's sakes, but for our own. We had reached an inflection point, I thought, the contradictions we had to live with were too great, and in the interest of obscuring them we had abused language to the point that we could no longer speak to one another. We could scarcely leave our tribes.

"What does this have to do with Rhea and Elena? I don't know. I really don't. Except they began to seem a refuge, a corrective of some sort. Was this crazy? I mean, you've been listening. What had they done but make me unfit to live? Unable to countenance the petty, impoverished, glib, bankrupt, unfeeling, and passionless world that stalked our streets and invaded our hearts? And still they felt like some faint hope amid the spires verging up into the sky, some forgotten possibility under the soles of our feet."

I *was* listening, of course. I had been. I thought I knew the hope Tanner meant and the peril that lived inside it. Had I found a voice to speak just then I might have reminded him that it is the nature of a refuge to leave us less fit to live and that we do not blinker ourselves for the fun of it. It is out of necessity, rather—the necessity of living within ourselves, feeding our hungers, crediting the worthless strength of our emotions. In the days before I gave up my artistic ambitions there were moments, I thought, when I had caught a glimpse around the blinders, and what I saw was the landless gray expanse of a northern sea, that emptiness of pewter ribbed in wind and sun. There was no channel marker I could find. No shore to crawl up on. I simply could not concede my life anymore, my centrality to it, nor the privilege I gave to the insular language in which we invented ourselves, the endless stories that, if each were only a degree off true north, put end to end added up to a world turned upside down. It seemed to me my only choice was between complicity in this boundless small perjury and the sort of honesty that becomes self-negating.

"I couldn't help thinking of Rhea's smile in the weeks that followed," Tanner continued. "How had she given me to Elena so peaceably? Of course maybe she cared for me little in that way or cared for Elena in a superlative sense, loving her sister's happiness more than her own. But I thought there was something more here too, that perhaps this augured a new relationship to the world of things, a correction to the awful harm embedded in our idea of possession.

"But I didn't have it in me to go as far as the sisters. After a month Elena said to me, 'You miss her. Go.'

"'I'm happy with you,' I said, although this wasn't exactly true.

"'Look,' Elena said a little sadly. 'Rhea and I made a trade-off early on, not explicitly, but in the way siblings do, and perhaps especially sisters. I agreed to see what was in front of me, see things for what they were, so that Rhea wouldn't have to. So that for her, meaning and motive never split, if you understand what I mean. So that language stayed intact. But it means she doesn't keep some part of herself for her alone, do you see, the way the rest of us do. And for my part I am too disabused to believe a lie, even a small one, and I would rather you leave than start telling me falsehoods. In the end you can't fool me anyhow."

"So I did go. I left. I went to Copenhagen. I got a studio in Nørrebro, across the canal from the center of town. I started painting. I lived on almost nothing, coffee, bread, a little herring. I walked the city and painted. Rhea was shooting a new film, documentary, soundless. She followed foreigners through the city filming them, immigrants, men smoking in bead-curtain cafés, professors at chalkboards, cannery workers, roustabouts on the docks. I spent my nights with her, watching the footage she had shot. I found it mesmerizing, the *neutrality* of its attention, and although it was always silent I often thought I heard a sound running through it all the same, an expectancy at the edge of silence, the pregnancy of a fermata, a sound like wind passing through apertures in the distance.

"I was painting color fields during the day, gradients of bleeding hue tinged with washes and drizzles. Derivative, amateur AbEx, but I enjoyed it. I walked through Strøget at dusk, a ghost among the waves of purpose. I had a vague notion that I could fade slowly into the latticework of the world, like an image dissolving in the evening light. And I might have, had a disarming thing not occurred.

"I was settling down to paint one day when I realized I'd left a book of mine at Rhea's. Blake's engravings. I wanted to steal a color arrangement of his for the piece I was working on, so I hiked back across town and let myself into her apartment. I was wiping my feet in the foyer when it came to me that something was wrong. I don't know whether it was more than an intuition, but I felt compelled to creep through the apartment to Rhea's room, where I found the door ajar, a soft, plangent music issuing from inside. I peeked in. There were Rhea and a young woman, naked in bed. The woman was ugly—truly hideous, I realized later—but all that I re-marked on in that moment was the look of earnest hope on her face, a look I recognized, that stopped me cold. I froze, or rather I saw the part of me supposed to feel anger freeze, like a person at the periph-ery of a black hole, and moving away from that person, floating away to a different vantage, I felt instead a kind of joy, a sense of possibility embodied in the act, written on her face, and ferrying them beyond the jealousies of time. Just then Rhea caught my eye. She smiled at me, and I . . . smiled back. It's strange to tell you, but it's the truth. Before that figure posed at the edge of eternity recalled me, I smiled. Before the suspension broke, before the bardo state collapsed, for a few seconds Rhea and I grinned at each other. I don't think I've ever been present with another person as deeply as I was in that moment. And then, like a plunging anchor that finally con-sumes its rope, the childish hurt and anger I had been expecting returned to me, tugged suddenly at my stomach, and I shut the door and left quickly, feeling very stupid and weak.

"For a long time I walked. I walked to the edge of the Øresund, to the water, where I watched for hours as the day moved to comple-tion, a coarse gray sheet shaken out in a motion so slow you didn't notice when it settled over you, entombing the light beyond. I thought many things. I thought I had heard the Sirens' call, driven bereft against the rocks, drunk on beauty and madness—or, fuck beauty—drunk on the kaleidoscope of involuted moods, the infi-nite divisions within everything, the moods within their song for which we have no name. I had been crippled in the deepest way, I felt—past the point of *wanting* to be healed. But then not entirely, for within me still was some corrupted anger, of righteousness or me-ness, some ridiculous self-importance. And sure enough, when I got home that night, I found I hadn't thrown out my credit cards or passport. I still had an old phone with friends' numbers on it, my parents' numbers. My hair was a disaster, but none of it was hope-less. I had never committed, see, never stepped out with both feet.

I had been *playacting*. I could get on a plane and come back. And now that I'm back, confused, adrift, in some sense unviable as a person, I have this one thing, I know this one thing about myself: I am a playactor and will never be anything more."

Tanner fell silent. My bladder was going to burst, I feared, but I was past the point of interrupting and hadn't signaled to our waiter in forty-five minutes. Our wine was gone, as was the water in my glass, and although the evening had grown cold I noticed that my back, pressed against the iron chair frame, was coated in sweat. It is not hard to say what I felt, although in another sense it is hard to say it in fewer words than it took Tanner to tell. I had the familiar feeling of being a cracked vessel refilled by blind servants. And although this was not a pleasant self-knowledge to possess, I reconciled myself, to carry the metaphor further still, with the notion that all this water was being gathered to drown a prisoner who was free to leave. Which is all to say *better* cracked than whole.

But maybe I am just more oblique than Tanner because I have more cause for self-protection. Or maybe I have lived longer in the jeopardy he describes. *Or.* Sometimes I think we might define ourselves by such simple words—"and," "or"—and that I merely side with paralysis over fabrication.

"So you're back," I said.

Tanner looked at me sadly, seeing, I guess, that I did not understand or couldn't say aloud how much I did, that this is what it meant to playact, to have bought in or sold out—never acknowledging how much you understood.

"I'm not back," he said.

He got up, laid some amount of money on the table. I didn't count. I didn't offer to chip in.

"What, is that it?" I said.

"I'm tired." He looked away. "Another time."

"Soon though," I said.

"Sure," he said. "Soon."

When I returned from the bathroom Tanner was gone. I wouldn't see him again for many months.

When I did see Tanner next he had begun to fill back in. His hair was clean, his scruff shorn to a handsome stubble. The clothes he wore looked expensive and fit. He joked about our previous meeting, saying how he'd been in a state. "Overwrought" was the word he used, I think, and he described the intervening months as a *rappel à l'ordre*. We were at some insignificant party, on the roof, drinking cocktails out of Mexican glasses and gazing across the river at the city that loomed above. I watched Tanner as he laughed and made his way through the crowd, watched as he leaned in to make a joke or bent to catch a private word whispered in his ear. He seemed his old self and so I was surprised, later, when I saw him gazing at a print—*Ruggiero Freeing Angelica*, I believe—to catch a far-off look in his eye, a look he didn't mask right away on registering my glance but shared with me, letting it settle briefly in the wry despair of officers who, without a word, tell each other they know their city will fall. It was too much for me, this brief window on the shoreless sea we carry around inside us. I said my goodbyes hurriedly and went home, settling in the living room as voices in the dark around me wove a thin fabric from the tatters of what we have been taught to call our lives.

Perhaps you will not be surprised to learn—perhaps it is already clear—that Tanner and I had ceased to be different people. We are different in the sense that we look different, have different Social Security numbers and addresses, and that I never met the Magnusson sisters. But in another, and the more important, sense, of course I did, I *have* met them, and it has been the great joy and misfortune of my life.

My memory is not perfect, nor would I hope it to be, for if my perception isn't either this would simply be the faithful transcription of a mistake. But I can still hear the voices that spoke to me in the dark living room that night saying, "Once, when you thought she was caring for you, your mother was walking the fault lines of a perilous terrain. When you see the spires fall, you will know we are singing to you. It is a melody constructed from the martyrdom of a swimming pool filled with drowned cowards. The earth was ripped open so that you could fall in. It is we, the sisters, come. Come join us at the bottom, and sing!"

Summer 1984

There is a gun in Act I. I have put it there. I am one and a half when this happens, when Michaela's story takes place, an age when the literature tells me the child's personality has begun to emerge, a sense of independence, and the imagination too. When children first pretend to be people they are not, characters from books and movies, and when they may begin to mimic their caretaking on dolls. Because I am a boy-child I have no dolls. Many years later I am fascinated by the claim that "violence is essentially the form of the quest for identity." I leave the conclusions to you. At one and a half, my parents tell me, I was curious, baffled, intent. I liked car rides, the quiet displacements beyond the glass. The simple magic of vision, the reality of space. I liked going home.

MICHAELA'S STORY (AS TOLD BY HER)

I signed on with D.H. for a second summer because it was a sure thing and I needed the money if I was going to Nicaragua. All summer my dreams would be dark coiled things sprung from a wilderness I didn't, or hadn't yet taken the time to, understand. I was back from college, living at my mom's, trying to get through Paulo Freire. I was reading too much news. Central America had become an obsession with me, I couldn't get enough. I read articles on breaks at work, bought magazines and dailies on my nightly walks. There wasn't much else to do. My sister Tatiana—the youngest after me—had finally done what Kiki, Viola, and Erin had all done, which was to leave. She wanted to go to the far side of the continent and ride motorcycles through redwood forests with guys named Bruce, it turned out. So that left me. I was glad D.H. took me on. Tatiana and I had set a record the summer before, painting four dorm rooms in a day, and I guess that was résumé and interview.

I worked with Mellie wallpapering the first week. Mellie was twenty-three. She put me in mind of a tomboy who had grown up prettier than anyone expected and I'm not sure she understood her effect on people. A lot of what she told me had to do with her boyfriend Judson and their sex life, a semipublic affair inflected by some exhibitionist hankering. Mellie could be racist too, but these failings aside, and I certainly counted Judson a failing, she was my favorite on the crew. I granted her a good soul that had come under a bad influence, which was probably granting her too much, but I liked her so that's what happened.

A Mellie vignette: *Sometimes we'll be out, and Judson'll tell me to go wait for him in the stall. Just get ready and wait. A few minutes later he'll come in. I'll be turned away, but I'll know it's him by how he's breathing. I'll feel his eyes on me. It's the most exciting thing, Michaela, that moment, right before anything happens.* She'll have stopped working, the seam roller in her hand hovering at her shoulder. Her gaze will drift to the window, like out there somewhere is her real life . . . *I'll feel him looking, and sometimes my heart just catches it's beating so hard. Do you know what that's like, just surrendering like that?*

Show me again how to get the bubbles out without it creasing, I might say, just to say something. And Mellie would give me a look like my big sisters used to and say, Ah, you're too young to understand.

But that didn't seem to me to be the problem. I kept imagining the poor person trapped in the stall next to theirs, listening to the bullish exhaust of Judson's appetite. Clearly that was part of what thrilled them, though, the possibility of being discovered, overheard, *seen*. I was back to painting the next week, anyway, and that was the end of Mellie's stories. I had to work with Bobby, but otherwise I preferred painting, which was mindless and voiding. We'd been contracted to do the sports facilities that summer, the basketball complex, the doorframes, chairs, the mascot logo at center court. Don't let that idiot near it, D.H. told me, meaning Bobby, meaning the logo. So for a few days it was just me and that mischievous grinning face, eye to eye.

The coach stopped by one day to see how we were making out. It was pretty decent of him, I thought, given his status in our town, which compared favorably to the Messiah. He had a growth on his head. It caught me off guard and for a second I thought it was a trick of the light, but then I looked again, without really meaning to but also shamelessly, and there it was, wan and hideous like a tree fungus. He flinched. His hand leapt to his head and he brushed his hair back.

Let's hope this heat breaks, he said.

Oh! I said, which wasn't what I meant to say.

Our work began early and ended in the late afternoon. Every day at four we trickled into the basement room by the lockers: me, Mellie, Bobby, Carl, Radar, Stan, Ellen S., and Ellen V. Because we couldn't leave until everyone was there, we sat around chitchatting, changing our shoes, and watching Bobby pick the calluses on his feet. Most days I rode home with Carl, but when luck turned against me I was stuck with Radar and Stan.

They were cousins of some sort, that's what they said anyway, but if they shared anything it was an omission, I thought, the absence of a trait necessary to the composition of a full human. They are missing the chromosome on which God placed love, Carl once said, seeming to pluck the idiotic phrase from the ticker tape homily of his mind. Radar was short and round, Stan tall and gaunt. Together they made a backcountry Laurel and Hardy. When I rode with them, always in the back, they seemed to forget I was there and told stories that might've even made Mellie blush.

So down to the motel, Radar said on the Tuesday after a long weekend, me and Derek are out drinking beers by the pool. And there's this girl, she wants to go swimming. She's maybe eleven or twelve, I don't know, and the thing is, and you can see where this is going, she doesn't have a suit. Well so the mother says, Ah, you don't need none, just go in. And Derek and me's looking at each other like, did we just hear right? We've maybe had a few at this point. The girl's stripping, Derek's cracking. And thing is, she like . . . *likes* it, you can tell. She's, like, *showing off.* Stan hit a fist against the doorframe. What's the mother thinking? Fuck, said Radar, for all I know they're nudists. His voice took on a sudden sober conviction. I'll tell you this though, boy—she gave us a *show.* Bet you saw a little pink button, Stan said. Shit, said Radar. Size of my pinkie.

It amazed me in those days how quickly my presence, my very existence, seemed to disappear from people's minds. I got to the point of daydreaming so deeply, dreams empty of any content, that I began to think myself some astral walker, present but on a different plane, and when people spoke to me it often took me long seconds before I could remember how to speak. And yet even as I entered states of attention so total and immediate as to purge my mind of thought, I found I could later recall what had taken place around me, indexed with emotions like the colors on file tabs. And what I felt recalling Radar and Stan, with the benefit of some distance, was not disgust, though they were gross, but the tragic smallness of what they needed and still could not get, the smallness of their need next to the need that drove others not so very far away, the people whose stories I read daily in the news, to martyrdom and murder in conflicts that stretched into other lifetimes. I don't mean Radar and Stan were pathetic. I mean I couldn't reconcile the scales. And I knew nothing of sex then. I'm still mystified by its true nature, whether it is an itch to scratch, an exercise in power, in pleasure, a form of togetherness, of renewal, an act of reckless hope, slavery, or freedom. All I feel confident saying, I suppose, is that you act differently when there are eyes on you. You undress differently observed.

My mother worked odd hours at the furniture factory. She was never around when I got home, so after checking on Mad Max, the screech owl that flew freely in our house that summer, and sometimes picking a cicada for him from the pear tree out front, I set out into the endless summer evening, cutting through the developments next door, that creeping mold of selfsame houses and curving roads, crossed guardrails and culverts, dirt lots and light-industrial blight, past baseball fields where kids called to one another in the hot, low sun and the dust rising from the infield was gold powder, all the way to the rutted path that traced our little river, a river of rocks that summer, which I would follow until it turned off into the nicer part of town.

It was there, in one of the cafés, among the antique shops and sycamores that I first saw her. She was a woman of some dignified middle age, in an elegant sleeveless dress the color of the sky before, or maybe after, a storm. She had short hair, silver earrings, a cup of tea before her, and a piece of white cake she was eating slowly. Looking back I don't know whether it was her appearance that made me glance at what she was reading or what she was reading that sensitized me to the air of loneliness, or incongruity, that had settled around her. It was a magazine article I'd read a few days before on El Mozote, about which great controversy then raged. It was enough, anyway, for me to take note and then recognize her a week later in front of a house, trimming sundrops and coral bells in gray gloves. That was early evening. The sun coursed down like a river, washing over her and the house's weathered brick all the way to the rhododendrons in the back, which stood guard at the border where her yard abutted a small park with a pond.

I had no history of spying on people, no buried desire in this direction, I think, and I did not, even much later, consider my curiosity a violation, although it was in its way. I did not—here was the thing—I never associated what I was doing with the sort of furtive spying you saw in movies and on TV, which grew out of some disorder or perversion and went by the name of *peeping*. I simply fell into the habit of passing through the small park on my nightly walk and, when it was dark and I could do so unobserved, slipping through the bushes into her backyard.

When the lights were on I could see into the house. Sometimes I saw her in an armchair, reading, music playing at low volume, or else in the kitchen preparing a meal, an apron strung around her waist, steam rising from steel pots. The house looked like she might be expecting a dignitary at any minute. There was a mantel clock above the fireplace, long pretty curtains gathered neatly at the windows. I don't know what I hoped to discover. Possibly I was just bored and this opportunity had fallen into my lap. Someone seemingly as alone as me, and yet completely different. Or maybe I convinced myself that the secret of the massacre lived in this house, whatever that might have meant.

I didn't drink then, I already found the world confusing enough, but Bobby drank, and as June wound into July he began showing up to work drunk and then drinking on the job. It meant I had to work harder to keep us on pace, and laboring amid oil and epoxy fumes I got terrible headaches. Head rushes swept over me, leaving my vision abuzz and scattered in blocks of color. At times I had to lie down to let the nausea pass.

D.H. found me like this one day, on my back in the bleachers. Michaela, he said, you're a good painter: you're fast and you're precise. But if I catch you lying down on the job again, I'll fire you without a second thought. I couldn't respond; the moment had come and gone too fast. Woo-*ee*, Bobby said when D.H. had left. Look who ain't long for the world!

I tried to talk about it with Carl on the ride home that afternoon. In a fair world, Carl philosophized, I'd say rat out the drunk. But we don't live in a fair world, and it's probably worse to be thought a snitch. I just don't see why I *care*, I said. Carl smiled. It's all for naught, he said. You know what that means? I blinked at him so that I didn't hurt him. Who didn't know what *all for naught* meant? He said it all the time, anyway, like a ludicrous mantra. In his thick accent it sounded like he was saying *it's often hot*—which was true, it was.

But it wasn't all for naught, not for me anyway. I needed the money so I could leave, like my sisters had, so I could fly to Nicaragua, or El Salvador, and begin what I imagined to be my life. I had already told college I wouldn't be back in the fall and part of me doubted I ever would. College was fine. It was just fine.

When I got home from my walks, I often found my mother on the sofa, watching reruns and drinking Stroh's. Sometimes Max would be perched on her head and turn his eyes on me, fixed in their dead-ahead regard. Something was wrong with him, I'd say a broken wing if that didn't sound so stupidly symbolic, but his summer in our house anyway was a convalescence.

One night my mother asked me to come over and sit down, and before I knew it she'd cut a lock of my hair with a pair of scissors. For Max, she said, who needed the roughage for his digestion. You could have asked, I said. And what's wrong with your hair? You don't want Max eating *dye*, she said aghast. She cut a raw steak into small pieces and wrapped them in my hair. See how much he likes it, she said. He seemed to like it the exact amount he liked everything.

In those moments when our eyes met, I thought I saw my mother's wobble, unable to fixate or lock, as though steady gaze and the picture of the world it offered were a thing she'd given up, a thing taken from her or traded away, and in those moments I had the urge to flee and never come back. I sometimes thought I heard goats bleating out back, before I remembered that we no longer kept goats, that it had been my father's idea to keep goats, before he left us and left us the goats, the asshole. I didn't intend to forgive him, even as I forgave my sisters, wordlessly, without a second thought, knowing that in their shoes I would have done the same. You save yourself first.

My only companionship that summer was my college friend, Linda. She was a camp counselor in New Hampshire, a thousand miles away, and for the first half of the summer we wrote each other diligently. Having nothing to report myself, I told stories from work. *The Dynamic Duo*, I wrote, which was the name I'd given Radar and Stan, *recently hatched a plan to knock over a convenience store called Binny's. Now Binny's is possibly the saddest convenience store on earth. I don't know whether they accept or have ever seen paper currency, but well, the boys, they're like Sonny Wortzik and Sal when they get plotting (remember when we saw that at the Nugget?). They think it's a cinch because it's all stoned teenagers working there over the summer, but what about me? What do they think I'm going to say to the cops? If I die under mysterious circumstances please show them this letter.*

Linda began most of her notes by telling me how *crazy* and *hilarious* my life at home was; then she'd tell me about sailboats capsizing on the lake, taking ticks off campers with blown-out matches, girls getting their periods for the first time, convinced they were diseased or dying, campers who got so homesick their parents had to come get them. Homesick? I thought like love this referred to an emotion I lacked the sensitivity to pick up. Late at night, Linda said, she and the other counselors snuck out to meet up with their counterparts from the boys' camp nearby. *I may have done a certain something with Hot Josh,* she wrote. *Aaaah! I feel crazy!* I skimmed for a couple of pages until Josh's name stopped appearing. I didn't know this Linda. Foucault had died and she hadn't even mentioned it.

As much as Linda described it I failed to understand what camp really was. I kept thinking, You do *what* all day? sure I'd missed something. It wasn't envy I felt. I felt the way I did when I read about Buddhist monks walking barefoot on hot coals. I felt: *Why?*

On breaks at work, while the others smoked, I skimmed the papers looking for news from the south. People were killing one another here in the U.S. too—at McDonald's, in San Diego, in Alaska. That was different, I thought. That was despair. They wanted to *kill*. To kill *intransitively*. That was how the AIDS virus killed, science had just told us, so long as you agreed it wasn't punishment from God, believed it followed the thoughtless compulsion of its biology or chemistry or whatever clockwork urged it on, like the freak tornado swarm that had swept through just east of here while I was at school, killing dozens and wreaking its fantastic havoc. People still spoke of the tornadoes in low tones like fate were listening. Violence of this sort unnerved me. It didn't believe in the world.

At work Bobby sometimes asked me to tell him again what it was I was studying in college.

History, I said. Latin American history.

You, he'd say, shaking his head. *You* I do not understand.

But the truth was, if there was a truth, that thin strip of umbilical land between Mexico and Colombia turned out to be the only thing that could hold my attention: Nicaraguan land reform, Panzós and the Spanish embassy fire, Rigoberta Menchú's memoir, the assassination of Archbishop Romero. I read article after article on the unfolding revolutionary chaos, the power seizures and coups, the juntas, the leftist turns against the juntas, the brave stands taken by peasants and clergy. That spring in São Paulo, a million and a half had gathered in the Anhangabaú Valley demanding democratic elections. And though the vote had failed, things seemed to be changing, the impulse spreading—the impulse to *change* everything, to take every mistake and inevitability that went by the name of life—as in, *that's life*—and erase it, like footprints in the sand, or to cut it off like chains binding us to the past. I had no real clue what I would do if I made it to Nicaragua or El Salvador, but I knew that I would never forgive myself if I failed to see what was happening firsthand. If I failed in whatever small way to participate. History still existed there and it had dried up here at home. I don't think I put things to myself in those terms then, but I sensed a fissure in me that would otherwise never heal.

I thought about the reality of these distant countries as I gazed into the woman's house, the soft lit world beyond its panes. I imagined the woman's husband returning from the revolutionary tropics, from some grim mission attending to American *interests*, as they're always called, coming back to this snow globe world and giving in to the delusion that the two worlds did not exist in one continuous reality, separated only by permeable space. Maybe he was the dignitary she was always expecting. Or maybe the house was just her way of curating that delusion.

Of course I didn't know the first thing about her husband—whether he was alive, where he was, what he did, if he existed at all. I knew only that she wore a ring, a silver band, and the name she spoke the one time I heard her speak might have been anyone's—her husband's, a child's, God's. Probably not God's, but you never know. It was a July night full of plant heat. The day had been suffocating too and crowns of vapor fringed the lights set to burn in the dark. The woman had her windows cracked and when the phone rang the sound passed out into the yard like the trilling of Max's birdsong. She disappeared and I went around to the other side of the house where, standing on the metal lip of a window well with my hands on the sash, I found her again, a silhouette across the unlit room.

She was standing in a small interior hall, partly obscured by the doorframe and turned away from me so that I couldn't see her face. Light from the kitchen washed dimly into the hallway. I couldn't make out her words at first, only what sounded like distress in them. An old distress, I thought, nothing unexpected. An unscabbed wound.

I strained to hear, pressed against the mullions, then the window lurched in my hands, opened under an upward pressure, and I heard her say, Gabriel. *Gabriel.* A pause. Hold on. Hello? she said in a loud, timorous voice. I held still, my head ducked out of sight, waiting, letting the very faintest breath escape me while my heart drummed mercilessly in my chest. In the silence the static of the crickets rose up, so loud I couldn't believe I hadn't noticed it before. The sound was deafening. It seemed to pulse. I thought I heard the insects humming in the fluid skin above the pond. Then I heard her say, Nothing, I guess. Two dozen? Too many. What about— Well, how does it run? Uh-huh. Uh-huh. She laughed. Karen? *No!*

A few days later I got a letter from Linda telling me how madly in love with Josh she was. *He's thin, but he's strong too,* she wrote. *Sometimes, when the stars are out and everything's quiet, I rest my head on his chest. I listen to his heartbeat and the frogs by the lake, and I think I'm hearing God. I think, This must be what people mean by God. That the universe is listening, that you're listening to it. I know it sounds ridiculous but that's what I think. I think: God is everywhere . . . Oh, Michaela, what's happening to me? I almost let my girls retrieve their arrows before everyone was done shooting. Someone could have been shot! I'm distracted all the time. I cry for no reason. I think about marrying Josh . . .*

The letter was eight pages long. I didn't read the whole thing. I concluded that Linda had gone insane and I put the letter back in its envelope. I considered writing Return to Sender and dropping it in a mailbox or possibly burning it, but in the end I just lost it.

At work Bobby said, What do you think it's like to kill some-one? That depends, I said. Okay, said Bobby. There's lots of ways to kill someone, I said. You could choke someone to death, look right in their eyes. You could be one shooter in a firing squad. You could get the order to drop a bomb. You could *give* the order to drop a bomb. You could kill someone by accident . . . I'm talking about face-to-face, gun to the head, *Bam!* Bobby said. One second they're alive, next second they're dead. I looked at Bobby. He was covered in sweat. Actually, I don't want to talk about this, I said.

I didn't realize how much I didn't until I got to the women's room and found I was shaking. I felt sick, like a summer flu had exploded inside me. I opened the window. The air was even hotter outside, as sickly moist as dog's breath. The sun fell through the window like scalding water on my skin.

Fucking, cocksucking, Mellie muttered, banging through the door. When she saw me she stopped for a second. Hey, she said, you know that fucking asshole Randall, the supplier? Fucking spook's joking around with Radar and Stan, looks me up and down, takes his *sweet* time, and I'm like, Take a fucking picture, why don't you? And he says—I don't even fucking know—some slimy shit, and Radar and Stan and him are all cracking up. I swear Judson would *kill* that—

I had my hand up. The heat, the shouting—it was too much. Part of me maybe had a crush on Mellie, but just then I could have smashed her head through the porcelain sink. I thought I saw the tragedy of her life in that one instant stretching off like a highway that ends in a hopeless desert. I was feverish the rest of the day. I drank water and imagined it was paint I was pouring into me. An unabsorbable plastic substance embalming me from the inside out. When I went to the bathroom for the fourth time Bobby winked at me and said, Time of the month?

When our shift ended at four o'clock and we'd gathered in our circle I was ready to come apart. You don't look so good, Carl said. You look, as the saying goes, like death. I feel cold, I said, though I was sweating profusely. I feel terrible, actually. I felt cold inside my bones.

That's funny, Bobby said, addressing no one in particular. I was just thinking how it's going to be a wonderful day. He was smiling up at the ceiling like he'd finally lost his mind. I was just thinking how everything's *coming together*. How it's going to be a . . . a magical, wonderful day! We were all staring at him. He laughed and started coughing. I don't know when we saw the revolver in his hand, but we must have all seen it pretty fast. You could feel something change in the room, the air come alive with what may, in fact, have been a kind of magic. It was air in which things could now begin and end. There were recesses in the space around us; the space itself had become more capacious. I briefly thought about dancing, there was so much space! The past disappeared. Maybe it's truer to say it flowed into the present, lingered on around us longer than it should have, until it became self-aware and consumed itself like burning paper on the air.

I feel, Bobby strained to find the right words, just a tremendous sense of *hope*.

His face gleams as he says this, says, I was watching that *Sudden Impact* movie the other night. Great film, *great* film. You know what Dirty Harry says? He says, Go ahead. Make . . . my . . . day. Just like that! Isn't that great? Bobby cocks the gun and points it at Stan. Make my day! He laughs. Stan stares at the floor, eyes like a drowsing drunk's. Or how 'bout you, bucko? Buddy, buddy, buddy, Bobby says, turning the gun on Carl. Go ahead. Make. My. Day. Carl's looking off to the side of Bobby. It's a strange look on his face, like something almost funny's going on in the corner of the room, and I think I hear a kind of warbling sound come from him, but I'm not sure, and then it's my turn, anyway, Bobby's pointed the gun at me and asks me, or encourages me, to make his day, whatever that really means. I look at Bobby. I can't look down the barrel of the gun, so I look Bobby in the eye and with a particular intensity, because part of me knows this may be the last thing I ever see. Bobby's face is round and red, glistening in the light. His thin hair rests damply on his forehead. There is a faint colorless fuzz in his pockmarks. It might as well be the first time I've looked at Bobby. And then it's very funny to me all of a sudden that someone like Bobby, on a day like this, a day that means nothing, can hold my life in his hand, in a tiny displacement of his finger: resting on the trigger, squeezed. But the thing I want to say now is that we are all people like Bobby, each day is crucial, meaningless. And I think of my father for the first time in years without hate and wonder if the news of his daughter's death will reach him wherever he is, and if he'll care; and that's when I know I'll never see him again, even if I don't die this day, I'll never see him again, and I laugh to think my mother will cut the hair from my cadaver to feed Mad Max.

By the time I have every last one of these thoughts Bobby has moved on, to Radar and Mellie and Ellen S. and Ellen V. I don't feel sick anymore. Something else has risen up in me, and I think Bobby's right, it *is* going to be a wonderful day, what's left of it.

When he's done he opens the chamber and dumps out the bullets in his hand. We sit there, slow to move as he wipes the gun with a chamois cloth. He looks at the bullets in his hand, then at us, then back at the bullets, counting.

One of you would have lived, he says.

That August I flew south.

•

The gun does not go off. Michaela and I meet thirty years later. I am grown by then, having passed through the appropriate stages of development, or so I hope, having grown more fixed in myself, set in my ways, and more open to inhabiting another's life, I think—an irony which, like all ironies, must resolve somewhere in a deeper truth. Michaela tells me her story, gives me permission to use it, and I do, I write what you have read, something quite different from what Michaela told me, her name, of course, not being Michaela at all, which means "who is like God."

A meaningful detail? I don't know. Don't ask me to go on the record. I named her that; my attention went to other things. I liked the name, I kept it. What is my responsibility to any of this, a face pressed to the glass, peering in? A ghost, a spy. Let me be the trellis of vantage points, I might say, the lattice hidden everywhere in the leaves of another's story. Probably not the way it works, but what do I know.

Well, this.

In the summer of 1984 there are consolations ahead that Michaela can't know about. Five years after Bobby points a gun in her face and says it is always and only *today* that a thing begins or ends, the movement that began as Diretas Já succeeds in bringing democratic elections to Brazil; Joe Moakley, U.S. representative from Massachusetts, the state to which I have just moved at the time, travels to El Salvador to investigate the killing of six Jesuit priests, their housekeeper, and her daughter; the history of evil is being disinterred, recorded, and the creeping vines of complicity will stretch from the fine verandas of San Salvador to the banks of the Potomac. There are setbacks too, of course. What comes to light, like everything so terrible and pointless, is destined for a living burial in summaries, figures, and paragraphs. In the way our attention drifts. The acid bath of bald numbers is always the second death in which people, as individuals, melt away. But first the stories will be heard, the people will seen, and that much alone will cost lives.

The harbor town where Michaela and I walk is protected from the sea. Still, it gets quite a lot of wind, waves too. It is winter, so—cold. Wind turbines turn across the bay. Lighthouses mark the points where land juts out. Some sweep through the night and some are just relics now. We pass the breakwater. Michaela is telling me a story, a funny story with bits in it that aren't so funny. We are passing friends in a moment, the sort that lasts a few months. It is odd, I think, how these intimacies happen, how we grow close in circumstances that promise only to abandon us, at first chance, to the estrangement where we began. Meanwhile Michaela might have been my big sister, and why not? I would have liked that, walking together like this, the wind off the ocean meeting us with its parcels of sea spray. And were I a child she might have told me, Once upon a time a ship full of people landed here. They were far from home and they were full of hope. This is how you tell stories to children, of course. *Once upon a time. Full of hope.* And the eyes blinking in the forest? they ask. The thick woods chime with green light.

What about them? you say.

Metanarrative Breakdown

As he lay dying, Icarius remembered something that had happened not long before. Dionysus had taught him how to plant the vines and look after them. Icarius watched over their growth with the same love he had for his trees, waiting for the moment when he would be able to squeeze the grapes with his own hands. One day he caught a goat eating some vine leaves. He was overcome by anger and killed the animal on the spot. Now he realized the goat had been himself.

But something else had happened that had to do with that goat. Icarius had skinned it, put on its pelt, and, with some other peasants, improvised a dance around the beast's mangled corpse. Icarius didn't appreciate, as he lay dying, that the gesture had been the origin of tragedy, but he did sense that the death of the goat was connected with what was happening to him, the shepherds circling him, each one hitting him with a different weapon, until he saw the spit that would pierce his heart.

—Robert Calasso, *The Marriage of Cadmus and Harmony*

To begin with, the house. A large house. Shingle style, on an island bluff in a northern American state. A handsome house, my grandparents' house—or so it had been, and that was how I first knew it. Once upon a time they had sailed up the coast. Once upon a time they had packed a summer's worth of books and clothes on their sailboat and set off with no more than a direction in mind. A sense of adventure. A muted good-burgher quixotism. After a month of following the bights and inlets of the shore, tacking upwind to round headlands and capes, from the calm waters of the bay they saw it glinting in the sun: their house. This is the story I was told. I don't question it because I like it. I forgive it dubiety and simplicity because this was a time when stories were easier to tell. When the arcs were cleaner and optimism cast like daylight into the corners of a June afternoon redolent of flowers slaked with rain. Was it on such an afternoon that my grandparents first arrived?

In later years, when they were feeling whimsical, or perhaps extravagant, they would fly a flag bearing our family's coat of arms from a mounting bracket between the second and third stories of the house. It was either a charming or an affected display because we had not the slightest trace of heraldic legacy. Our ancestors had been émigré Jews who arrived in this country penniless and built what they had out of daydreams and hewn wood: furniture makers, shopkeepers, gold rush prospectors, salesmen. They told a better story every year. The house was no different. It was a fantasy, a shoreside idyll. Before a legacy—always—a property, and the dull present.

My grandfather was still alive, but the house now belonged to my aunts. They were his daughters, my mother's sisters, Cynthia and Ruth, and although they all lived together in the summer, they lived apart. My aunts had remodeled the house to accommodate the sense of grievance that lingered between them and their father, a change undetectable from the outside but which divided a building constructed in a style preoccupied with unity into two distinct living spaces, two *houses*, so aesthetically incoherent on the inside that moving between them felt like passing between eras, temporalities, consciousnesses—a seamless entanglement of discontinuity that called to mind nothing so much as exotic species grafted onto each other, a vaguely ouroboric and labyrinthine autophagy, like knotted cities in a China Miéville novel.

It is not for me to say what wounds of childhood, parenthood, or time had scarred over in this prickly intimacy. I don't know. If this were a different story, my mother would be the youngest daughter and the only one to love her father with his due, my aunts would be wicked and conniving, my grandfather gripped by a vital senility, raging against the cruel terms life and love have to offer at their best. Things aren't like that, of course. People aren't often good or evil, and it's no different here. There are no Kents disguised as Caius attending one's madness on the heath. No good father, no bad daughter. There are paid nurses, caretakers from the West Indies. Pricey doctors titrating statins from cities down the coast. There are housekeepers, maids, gardeners, cooks. Because there is money, there are these things.

It was in this house, this summer, that my grandfather was dying. I got the call from Ruth late one night at a wedding I was attending on the West Coast.

"But aren't we all, in a sense, always dying?"

"Don't be smart. We may be talking hours."

"But if you break the years any of us have left into days, and the days then into—"

"Goodbye," Ruth said.

Her unwillingness to get philosophical with me put me on alert, and I lay in bed in my hotel room on the far side of the continent wondering where I was, or where I should be, how from here on out I was to *know*, and whether, with no little anxiety, I would get to see my grandfather again alive. In the building across the street a single apartment was illuminated. It glowed the primitive orange-red of the sun osculating the ocean out here. Why had I come? What was I doing at this wedding? I had stumbled on a bit of good fortune that summer, a first nip of success, and between the travel and this ramifying wave carrying into every last recess of my life, I had lost a sense of what affixed me to one reality over another, what my points of contact with the world really were. I no longer felt certain that I knew anyone, or perhaps I no longer felt certain anyone knew me. In the deep sense, I mean, past the flitting projections we cast onto the screens of our bodies. The people in the apartment across the street were just shades in the luminous vermilion, attenuated by some trick of the light so that they resembled Giacometti sculptures. I thought about calling Misty, but it was late on the East Coast, and we hadn't spoken, I remembered, since I'd had my good news.

What had happened is this, it's very simple. After years of being to friends and family a writer in no more than name—indulged, in the best-case scenario, as a romantic layabout—I had begun publishing work and as a consequence I'd sold a book. Two books, in fact—it looked like I might make a go of it. I was by no means moneyed; it was not an immoderate amount of success, but it was enough given the fecklessness and apparent neoteny of my life before, enough to rob me of the ritual dissatisfaction and single-minded struggle that had *been* my story, and in a way my comfort, enough for the people in my life to begin treating me oddly, tentatively, or so I felt, like I were a lunatic man living on an island of bridges, carrying dynamite with him everywhere, enough that my grandfather in our phone chats had taken to saying, "I start to think it was all worth it," where the respective "it"s seemed to refer (troublingly) to his life and (hyperbolically) to this business of living. So in a thought no doubt as perverse as it was self-important, in addition to everything else, I feared that I might have given my grandfather permission to die.

After wandering the wedding grounds the next morning and settling on a small dock by the pond, I did call Misty.

"So now you're famous," she said by way of answering.

"I'm not famous."

"You're an asshole."

Caterers dressed in black hurried across the lawn behind me, arranging champagne flutes in neat formations on card tables draped in cream-colored cloths.

"It's nice to hear your voice," I said. "Are you there?"

"I was already there. It's called 'here' where I am."

"What happened to grad school?" I said. "Actually, never mind."

Misty was Cynthia's daughter, my favorite cousin. Although we had traditionally kept track of each other's goings-on, in recent years we'd drifted into the drab adult preoccupation of paying rent and fallen out of touch. Or maybe I just mean that I had. I'd lost track, at any rate, of just how many master's programs she'd abandoned and what it was, again, she'd left art school for. Urban planning, I thought.

"The question is," she said, "where are *you?*"

"I'm at a wedding."

"And geographically?"

"I don't know," I said. Of course I did know, or I knew where I would catch the red-eye from that night, but not knowing seemed closer to the way I felt.

"Are you on drugs?" Misty said. "Don't start doing drugs just because you're still a fuck-up but can afford them now."

"I think I did meth the other day by accident." I said this a bit distractedly, the noises and movements of the pond, the burble and chatter of water and insects, briefly claiming my attention. A turtle stretched its head into the chalky summer air.

"Only you." I could all but hear her shaking her head and it made me miss her.

"I was with Gabrielle. I'll tell you when I see you."

"Hurry up. There are bats everywhere."

"Bats?" I said, but Misty had hung up.

The wedding was very pretty and sweet. I watched, standing off to the side, beset by a sun that seemed to want a confession from me. I tried to stay in the moment, a moment that was rightly not my own, tried not to worry about what time it was or whether the cab would find me so many miles from the city: whether I would make my flight. The groom was a college buddy. We hadn't seen much of each other since he'd moved to the West Coast, and now we wouldn't have even this. I was a ghost, a visible form that would come and go without explaining its presence; and as I watched the couple kiss to seal their undying love, at least a stirring faith in it, as I understood just how different my day's narrative was from my old friend's, a sense of my ineluctable subjectivity came over me, a sense I had been on increasingly intimate terms with that summer, a vertigo of disconnection. It didn't help, good fortune aside, that my life stretched before me with little more than routine and new worries to enliven it, as though I were the medium of my success rather than its claimant. I saw my friend deplaning on some South Pacific island with his bride and embarking on the adventure of mutual life—and I was jealous. Not of his love so much as the novelty of this togetherness. I was stuck, it seemed, at the opposite pole of human experience, for in feeling estranged from the world around me I had ceased to believe myself quite a thing placed inside it. The spheres, inner and outer, had come unnested.

I thought about Gabrielle on the flight east, trying for a time to represent the long years of our friendship and our closeness, our conversation, and the delight we took in each other as a patterning of love as yet misunderstood, as yet unrecognized by the two of us, as though that sense of comfort, of someone getting you and you her, that sense of home, *were* love in all its modest glory and the rest we asked of it no more than the bullwhip of hormones, the gluttony of surfeit. She was one of my oldest friends. We had known each other half our lives, the half that counts, and the precise quality of our time together took something meaningful from the restraint we had shown in never dating or hooking up. She was an architect and she'd visited me a few weeks before on her way back from Rome. I'd been very glad she'd come. I wasn't getting much done and I needed a better excuse. But I was also just happy to see her. We had that rare capacity for *mudita*, I think it's called, the ability to take unadulterated pleasure in each other's triumphs, when with so many people, it seems, the unreserved love you want demands that you come to them in weakness, offering up that weakness in your hands. Something profound and harrowing had also happened during Gaby's visit, and no doubt sharing this, and then experiencing a deep aloneness after she left, had muddled my feelings. And still in my bones I knew that what I wanted from love right then was answers, and love is not in the business of answers.

There was another flight and a long ride in a hired car and then a ferry crossing before I saw Misty at the terminal, leaning against the dock's weathered wood and smoking a cigarette while she waited. She didn't move or wave as I walked over to her. Our eyes merely met, and I smiled at the struck pose, which was her way of joking and of telling me we would always pick up just where we'd left off.

"You missed it," she said when we'd hugged.

My heart skipped a beat. "Missed what?"

She tossed her cigarette in the ocean. "Game night last night. I taught everyone Celebrity."

"Jesus, Misty." I threw my bags in the backseat. The fishing boats in the cove shimmied in an echo of the ferry's wake. "How's the old guy doing?"

"Better, we think." She started the Subaru, gunning the engine needlessly. "He's quoting poetry—in Latin."

"He knows Latin?"

She honked a greeting at someone on foot I didn't know. "Are you listening to me? Look, prepare yourself. The house is a zoo."

I don't know why, but I had been expecting to find the house draped in a somber pall, the days drifting melancholically between the unplaceable moment an afternoon becomes sad and the cobalt fullness at dusk's last breath. What I walked into, however, more closely resembled a Great War hospital established in some British country manor. There were maids and nurses and respect payers and well-wishers. It took me a long time to get everyone straight. For a while I had to approach each conversation with the ecumenical delicacy of a store clerk. I failed—wildly, you might say—to calibrate my answers to the questions I got about who I was and what I did and where I lived, questions to which I had no good answers anyway. After half an hour, and asking after the family of a man who turned out just to be making a delivery, I found my way to the bayside veranda where my grandfather was set up looking out to sea.

I bent to kiss him.

"You made it," he said in a voice that somehow, at once, conveyed both boyish gratitude and a faint sense of betrayal.

"I wouldn't have missed it."

My grandfather ignored the innuendo in this, the sort I am helpless to make, wincing all the while. Perhaps he didn't catch it. He raised a quivering finger to point out a passing schooner making its way up the bay on a reach. An osprey scrutinized the stretch of coast a few hundred yards out, and at the foot of the porch flowers in the parterre had the full lavish beauty of their high summer bloom.

"Not too shabby," I said. And because I had been here every year since my birth, it was simply not possible to say how deep an impression this one bit of extravagant and stern beauty had made on my psyche, my longings, my fury, my hope.

It took my grandfather a while to collect the words on his tongue, but he managed finally, shrugging with a feigned cool. "If you like that sort of thing," he said.

Misty and I had the third floor to ourselves, a suite of seaward garrets out whose windows we smoked, monitoring the comings and goings below. There was a rotation of nurses, daily shifts and weekly substitutions; as we were on an island, they stayed with us and slept in the house. The stream of visitors my grandfather received was unending, social acquaintances from half a century of summers here, people committed to making an appearance but with little idea, finally, what you said to a ninety-seven-year-old widower in manifest pain, for whom speech had become an unpleasant game of recollective hide-and-seek. Cynthia had set up her easel on the back lawn, painting for hours with the imperious, imperturbable air of a cultist. Ruth, as far as I could tell, spent her days with a cordless phone wedged in the crook of her neck on calls to New York, holding up an index finger and walking away from anyone who talked to her. I loved my aunts, and beyond that I liked them, but I did not at heart understand what had come between them and their father, the irritations that had grown with age and then mapped themselves onto dynamics of grievance, of insufficient or misapplied love, rooted somewhere deep in the past. Perhaps nobody can respond to you exactly the way you want. Family is no doubt a pier glass for one's own self-contempt. But for all my regret that this should happen now, for all my frustration and incomprehension, those feelings, I knew, had to be set next to my own meager participation in these lives, the implicit idea that it was enough for me to show up now and again for a few days and assume the unencumbered neutrality that may, in fact, have been no different from my habitual absence.

"Do you like what we've done with the place?" Cynthia asked.

I had wandered over to her easel barefoot with a mug of coffee.

"I like that you've found a way to live together under one roof," I said politically.

"I wish your mother were here."

"She wishes that too, I'm sure."

We looked at the bestrewn islands of the bay, the mainland hills beyond, which at twilight took on the glaucous sheen that gave them their name. Although it was morning Cynthia was painting a night scene, bright buoys and ship lights overexposed on a dark sea.

"Do you know why I paint facing east?" she said.

"Because it's the direction with the view?"

She looked at me until every last bit of levity had drained from my remark. "Because that is the direction the Vedas designate for the gods."

"Ah."

"Where the sun comes from. *Dawn Land*. That's what indigenous tribes called this region."

"I didn't know."

"Yes," she said. "Ancient people all over the world knew that everything begins in the east. I find myself wanting to focus on beginnings."

I had dealt with death before, of course, but I had been younger then—more certain, that is, that the important experience being undergone was my own. I couldn't and wouldn't have wanted to summon this illusion now, and still I had only my own subjectivity to refer to. If I tried to imagine my grandfather's first-person experience of his own enfeeblement, helplessness, and mortality, I could do this only through an awareness of myself making the effort, *choosing* to make the effort, and so with a trace of self-congratulation spoiling the act. Nor was I even certain that this kind of transpersonal projection made up a worthy or compassionate goal. It verged on pity, and pity looked an awful lot like just the displaced fear of the same happening to you. My grandfather and I were separated by the impregnability of two skulls. I had taken to kissing him, more than I had ever kissed any relation of mine, his balding head, his sallow, sunken cheeks, but even I knew this was no more than symbolic pretense to the notion that we were of the same flesh and that nothing would undo this. He was my last living grandparent; I watched daily as he shrank into himself, able only to wonder, from my remove, at the indignity and terror of having your body desert you, of finding yourself trapped in the play and apperception of a still-lively mind while the words that gave thought form floated beyond your reach. I read to him mornings and evenings about Galileo and Janet Yellen, the plump little gibbous moon where our spheres of interest overlapped. He tired quickly following the movement and subordination of the written word. He tired when we spoke too. And through it all he groaned as waves of a great, unnameable pain came over him, saying merely "I'm fine, I'm fine" when we asked, bouncing a hand to shush us, like we'd grown histrionic.

The worst was at night. My bedroom was right above his, and he seemed no longer to sleep but to drift in states of an unpleasant semiconsciousness, moaning with a periodicity just irregular enough to keep me on edge. When I couldn't take it any longer, I wandered into Misty's room to drink her vodka out of a red-wine glass and share a smoke above the moonlit sea.

"Denise's husband is dying," Misty said. She made a fishlike face, letting the smoke float out of her mouth. "I don't know if you knew."

"I didn't," I said. Denise was the chummiest of the nurses and had a way of speaking, a delicate soprano whisper, that after having spent a good portion of the afternoon just fucking *rapt* as she described the uses and pitfalls of a medication called Coumadin I had begun to worry she was giving me ASMR.

"He has cancer," Misty said. "Lung that spread to the brain."

"Christ, and she's looking after Granddad."

"And we're smoking."

"Same guilt," I said, hating myself for smoking and smoking mostly out of self-hatred. "Thumbing our nose at the metanarrative, you know. The stupid tax we pay on how loathsomely important our privilege asks us to take ourselves."

Misty explored the offensive possibilities of literal nose thumbing. "What's the metanarrative?"

"Oh, this thing Gaby and I were throwing around. The narrative logic that sits behind a story, I guess. Whatever distinguishes narrative from, like, litany. Or accident."

Misty ashed out the window. "Are you going to tell me what happened?"

"You are too young, my dear. I shall tell you when you're older."

She looked at a make-believe watch on her wrist for a few seconds. "There," she said. "I'm older."

When I had asked Misty whether she was all right, the two of us drinking on my first night up, she said she was, why did I ask? I don't know, I said, the grad-school thing. First of all, it was summer, she explained, and her apparent listlessness was an insufficient ground to assume she'd dropped out of school; but yes, as a matter of fact, in the second place, she *had* left urban planning behind because, well, it was your typical M.A. utopianism, without the faintest hope of meaningful praxis, preparing you for little more than the enviable future of fighting starved pit bulls for jobs in municipal administrations that amounted to years of testing a brick wall's material durability with your head. I told Misty I'd never known her to let practical considerations get in the way of a rash decision. She sighed. "I guess I'm looking for love," she said. And I was about to say, Sure, but do you think it's just going to walk in the door one day? But what did I know. In my own way I was waiting for love too—not an object of love, not an instance of it, but perhaps love itself.

It was bright and sunny the next morning when Misty and I took the whaler out to the islands to hunt for chanterelles. On the way we passed skerries of sunbathing seals, as dun and tubular as slugs. They turned their heads to regard us. Misty sat up front and by the time we arrived the cigarette in her lips was wetted to extinguishment in the spray. I told her to throw the anchor in, and we watched as it sank into the emerald murk. The rope uncoiled, chasing after it, then slipped discreetly over the gunwale and disappeared itself.

"Whoops," Misty said. "*Shiiiiiit.*"

We regarded the traceless surface of the ocean for a minute, then we sat there and laughed. We laughed for a good long time. Finally we dragged the boat up onto the beach, tied the painter off on a large rock, and did our foraging.

Later, when I told Ruth what had happened, she said, "So we lost an anchor. Forget it."

"I think we can find it," I said. "Wait till it's low tide, you know."

"Okay. But why?"

She was right, of course, in the sense of prudence or necessity, but I felt a poignancy about the anchor, a desire not to let things slip away. I can't explain it. I couldn't quite bear to think of our trusty nine-pound Danforth lying there for centuries, millennia—*forever* perhaps—wondering when we were coming back for it.

I thought Cynthia might understand, but when I told her she just said, "You're an idiot."

And yes, she wasn't wrong, but where would we be without idiots? When would we laugh?

By evening, when the bats emerged, Misty had organized a betting pool in the house. You could bet on our finding the anchor or our not finding it. Everyone wanted in on the action. "Your grandfather's doing a little better tonight," the nurses would tell me before slipping five-, ten-dollar bills in my hand. "Against," they said.

Percy, the longtime gardener and groundskeeper, said, "There's no way to orient yourself. You're not going to know where to look. Shore's night and day at different tides."

"Care to make it interesting?" Misty said.

"That's all right," he said. "It'll be plenty interesting when I have to fish you out."

In a subtle way the house, which had been merely busy, came alive at the prospect of this unnecessary act. We had something to talk about, to grin about, something to anticipate that in its silliness, the pointlessness of its derring-do, resisted the seriousness of death. I told my grandfather about the endeavor and he nodded a little, like what I was saying made sense, but then, as comprehension set in, he raised his eyebrows and shook his head, echoing Cynthia's verdict in his way.

"Why?" he said.

"I don't know," I said. Why anything?

The issue with the bats was that we had no idea where they were getting in. That and they upset the nurses. You could track their progress through the house by listening to the nurses' screams, then judging the direction and the muting interference of the walls. They seemed to know when we ate dinner too, for it was most often then that Misty and I had to excuse ourselves, dabbing mouths with napkins, and cross into the old wing, where a nurse would stand pointing dumbly to the site of our present visitation. They must have been coming in during the day, hiding themselves in curtains and crown moldings until it was dark and the time had come for them to cast about the house like inebriate demons.

The bats were one more act in the circus our lives had become that summer. A fey carnival cast in shadow. The particularity of moments, the deceits of memory. A Chris Marker mash-up. *Cirque Sans Soleil*. There would be emus in the zone. I am sure it was only me who felt this. I had a way of digressing into minutiae, fixating on the feel of confluent ephemera while the world moved on. Ruth correcting the newspaper in red pen; Cynthia video-Skyping with her dogs in L.A., neurosis-ridden rescues who suffered crippling and dysphoric separation anxiety (or so she claimed); Misty's habit of hiding framed pictures, marshmallow men, and beetle carapaces in my bed. I relished missing the forest for the trees; it was a significant part of why I had become a writer, all the stillbirths of pregnant moments. And yet in the weightless disconnection I felt that summer from all we have been taught will sustain us, I saw this tendency of mine achieve a kind of apogee, this inability or refusal to distinguish between *studium* and *punctum*, until all I saw everywhere were the dissipating freeze-frames of life, instants of salient and perverse meaning, of felicity, contradiction, the inexhaustible poetry of juxtaposition, the eclecticism that with acts of curation becomes sensibility. Sitting on the stone wall below the crab apple trees, the pale decaying fruit scattered at my feet, in the right light, the sun still crisp but low enough to sieve through the west-lying trees, I could convince myself, for instance, that I was not a person, or rather not the specific person I enacted within a web of expectations and memories, that Cynthia was not an "artist" or Misty a soul adrift, that the present did not situate itself inside a time or date, that these were instead phantoms imposing themselves on the ceaseless flux, the *ever-becoming*, and that my grandfather was not dying but simply living another, different day, was not *my* grandfather, was not who I believed him to be, certainly, but was also an elusive quantity to himself—that, in short, all the words we had for everything added up to a catalogued death sentence of the discrete, turning the raw matter of experience transactionable at the cost of making experience itself inaccessible.

The night before Misty and I set out for the anchor I awoke in blackness to a cold wet breeze flowing in through the window. I wasn't tired, though I couldn't have been asleep very long. I didn't check the time, knowing instinctively that it was hours before I could reasonably get up. I heard my grandfather in pain below me, the ebbing and flowing of an irrepressible ache. And what are you to do with that? What really can you do? Did I wish him to feel released, in the manner of Montaigne, who says we should pass from life to death with the equanimity with which we first passed from nonexistence to life at birth? Was it loving or selfish to wish him that? Loving or selfish to want him to live just as many of these gruesome days as he could? I wanted both for him, even as one wish negated the other, and what I wanted most was just to believe he wasn't alone in his pain, in the inner confrontation with his own dissolution, I wanted to believe there was someone watching, keeping vigil with him on the level I couldn't.

The lights were off in Misty's room.

"Mirabella," I said with a small coloratura, knocking gently.

"I'm asleep." I could just make out a lump under the quilt on the far bed. "And please don't call me that."

I poured some vodka in a glass and sat on the cushioned chair across from her. "Don't you think this rejection of our given names bespeaks a certain juvenility?" I said. "A not wanting to grow up?"

"You're the expert in that."

"My, aren't we just a pepperbox of wit tonight."

She might have shrugged under the blanket, but I couldn't see. Beyond the window the moon painted its glissando on the bay. It was my grandfather who had taught me the phases of the moon, I remembered, the spherical dance that gave rise to them; he had once been a scientist and delighted in teaching us, his grandkids, about the composition of the world around us, the dynamics of its interactions: tides, stars, the aeronautics of sailing, the geology of the coast.

"I'm sorry," I said.

"For what?"

For what. It wasn't for teasing her, of course. It wasn't for anything I could very well name. Misty was sitting up in bed now. She leaned her head to one side and then the other, stretching her neck. She looked at me. I wanted to tell her that she could say anything to me, that she could cry or stop enacting herself however briefly, that everything was going to work out, although I didn't know that it would, that wherever I was going she was coming with me, although she wasn't. I had no business advising anyone on how to live. My own life, far from coming into focus with success, had blurred to the point that I hardly believed anymore in the concept of "a life." Whatever ongoing first-personhood I continued to experience seemed more a fantasy or structureless joke than a project in integral coherence, and the untethered feeling visiting me that summer might have been no more than the confirmation, on realizing certain far-fetched dreams, that there was no track governing life's direction, life was indeed surprising, and if it was full of more good than you could anticipate, by implication it was full of more bad too. And yet, all the same, in spite of my dubiety of the stories we tell about who we are, starting with my own, I *was* writing at the behest of some inner scream, some reckless anger and love far too specific not to originate in me, in whatever idiosyncrasy distinguishes all the me's that appear to be just fucking everywhere in the world. And the form this anger and this love took could perhaps most simply be described in the metonymy of Misty, her weirdness, the child she once was, the desire to nurture that person, and the rage I felt at anything and everything that did not lift her up.

"I know you are," she said at last. Her eyes in the dark held dabs of moonshine. And what, really, was the chance some one ray of light would leave the sun and carom off the moon and continue to the tiny sphere of her eye, so far away, and leave from there to enter my own?

"Do you want to hear a bedtime story?" I said.

"Tell me what happened with Gaby and the meth," she said.

"All right," I said. And I told her.

•

Misty had known Gabrielle since my freshman year of college. This was when Gaby and I first met, founding the closeness that would carry us through the next four years of school, a closeness that had come at such a critical juncture in our intellectual and social self-orientation that our friendship, in later years, seemed more a case study in comparative morphology, pointing back to the time when two species were one, and our minds, which had formed during countless hours of decoding and reconstructing the world, in how they moved to the same language and ideas, resembled constructivist projects, or so I thought—in the architectural sense, in the artistic sense. And now I was an artist. And now Gabrielle was an architect.

When she got back from Rome and came to visit me at the cottage where I was house-sitting, Gaby was excited about what she'd seen. She had a notebook brimming with sketches: buildings in profile and perspective, details of decorative flourishes, felicitous proportionalities, stabs at capturing the subtle enmeshments of public and private space. The only thing getting her down was Rome's implicit critique of contemporary practice, which had come, she explained, to privilege concept and style over what she termed the *experience of space*. The experience of space was harder to talk about. It was largely private and rarely came across in images or floor plans. The true experience of a space, she said, might only reveal itself over time, months—*years*—of being in the space and using it.

"And it's emotional too, right. How does this space make me *feel*?" I said.

"Which could have to do with sunlight or shade. How a building frames its views, works with a landscape. Which could simply be the *absence* of nuisance. So not necessarily things people even notice."

"Art should be *habitable*, not merely visitable."

Gaby grimaced. "You need some new quotes."

"What's wrong with Barthes?" I said. "Barthes is cool."

"Really? No, you know this. There's this very clear statute of limitations on invoking post-structuralism after college. It's like three years. After that you're the unreconstructed guy who lives in the lobby of some film archive with his sweater on backwards."

"That's the opposite of a statute of limitations."

"What do I mean?"

"A grace period."

"Yeah, well, you're out of grace."

We spent the first few days of Gaby's visit drinking and smoking into the early morning on the second-story balcony overlooking the field. Our catching-up had less to do with new information, generally, than with returning again and again to our reservoir of shared stories, comparing perspective and interpretation, amending and gently challenging what had set as memory, and testing new conceptual frameworks on the before and after, the ever-expanding context, the ramifying that never ends, until it does. The idea that started taking shape in me as I listened to Gaby talk about Rome and its built textures, the textures that gave rise to the experience of its space and that in a sense therefore *were* Rome, was that we might correspondingly describe literature as an *experience of information*, one with its own utopian aspirations to improve on the assaultive chaos of existence, to give it form, to act as docent in this makeshift exhibit culled from fleeting and desultory scatterings. Just as we needed and relied on more conscious order in the spatial dimension than we often realized, so too when it came to information— for whether we realized it or not, I now hypothesized to Gaby, without some pretty robust structuring principles our experience of information was going to be inarticulate mayhem. It was just that we didn't see these principles when they were working, the same way, as Gaby had said herself, you didn't typically remark the endless potential inconveniences always passing you by, always *not* happening. We rarely noticed the narratives we had let slip into place until events conspired to thwart them.

There are many examples, on varying scales of significance and disruption, but at its most simple, I expatiated, you might think of having a carefully scheduled day ahead of you and blowing out your tire at 10:30 a.m. Or similarly, taking a long-awaited weekend trip and arriving at your rental to discover that the roof leaks and you can expect thunderstorms all weekend. The inconvenience is annoying, yes, but what is really upsetting, what is *emotionally* trying, is seeing the story you've been telling yourself collapse and having to start again on the tiresome process of building a narrative to give shape to your day, a plausible little ecology of plans and hopes and chores. I don't mean by these examples to suggest that this is a first-world problem, either. It is a consequence of living in the dimensionless present, and the size of the disruption entails the scope of the revision. Gaby and I brainstormed some lugubrious options—accident, illness, or perhaps discovering after a childhood of abuse from old Russian tutors and devoting yourself to the minute beauty of the game that a computer will always beat you at chess. That technology has supplanted your life's work. Or to take an exceedingly trivial example, but one Gaby and I discussed at some length, the time I visited her when she was studying abroad and walked her friend halfway across town late one night only not to be invited up.

Me: We'd been flirting all day. She lived in the exact opposite direction from you. I mean it's understood, right, what offering to walk someone home in that context means?

Gaby: You thought the walk was a euphemism.

M: Indeed.

G: But then it wasn't.

M: It was not. That is correct.

G: And when you realized it wasn't a euphemism, was just itself . . .

M: Look, you don't want to fall on either side. You don't want to be the cynic who disallows the possibility of sincerity. You also don't want to be the rube who doesn't know when something's a joke.

G: Mm-hmm.

M: I'm not going to lose sleep over it. We were in different stories is all.

G: It sounds to me like no one was going to lose any sleep over it. Everyone was going to get to sleep *nice* and early, and wake up refreshed and—

M: . . .

G: You were in different stories is all.

M: I was in a different story. I had to throw out the whole plot arc I was working with.

G: Which was?

M: I was talking in this gentle, breathy voice, trying not to say anything too weird.

G: The voice you do when it's a girl on the phone.

M: The part of the dramatic structure narratologists call "rising action."

G: Eww.

M: That was funny!

G: How many narratology puns do I get to look forward to in this conversation?

M: How many is too many?

G: So you're walking along, telling yourself some story that ends in sweet, foreign, dawn-welcoming butt sex . . .

M: Go on.

G: And then you reach the front door, hang out there—what?—I'm guessing five, ten minutes trying to feel out the situation. And finally she says she's tired, gives you a kiss on the cheek, and goes in. And you have to walk home. And your story has come crashing down. And your life has no point—

M: No, that's where you're wrong. My *life* was fine. I had to start telling myself a new story is all.

G: Which we do all the time.

M: Which we do all the time. And which is fine so long as the metanarrative endures.

G (*a beat, squinting*): And the metanarrative again, just so we're clear?

M: What it sounds like, I think. The fundamental Platonic form of narrative. The prime fabric of meaning.

G: What has significance for us. What we're about.

M: Yeah, sort of. Though maybe more like a scaffold. A particular shape in which any one narrative has to fit.

G: And how do we know if one fits?

M: That's what I'm saying, I guess. It's more like a feeling we get when something *doesn't* fit. Then we worry the thing until it does. But some things come along, right, that just refuse to fit, and in defying the scaffold they wake us up to the whole apparatus.

G: Like you've been on autopilot, yeah, without taking the time to figure out what the metanarrative is, just sort of assuming that if you do more or less what other people seem to be doing it'll figure itself out?

M: Right.

G: Then, boom! You just gave the ten best years of your life to corporate law.

M: And you realize nobody really cares. Nobody's, like, proud of you. The world's kind of done patting you on the back, scratching behind your ears.

G: But you're not broke.

M: You're not broke, it's true.

G: You have a lot of television options to scroll through

while you're wondering if maybe musical theater wasn't
your passion all along.

M: Some totally decent scotch.

G: And you get drunk and bone a stranger who's not your
type and— Surprise, that didn't help!

M: And you quit your job and travel in India.

G: Ashram, roshi, et cetera.

M: And you come back and volunteer at a hospice.

G: Which is actually a *really* great thing to do.

M: I have, you know, zero doubt.

G: But corporate law is just the low-hanging fruit, right?

M: Yeah, no, it's all of us.

G: It just comes in different forms, at different times?

M: One that happens to most of us, I think, is the moment
when you're getting older and it hits you that you don't
really have a "home" anymore. And you think: What is
a *home*, really? Did I *ever* have one? Do I need one?

G: The difference between a house and a home.

M: Mm . . . Say more.

G: The house is the physical object. The home is that object
inside a narrative.

M: The difference between a walk and a *walk*.

G: Between mushrooms and *mushrooms*.

M: Are you feeling anything?

She nodded. I was beginning to feel something too. The psilo-
cybin had begun gently thrumming the surface of the day. The field
below us, blanched in sunshine, was not changing exactly, but it was
taking on different emphases. The conceptual had begun to recede,
so that the trees, for instance, appeared to me more as the visual ele-
ments that made them up and less as the thing we call "tree." A
patch of reddish berries, which I had never noticed in the leaves
across the yard, were now the first thing I saw each time I looked
up. They seemed to push into the visual field and as the effect

deepened, faint mists transpired before me, as though a haze disclosed by the light, the day grew brighter, the clouds spun and broke apart, piercing white, an animate lace whose definition at their wispy edges could only be called preternatural. I laughed, and then I wasn't sure why I'd laughed. Gabrielle said that it was in this state and this state alone that black velvet art began to make sense to her.

The thing that happens to me most profoundly on psychedelics, the reason I occasionally do them, in fact, and what happened to me that afternoon for a good two hours or so during the deepest part of the trip, is that my sense of connection to the metanarrative deserts me. Maybe it's more accurate to say that in seeing the possibility of this connection foreclosed, I become aware of something I didn't know was taking place, an unconscious process, a limbic subroutine, an autonomic *checking-in* the brain seems regularly to perform to square what you are doing with the context of the day, the week, the still broader context of the year, your life, what you care about and hope to achieve, how you see yourself and how you hope to be seen. It is in watching this process break down that you become conscious of it, the failure of some mechanism to catch at the appropriate point, and the sensation is not unlike waking repeatedly from a dream without having realized you were asleep.

This has been my experience, in any case, and it isn't exactly pleasant. It is instructive, though, I think, to step outside future-directed life, to feel the past slip away, and to confront who you are unmoored from history and intention. It can be frightening. You're left with very little when these things go. But it opens some brief window on the phenomenology of being alive, of living inside a head, and it offers a fleeting glimpse of the metanarrative unmasked as demiurge, as idol, which if you're like me you must punish from time to time, smash and sweep from the Ka'aba. The pristine emptiness, when you've done this, can seem to verge on holiness.

The worst part of a trip, we can probably all agree, is the moment when you've come down enough to realize you are not down all the way. Gabrielle and I are throwing a Frisbee in the yard, watching it glimmer metallic shades as it zips between us, when this moment comes. Gaby lets the Frisbee fall behind her without making any effort to catch it.

"I'm going to do yoga now," she says.

"Okay," I say, and because I dislike even *thinking* about yoga, I decide to take a walk instead of chatting with her while she limbers up. I put on a shirt. I get my phone, some earbuds. I pick out a podcast to listen to. I feel briefly lucid as I set off down the street. It is a lightly wooded residential street, with a few people out front watering their lawns. The occasional car passes slowly by. Once I see the people on their lawns and in their cars, however, and realize they see me, I am flooded with the certainty that they know I'm on drugs, which now that I've left the equivocal sphere of the house it seems I really am. But I compel myself to focus on the podcast, on Terry Gross's familiar voice, her warm, brisk personality, and for about ten seconds I feel fine. I manage to smile at a father and daughter playing catch without, I believe, appearing unambiguously psychotic. And yet I can feel a small worry taking shape in me, a worry I can tamp down but not entirely ignore, and which takes the form of the following question posed to myself: Haven't I been walking on this street an insanely long time? The right way to put it is that I have no *idea* how long I've been walking on the street, and being unable to reconstruct the experience with any temporal dimensionality feels akin to having been *always* walking on the street. It is not a long street, I know this for a fact. In either direction it runs into a perpendicular street and ends, measuring along its entire length at most eight hundred feet, a distance a world-class sprinter could cover in under twenty-five seconds. But because my walk is an iterative action and not a coherent experience—because it is not a *walk* so much as all the component parts of a walk—it does not seem possible, or at least inevitable, that I will *ever* reach the end of the street. And the more anxious this realization makes me, the more closely I attend to my progress, the rate of which, as a consequence of this heightened attention, seems correspondingly to diminish. And it is right around this time, experiencing the first licks of panic, that I realize my walk has become Zeno's paradox.

I don't remember how I made it back. I must have turned around, but honestly it's all a blur. A blur not because it went by fast, but in the sense that the recording of a voice slowed down sufficiently no longer resembles a voice. I credit Terry Gross with getting me home, the grounding cadence of her speech, a metronomic standard by which my subjective experience of time was kept from veering into a fatal adagio. And soon enough—or, you know, whenever—I found myself back in the sunny yard, watching Gabrielle articulate her body in serpentine asanas, listening to Terry interview an author I like, and then an actress I like, as happy as a puppy and at peace, because what I understood just then was that Terry Gross's voice *was* the voice of the metanarrative, demotic ur-parent, Catcher in the WHYY, the call of the shepherd returning me to the pastures of solicitude and moderation, that cultural plane on which the day's horrific news—ecocatastrophe, civilizational conflict, postcolonial scarring, and our legacies of violence and extortion—was not diminished or ignored but existed in a strange vaporous adjacency to yuppie mores, triumphalist life narratives, midcult art, and an anachronistic fixation on jazz, this narrow-bandwidth refugium for temperamental decency and civic virtue and a heartbreaking reasonableness that seemed less and less like the earned wisdom of life than a tragic hope laid over it.

You should not have grown wise before you grew old. Was it my grandfather speaking to me, telling me to persist in my folly, the best way out being through, unless you happen to be standing right by an exit? Is what inaugurates an avant-garde really more than the moment when how it feels to be alive has deviated too far from our operative metanarratives, from what we have to understand and draw significance from the ceaseless welter before us, and when it seems no adult or authority is any longer capable of restoring order or putting things right because we lack even a language with which to name the problem, to place it before us, and to talk together as friends?

That afternoon, as the mushrooms left me gently in the sunlit grass, as I felt the old hierarchies reassert themselves—so that the things I could act upon came forward and those I could merely contemplate fell away—as time regained its normal speed, a speed that seemed almost a trance or deadness, the returning cognizance of how my life was changing felt to me like waking up into a dream. I would write books; people would discuss what to that point had been figments and private reveries, idle inventions—or so I hoped. And I do not mean dream in the sense of nightmare's obverse, not a long-awaited joy or fantastical delight, but rather dream as pseudo-reality, as what resembles life but has no commerce with it. For if the substance of my work purported to be communication of some sort, the exploration and expression of what I found meaningful, my unshakable premonition was that its result would only be to clarify my perversity, deepen my sense of being misunderstood, and thereby accentuate my loneliness. If so, the prefigured fantasy was just a false dream of home. And I looked at Gaby, wondering again whether I hadn't attached the wrong labels to my emotions long ago, as though I had puce and mauve backward, had never been corrected, and now were chasing some impossible chimera because I failed to see that all the things I felt for Gaby *were* love, full stop.

But it was not a moment to make reliable judgments, I suspected.

We spent the night in a nearby city, a pretty harbor town where, truth be told, I had once been born. We drank Belgian dubbels in a cellar bar where the decorative stonework peeked out of the walls and made a piping over low arched passageways. We discussed fame, celebrity, renown, what these things were and why we sought them. The beer had washed any last hallucinatory tincture from us, trading mistake for imprecision, and because we had both failed to read *The Power Broker* for the same class in college, an omission that ever after established Robert Moses as a favorite figure of informed discussion, I now raised his example as a perhaps-instructive case.

Me: Moses was a famous person. Powerful. People would have known who he was when he walked in the room.

Gaby: People were interacting with the idea of him as much as with him. Maybe even more so.

M: Right, and that's clearly an important aspect of fame.

G: You're a representative of the idea of you. Not the other way around.

M: Which is pretty fucked-up.

G: Especially when you consider that you're probably only fractionally responsible for that idea.

M: But with Moses, right, short of his leading some truly lurid private life—which, having read the Caro, I think we can agree he did not—it's not like people wanted to buy magazines to read about who he was dating, whether he'd gained or lost weight, his taste in vacation getaways.

G: Some of that was the era though.

M: Maybe.

G: —and you know the blinding glory of city-administration work.

M: My calendar this year, by the way: our nation's top comptrollers, topless.

G: Ooh. I hear March is a total CPA's wet dream.

M: He's posed with like a lamb, a lion cub, and a double-entry ledger.

G: In a hammock.

M: In a windowless municipal alcove.

G: But so you're saying people didn't feel on intimate terms with Moses. His fame wasn't bound up in enacting a social persona.

M: Which is probably *exactly* the difference between celebrity and fame.

G: And which is funny because a lot of what makes us interested in the celebrities as real people, right, is their always appearing to us as fictional people.

M: We want the fantasy. We also want the fantasy to be real.

G (*with a mischievous relish*): And we want to see them crash and burn.

M: Yeah. We want to see them crash and burn so we know they're like us. And we want to see these perfect façades so we can imagine there's some more exalted life out there.

G: A paradox.

M: Yup.

G: But there's another contradiction too, because the more we tune in to this celebrity gossip, the more we realize they aren't different from us, aren't experiencing some, I don't know, transcendent spiritual election.

M: Well, I think this is sort of where the dark turn comes.

G: I just got chills.

M: Because at some point it's not about the fantasy anymore, right? It's not about the thing we're looking at. It's about *the fact that we're all looking*.

G: The most photographed barn in America.

M: Exactly.

G: And we want to be the barn.

M: It seems better than just staring at the barn.

G: Barn watching, the Amish call it.

M: Right in that sweet spot between hobby and venial sin.

G: Very strong prohibitions on coveting thy neighbor's barn.

M: Thirteen-year-olds sneaking *Architectural Digest* into the outhouse . . .

G: But then why do we want to be the barn if we know it's

all bullshit fantasy? There are plenty of other ways to make money and get laid, right?

M: I think it comes down to a sense that if God's not watching, maybe thirty million Americans are the next best thing.

G: That's the dream.

M: Not necessarily a dream we quite articulate to ourselves, but yes.

G: So the longing behind celebrity worship, if I'm understanding you, is for proximity to God.

M: One way to put it.

G: Or . . .

M: Proximity to God's absence. The innermost circle of our aloneness.

G: Ooh. You make it sound fun.

M: Dante's ball pit.

G: I don't think I made it to that ring. I got stuck with a gargoyle in a Velcro maze.

M: . . .

G: But is there comfort in this inner circle? It doesn't relieve whatever loneliness or despair drove you there, does it?

I told Gaby I didn't know but I assumed she was right; I was pretty sure the aloneness was only deeper at the center, where you could hear it echo, where enfolding the contingency of your existence always was the weightless, transparent envelope of the *idea* of you, a public action having expropriated part of you into the social body, culture's eminent domain exercising its claim on your soul, when all we really wanted were resting points, or so I thought— God, celebrity, accomplishment, sex—weren't they all just pleas for arrival, for the moment sufficient in itself, that feeling of *getting there*, dropping your bags, pouring yourself a drink, and sitting down with an old friend on the porch? The spiritual equivalent of saying, Ah, here we are.

Gaby thought about this for the span of two unhurried sips. "But then the morning *after* the day of arrival."

"Yeah. I know."

I did. I was not only coming down off mushrooms just then and getting drunk, but also, due to a mix-up in my prescription, going off the SSRI I usually took. It had been five days since my last pill, and as we talked and drank I felt an increasingly tenuous line connecting me to my life, a line I imagined as the tether that keeps astronauts from floating away on spacewalks; I was floating, letting something go, possibly myself, possibly because I was in a different story and felt the need to sever ties with the old, test the tensile strength of the new, even as the game of musical chairs I seemed to be playing with my somatic chemistry had set off a sort of inner vibration in me, starting in my abdomen and radiating outward, a proprioceptive fuzziness, like the atomization of my cells experienced from the inside out, the feeling of what it would be like for them independently and all at once to question whether they belonged together, whether we could come to some flawed consensus that pooled our fortunes and coexist under an umbrella dispensation we would call identity. I trusted that I could ride this feeling out. I trusted that despite its buffetings I wouldn't decompose or unspool too far, that after years of holding myself together in what felt like an act of will I could unclench, release myself, and let the environmental pressure contain me, like the ocean depths, and that as long as I had one hand on the line, like a grip on Ariadne's yarn, I could find my way back.

I want to say that there was something comforting, liberating, ludic in this feeling, but I can't and remain honest. As we walked the cobblestone streets of downtown, where the faux-gas streetlamps scattered yellow bands in the shadows, and the colored lights jostling on the harbor water below us were flecks of candy on its jellied skin, it was rather placelessness I felt, an indifference to orientation, the way standing on the North Pole gives you only one cardinal direction in which to head; for through the darkness paneling my mind, what I saw at the far end of my tether, far from anchor or cleat, was instead a face, not the face of any person, but the aureole-enclosed fantasy of a smiling recognition, the face that is emblem and locus of celebrity, visible seat of the invisible being, so that rather than securing me to anything firm, I understood, like the velvet rope outside a club, this line was my invitation to the sanctum of celebrated space, my invitation to let go, that is, to give myself over to the *idea* of me, and like an acrobat transferring lines midair, to swing up up up into the divine and unanchored Valhalla of our debased world.

I admit that this may be somewhat overstated. Grandiose vis-à-vis the facts. I didn't mention it to Gaby, to whom, if this was true of one person on earth, I could say anything. But it was the endpoint of this train of thought, I think, that underlay the self-disgust and wretchedness that led me, when we'd shut down all the bars, to buy street drugs from a figure who appeared at my elbow calling himself Little D. I glanced at Gaby, who sort of shrugged at me, as though to say, Sure, why not? And I wondered if there weren't a bigger D out there somewhere, whether the adjective might not be relative, because our friend looked to me to epitomize male height.

"And this is MDMA?" I said.

"Um-hmm."

" 'Cause I don't know it from rat poison."

Little D looked disappointed in me. "I wouldn't play you like that."

"Okay, sure. But someone who *would* play me like that would say the same thing, right?"

"Nah . . ." He kind of swatted the paradox away.

And with the streetlights hissing their miasmatic fire and a deeper quality of night shaking out through the city, I knew my imp of the perverse had made its decision in accordance with the folk wisdom that says maybe it's better *not* to be, but to let yourself dissolve into the social body, the superorganism, enfolding ecology, the apprehensive moment itself.

I regret, D, that in your line of work you have to deal with idiots like me.

We watched him move off into the night, my fist clenched around the baggie he'd left there when we slapped hands, and at the last moment I called after him, "Hey, what's the D stand for?"

He turned. "What?"

"The D!"

"Ha *ha*." He grinned. "You figure it out!"

The substance in the bag, upon inspection, resembled a large misshapen pebble. We rolled ourselves smokes sitting on the patio furniture of some café and passed the compound back and forth, taking turns sniffing and licking it in those most primitive forms of chemical analysis. It had no smell I could discern and either no taste or was not soluble in saliva, which may come to the same thing. I found something minatory in its inertness.

We walked back to Gaby's car licking our little drug rock. Her car disappointingly did not seem to be where we'd left it. It was also true that neither of us knew where that was, precisely, and that technically it was her mother's car. But the most disheartening thing was that the downtown looked to have been *swept* of cars, and people too for that matter. A traffic light ran through its sequence without advising a single driver. The chill wind funneled down the street between the palisades of buildings. And I wondered why I was wearing a T-shirt before remembering that it was summer, almost two a.m. We wandered around for a while, contemplating what one did without a car and just a crack rock that was probably meth. It finally dawned on us to call the police. They were terribly helpful when we got through and didn't even seem concerned that the last thing we should be helped to locate just then was a car, and soon enough we were in a taxi crossing a bridge into the blighted outskirts of the city, a lifeless district saved from total darkness only by the sodic security lights of warehouses and irradiated signs of fast-food restaurants. Our cabbie, whose first name I had found reason to use no less than fifteen times on our short trip, did not seem as remorseful as I would have hoped about depositing us before a feral wraith of a man leaning against a colossal towing rig.

"Toyota, yep," the man said.

"Toyota's a pretty common car," Gaby said. "How do we know you have ours?"

"I got Toyotas."

Gaby and I glanced at each other.

"That's really not the most reassuring answer."

Now that he had stepped from the rig's shadow I could see the man's face. It might have been handsome if not for an elaborate pigmentary marking that gave it a marled look, streaks of dark nevi fanning out like comet tails below the stringy hair that fell across it. There was something vaguely regal in his bearing, I thought, a hunched, big-boned quality, like the awkward limbedness of a mantis.

"Can we just take a look," Gaby asked, "make sure it's the right car?"

"Can't open the gate until you pay me."

"I don't think that's true," I said. "I think you *won't* open the gate until we pay you. You can do whatever the hell you want."

"If you like it better than way," he said.

It came to $120, and Gaby and I had maybe $80 between us. I was regretting a bit the business deal I'd entered into with Little D, and, in a more general sense, the subjective experience of being alive. I had the urge to say to the man something like, How did we get here, how did this chain-link fence with its small padlock come between us, strangers, men, women, with nothing against one another, acting out the offices of far-flung and abstracted necessities, gutter kings, cursed and shambling exiles muttering an obfuscatory patois, recreants with no faith left in the conduit metaphor of language, abandoned to our preterition of cash transfers, synthetic highs, and a reflexive sabotage that may be at heart no more than contempt for the self-importance and medicalized vanity of other people, the more comfortably unelect, and yet content, it seems, to waste our lives in a pointless standoff at this insignificant gate? I was a bit skeptical of my ability to make myself understood, however, and so I did the one thing I could think to do, which was to take the crack/meth rock/crystal from my pocket and say, "You got somewhere you need to be?"

"You're looking at it," he said. He took the parcel from my hand and unscrewed a lightbulb from a string wreathing the lot, deftly picking out contact, stem, and filament with needle-nose pliers.

"What's your name?" Gaby said as he cleaned the bulb's cavity with a bit of towel and deposited some crushed drug inside it. He held the flame below the glass.

"Wendill," he said.

The smoke drifted up from the bulb as thick as milk.

The silence of the lot struck me at that moment, the moment of inhalation, the faint wind like a memory of elsewheres, the threnody of distance, and as the vapor replaced the chill in me with a lithe magma of hot blood, as the euphoria took hold, Wendill said, and I can only relate, not explain, what follows, "Now I will tell you the story of the human soul."

The Story of the Human Soul, Per Wendill

As you may imagine, I was not always as you see me now. I have lived, oh, many lives, gone by many names, worked all kinda jobs. Not that it's such a long way from claims adjuster to tugboat captain if you—ahem—catch my drift. You are not "before the law." The gate is locked, I assure you. Or maybe not. I forgot to check, I think. My memory . . . well. But what I mean is, see me as a friend, doomed for a certain term to walk the night, alas, but a father figure. I find you apt. Not like those egregious weeds on the riverbank. I spray and spray . . . But no, they will not shut up like a telescope. And I won't either. Ha ha!

Do you remember, in the Jungian sense, I mean, the sense of anamnesis, that day long ago when a slate sky dripped silver tears in the sky-painted lakes above the veldt, when you came upon the briar-caged creature and a man and a woman were one—androgynes, atmen, call them what you will—and a man and a woman and a blackbird were one? When the creature died on the hard point of a rock? How later you baited the briars with fruit, and when the man died and the woman died it was not different from when the creature died. Lush flowers fattened on their graves. And the men picked flowers for the women to remind them how life grows on the cusps of death, playing the B side of *Houses of the Holy* while everyone got laid?

And when the first jockey climbs aboard a creature struggling in the mud, and indestructible space foreshortens, might we not say the rider is the mind of the animal, the way a priest is the mind of the ritual, the way God is the mind of order and accident? The hippie boys and girls of North Beach, entheogenic rapscallions and the best minds of their generation, apparently, take soma to become the mind of the sacrifice. And order and accident have their uneasy marriage, of course, which like all marriages it would be pointless to try to understand from the outside.

That food in the briars begets more food is the initial form the offering takes. The offering is order's humility before accident. A violation brought to consciousness. A horse let wander for a year shadowed everywhere by a hundred young men who could really use some direction in their lives. Do you know what kids in Minoan Crete have to do? their moralizing parents ask. Dance with bulls—can you imagine? You have to follow this fucking horse around, but at least you aren't getting gored by bulls all the time.

And when the year is up, in some extreme unction, they coat the horse in butter, tie it to a post, and kill it. But you've grown fond of the horse over the year, haven't you? So: agenbite of inwit. Was the horse really *down*? You wonder, you perseverate. But perhaps, they say, perhaps it offered itself up like Odin, who hanged himself from a tree in

sacrifice to himself. Well, perhaps. The queen must spend a
night with the dead horse, anyway, sleep with it. The spirit
of the horse whinnies in the wind.

Are you with me? Have you drifted off, begun gnash-
ing your teeth and looking for something to obsessively
clean for the next few hours, because this is where the turn
comes, the morning sun stretches its rosy fingers into the lit
sky, crests mountain and hill, rolls the golden carpet of day
over sparkling sea and fruited plain, over man and woman
stilled of need, free of menace, stumbling into the light a
little hungover, shading their eyes, like: Not bad. Suppos-
ing that thing worked. What, the offering? Yeah. Worked?
(Shrugging) I dunno.

And so in fallow years, on battlefields against long odds,
on beaches dark with homesick siege forces, in the halls of
anxious kings and paranoid queens, inheritance-minded
princes, before the hearths of childless mothers, hapless
fathers, and on the rafts of enterprising castaways, the fire
set to consume the creature's flesh is a chemical transaction,
no more, a currency, an act not of subservience but of control, a way not to honor the gods but to enjoin them. A moment of fraud, for when we purchase something, let us be
clear, we do not call this act a *sacrifice*.

Where is the creature on its *Wanderjahr*, a hundred
shiftless youths behind it? We cannot say. We have lost the
creature. The horse now claims the land on which he tres-
passes for the king, as a wooden horse enters a walled city
to claim it for those outside the gates. Do not, as I say, see
me as a gatekeeper. See me as the blind man with a riddle
at the crossroads. Dispenser of an ambiguous viaticum. We
can await the barbarians long enough to become them,
because it is always a question of whose bidding we do.
And do not say, simply, our own. For is it then the bidding
of our hunger, our fear, our lust? Are we not ever in danger

of becoming slaves to what we merely can do, conscious procurers for our unconscious natures? Is it not always easier to gratify an appetite than to understand one?

The alternative? I confess I sometimes wonder whether it is not romanticism, or only hope, that leads us to imagine a time when spiritual life was more than ornamental garnish on material, a cult of consciousness, cult from the Latin *colere* of course (*colo, colere, colui, cultus*), to cultivate, to till, life spent in radical contemplation of the tidal nuance of a thinking-feeling involvement with all around us, the character, qualities, and rhythms picked out in reflection, so, like a shoreline seen from above, relinquishing shape and pattern on approach, the play of moods and shadings in a bright meadow, say, might evolve ever more complexly in the scrutiny of leaves and blades of grass shaking in the wind, the specific motion of each trembling, the tones in the arrangement of the day as things seek their fleeting equilibria, as branches rustle and petals fall, as the air makes its way through itself immured in the maze of its fluid pressures, bearing the grains of an endless pollination, as the vibrancies set off by stridulating wing or leg contour the static breeze, below the veined crags of mountain, monuments to the gravities that bind our ardor, skirted in tree and shrub running to the silt-swept banks, the plains where snowmelt carves silver fingers into humus and loam, where banyans and mangroves reach out like old hands rung in arthritic knots, berries gather the hidden colors of soil, where deer eat them, where the wolves eat deer, where the humans gather to eat, kill, fuck, and love, to stop and listen, pause within the violence and joy and take some measure of the unaccountable processes of which we are a part, and you might say, How I long to be a gypsy running free in the riot of my heart!, through tall grasses to the song of canebrakes, wild in the pleated dirges of a light knit from hay, sewn from straw verdure, the flaxen clothing of the evening, and those plucked frequencies of the day that sum to rapture. I could a tale unfold whose lightest word would harrow up thy soul, but—well, don't blame your mother.

We were quiet a minute. Then Gaby said, "You said something about our souls?"

Wendill laughed. "What do you think is that ludicrous dirigible in your hand?"

And when he said it our eyes went to our hands, which indeed were holding a length of poly curling ribbon, and from there up the line to the pair of Mylar balloons floating four or five feet overhead, balloons hungry, you could tell, for the very heights where they would pop, and on which, indeed looking rather ridiculous, were printed our own smiling faces.

•

Pop. Pop. Confetti. A blink. The swollen nighttime luster drifts. Lights return easy to their pinpoints and peel sleepily from the glass. The car recovered, the crack rock smoked, the meth—whatever. Gaby is at the wheel and I can feel her trying with all she has to keep us in the lane. The dashed lines converge at a point beyond the horizon and blink our way home. The road had become, I saw, the line of our lives. The yarn-path not *out* of the labyrinth maybe, but onward. If we could just follow it, it would keep us in our lives. But it was narrow, very narrow. One deviation and who knew? The highway curves, the macadam thread spinning off its distaff before us, yes, the chord in any circle being less than the arc which it subtends, but sometimes you're stuck on the arc, aren't you, and Atropos is posed there with her shears. If I could have I might have said, Parents, guardians of the metanarrative, *we* are the minotaur. Half child, half beast. Bury us in the heart of your maze. Hide the primal insanity of your culture from view. You will know us soon enough. We are the displacements of your wounds. Bundled lies sold off in tranches. Captured carbon shut up below the streets of Knossos. We are howl, destroying all you have given us to claim it fully—and *still* Gaby clenches, and I clench too, praying to keep on straight through the midnight highway, to find our way home, knowing all the same that if we make it back, we will be too joy-drunk on our improbable escape to remember to change black sails to white, too misted still in the amnesiac dawn of what Little Dionysius sold us to recall that when we got to the central chamber of the labyrinth it was empty, an echoing cavity, those Indian caves. We were the monster or there was none.

There is not much to say about drugs, hard drugs, drugs in combination, except that at some point you cease to exist. This is what you wanted, to sleep, to dream. To see the moment of your greatness flicker—out. That's it. Take someone else's word for it. It is unexciting and unnecessary. And that's the last thing I have to say about drugs. The day will come when we get to rest forever, no need to hasten it.

In the meantime the responsibilities weighing on us all—starting with the responsibility to take one breath after the next—are exhausting. They are also life. The day Gaby leaves we watch cats hunt mice in the overgrown grass behind the house. The crows watch from the field, sheening and idle lords who might be killing a few minutes between meetings. Lethargy in the heat interleaves with desire, tedium with panic. We laugh to keep the sadness at bay. I can feel it at the edges of my mind, waiting for its moment, the knowledge that I will soon be alone, that we are ever being left to ourselves, so that beyond simple aloneness a deeper architecture of loneliness exists, one obscured in the structures of identity and routine we build on top of it but laid bare in those structures' demolition, a feeling I hadn't sifted down through the rubble to meet since childhood, a full despair, as when, sent away and on your own for the first time, you see at last the sheer scope of the indifference hidden from you, the world's indifference, and how nowhere in the background of life hovers the metaphysical ghost of sentient care. It had been years since I'd considered that no one was taking care of me. The notion had no place in adulthood. I'd sloughed it off. But this is what I returned to in the days following Gabrielle's departure, as I stood in the middle of the field smoking, looking into the trees emptied of mystery, the red berries gone discreetly into shadow, the road beyond where the cars passed at the brisk, uninteresting speed they do, without the sluggish drama of film, the languor of prose. There was no one taking care of me. There wouldn't be any time soon. And I could fight the metanarrative all I wanted, slip its grasp for an evening, punish it for its tyranny by slowly destroying myself, but in the field that afternoon, among the stalking cats and crows, the rough dry grass and clover, under a sun too richly and heavily summered, dressing my exposed body in its violent cinnamon, it was me and the metanarrative alone. That even ticking beat.

You do not get to stop.

You do not really get to stop.

When I went back inside I put on *The Köln Concert*, got a straw broom out of the closet, and swept the house. I sweated. The sweat came in torrents. As Keith built in intensity, departing and returning to his theme, an elaborately toxic water spilled from me. I brought in beer bottles and cans, glasses with crushed lime crescents, viscid residues, the tan remains of onetime ice; I wiped down tables and knocked out ashtrays; I did laundry—clothes, bedding, towels—watered plants, washed dishes, knocked grit from rugs and doormats, took out the trash. Because I am a person I did these things. This is what a person does. You make peace with the melancholy. You invite it in. You say goodbye—to friends, to lovers, to family who are dying. To stray moments of understanding and of being understood. You clean, you shop. You go for runs. Sometimes you cry. Sometimes you want to cry and can't. You are too old, too big, the wrong gender; you have pushed away tears too long. There is a child trembling inside you but that isn't enough. No one cares. No one has time to care. People's lives are shot through with suffering, indignity, and privation you can't imagine. You know this. We all do. And still to say "people" is to refuse to see the child.

Who sees the child?

In the days that follow, it is books and books alone that make me not want to die. At school there was a class called Poetry Will Save Your Life, which we laughed at a little for its pomposity—because so many other things come first, I suppose, because art is always being asked to apologize for its inutility and superfluity. But I think it's true that poetry will save your life, if for no more than that I found it to be true that week, that literature was the only sort of arrival I could count on, an intimacy that wouldn't desert me, that didn't ask too much or fray fatally in the endless conflict of our competing needs, that permitted—or maybe simply *was*—the passage of experience back through us, our way of ravaging the endless ravishment of life. Heaven too is merely a dream of arrival, which we know from our inability to imagine anything ever happening in heaven.

So stop shortchanging poetry. Stop shortchanging art. Seriously. We're sick of it. Art has nothing to apologize for.

It is sick of apologizing.

•

A comedy ends in a wedding, they say. A tragedy in death. An epic comes full circle to end where it began, but—oh, endings!—take your time, I say. Come late!

Back on the island, my grandfather is living. I am living. The woods are living. Bumblebees as big as a child's thumb drift among living flowers. The harrumph of a lawn mower coming to life in the distance references the enveloping determination of growth. My aunts, lively in the morning, setting the coffee machine to burble, return from the garden with tomatoes, squash, parsley, chives, leeks, cabbage, zucchini, corn, thyme, rosemary, carrots, and beets, all of which, through the months of spring and early summer, feasting on the rot of soil, have slowly swelled. And if we are to believe

Greimasian semiotics, bound up in any sense of *dying* must be *living*, along with the *not-living*, *not-dying* rock of the coast, oil-black here and grained like a pompadour, the roll of seawater, the nescient wind that laps the flag with its fanciful coat of arms, stretches the cupped palms of canvas sails, splits on bird wings, and touches off the texture of the bay.

I sit with my grandfather in the morning. The day is chilly, with dark gray clouds portending to the southwest. My grandfather wears a baseball cap and a windbreaker over his sweater. There is no discerning a body beneath the clothes.

"When we sailed . . ." It takes him time to get his sentences out. "Sometimes the propeller got . . . tangled . . . on seaweed, you know . . . and I'd—I'd dive down with a knife . . ."

"Yes," I say, "and you'd cut the propeller free."

He nods. "That's right."

I've heard these stories many times before. He had an Aqua-Lung aboard the boat, which he used for difficult jobs. Often, though, he just went in in his underwear with a snorkel and mask, a six-inch pilot knife, down into the frigid waters of a strange harbor while his family roused themselves in the morning haze off the ocean. At least once he got tangled up, unable to break free beneath the boat, and had to dive back down to find the line gripping him and cut it before he drowned. He had nearly died thinking of his family just above him, humming as they prepared breakfast, so close and yet unable to hear him on the far side of that insuperable medium. Things must not be so different for him now. But he hadn't died that morning, of course, and he hasn't died still. And I take his choice of topic, in its elliptical way, to mean he understands my foolish plan to go after the anchor, the impulse to pit one's vitality against death, our heedless pursuit of what is always slipping beneath the surface. The first examples of writing, we are told, are inventories and accounts, records of the stores in granaries, the numbers in herds, trades, payments. *Bookkeeping*. A desire to keep track of things, to not forget.

I find Ruth in the study staring at an old computer, the monitor of which alone could flatten a corgi, and I knock on the doorframe.

"How do I turn a JPEG into an MP3?" she says.

"Hmm. I don't think you do."

"Francesca and Malcolm are coming tonight, you know."

"Yes." They are Ruth's children, my cousins; soon the house will be teeming with the full extant family. Bill, Ruth's husband, is flying in tomorrow from a work trip in Ireland. All these atoms of diverse energy, divergent lives and convergent genes, called together in these walls to confront the breadth of our mutual and utter incomprehension.

"I need you to take Denise to the ferry," Ruth says.

"I know, I talked to Denise. For the record, I'm not a big fan of the whole 'I need you to' formulation."

I expect Ruth to give me one of her lead-eyed looks, but her eyes are wide open and her face younger than I can remember it being in a long time. "It's all just really hard," she says.

"Do you want to tell me why you guys are still fighting?"

She shakes her head. "We forgot."

I am stubborn. I have lived long enough to know that. My aunts are stubborn. My grandfather is stubborn. We are a stubborn family; we don't agree, we disapprove, our esteem is hard to win, our affection hard to lose; our grudges linger even when we say they don't. And yet, if on the surface the dispute between my aunts and their father drew on those stock issues of family and age, of control and the disposition of *things*, the deeper grievance, I have to believe, was what it always is—that our children are us and yet not us, that parents turn from gods to men and women at last to children, that in describing our nearest boundary with the world our families also measure the distance, the gulf, and that love always comes with conditions, even if these are only the limits of love.

We can't forgive one another. To forgive our family would be to forgive the very strangeness of our being.

The sky has darkened and threatens rain as Denise and I wait at the ferry terminal. "You really going out there?" she says.

"I guess so."

"Jesus. Well, easiest twenty bucks I'll ever make."

I ask if she's going to see her husband and she says, Yup. How is he? Not good, she says, and because there's nothing else to do she laughs. It looks like he only has weeks left, a month or two at the outside, and she moved here initially for him, for his work and to be near his family. She doesn't know what's next for her, where she'll go. But then it's the kids she's really worried about. They've run off, disappeared into their young lives. They're at the age when they'd be leaving anyway, but now they're crashing cars, taking up with guys too old for them, fleeing to the far coast. It's too depressing at home, and she's not around.

"They don't know what to do. I don't either."

What to say? Kids are always running away from home.

"Don't ever think you've run too far to be welcomed back," she says. "That's what I'd say to them if I could."

On our way out to the island the salt water swept up by the wind might as well be incipient rain. I watch Misty's hair and jacket billow and blow around her, and it reminds me of a concert she and I once saw, the opening act for the band we'd come to see. It was some minor band I'd never heard of. The lead singer, a man with expressive lips and strawberry-blond hair, wore a full white-lace wedding gown and pallid makeup while he performed. The train of the dress swished around him as he danced and sang. He was in no way *cool*. This was what Misty and I had loved. Somehow you could tell he wasn't just laughing at himself. It could have been a gimmick and it wasn't. It was instead a kind of craziness, a kind of love. It was this or nothing—for him it was this or nothing, you could tell. And to writhe in a wedding dress and makeup before a sparse crowd there to see another band, to do this as a grown man, neither an idiot nor a clown, and to do it night after night without rising out of obscurity is the purest sort of conviction and bravery, I believe.

I am the one going in, we've decided. Misty and I trade places; she takes the wheel and steers the boat among the shallows by the rocks. I am already freezing in a thick sweatshirt.

"Can you see anything?" she says.

"No, it must be farther out."

The muddled seabed fades as the water deepens, the submerged rocks fade. The translucent olive water interposes itself like rippling screens bearing grains of light. After debating for a bit where I should go in we settle on a spot. I strip down to my bathing suit and for a second, standing in the boat, feel like the smallest pebble in an infinite pool, the bay waters in the distance seeming not to meet but to join the sky at some unbroken axis mundi in the smoldering gray.

"I was in the park the other day and I heard these twelve-year-old girls calling each other 'bro,'" Misty says. "They were like, 'Chill out, bro.' 'Sweet, bro.' 'Let me see your phone, bro.' It was hilarious."

"At the playground a few weeks ago, I heard this eight-year-old boy yelling, 'I'm tripping balls!' Just throwing it out there to no one in particular."

"We tripped some pretty serious balls when we were kids," Misty says.

"True," I say. It is true. "Watch me get hypothermia, bro."

I dive in.

For the first minute the water grips me like a cryonic gel, glacial, faintly pinguid, then a numbness starts to fill me and bit by bit I lose track of the water and my body until we are one substance slipping through itself. I dive down five, eight feet and turn to see the surface above me as just a lighter shade in the impenetrable haze, the hull of the whaler as white and luminous as a belly, recalling to me, for the first time in years, how I used to look up at my grandfather and my mother as they swam laps above me in the pool, a small, spindly child, ducking below them when they went past, captivated by the currents, the bubbles and roil, at their bodies, the wild, horselike look in their eyes, the oxygenous contrails streaming from their noses, the primal mystery of my connection to them. We can overrate blood, surely, the stepped-up bases of our inheritance, the avarice of our genes, but I want to believe that we preserve the things we love, that we mustn't glorify what is small, write our eulogies in the stars, or privilege any one scale to say that what befalls one of us befalls us all, or that we ever owe less than our attention.

My grandfather wanted to be a physicist, an astronomer, and although I knew him as a secular man it doesn't seem possible to me that someone turns his attention to the stars without a flicker of longing for the cosmos—the greater order of which our lives are a part—and the romantic's intuition that passion lives in a ramshackle outpost on the banks of the unknown. I sometimes wonder whether his forebears, German-Jewish burghers who lived not far downriver from Johann Peter Hebel along the Rhine, consulted the compendium in which the writer's *Kalendergeschichten* appeared, stories that alongside the almanac itself put forward the idea, and with it the mythology, of a world suited to the orderliness of the cosmos, a natural and social symmetry. I wonder whether this legacy then trickled down, for if Hebel's genius lies, as one great rememberer has written, in taking the perspective of the stars themselves, so that they tell not the emblazoned story of our grandeur but of our insignificance, as the life of the planet, seen from a celestial distance, settles into a music of the spheres, a tectonic fidgeting, a *not-living, not-dying* ecology, a word that means, most literally, the study of a *house*, a bound order, a family—we must all still take the house into which we are born, our mother's house, our father's house, and from the inside out build our own.

And if I asked Misty why she couldn't find her place she might say, "I was waiting for love," and then, laughing, "But don't think I envy lovers. Lovers are idiots. Only someone in love would name a child Mirabella." And if I saw my grandfather with Ruth or Cynthia in an unguarded moment, talking quietly in the study, I might know their grievance was no more than love, a wild rage at finity, at how we tell ourselves there will be time to mend our ruptures and know one another, and there never is. And if the intimacy Gaby and I share is more than one could hope for and still not enough, what then? What does this say? And if in eulogies we tell stories of the times we knew the deceased, hunting down the words to summon what they meant to us, is this remembering, a form of living, or is it only the sunyata of the dead, an unknown hollow we describe by the contours of a vacancy? For if true remembering were possible, would it not involve seeing the world through my grandfather's eyes, a boy born during World War I who could recall the milkman's horse lying dead on the cobblestones where it collapsed climbing their hill in the Bronx, who watched Murderers' Row—Ruth, Gehrig, "Long Bob" Meusel, Earle Combs—from the platform of the el with his own grandfather on his way home from school, his grandfather's hands, he would remember, perfumed with the oils he sold, bergamot, cedar, clove, and geranium, a man who as a widower lived with them on the steep and pastoral street at the end of which the shell-shocked veterans gathered at the hospital's iron gates, taunting and enticing my grandfather as he passed, that dark metal fence looming over his youth, one spent in thrall to science and to his idol, Frank Oppenheimer, five forms ahead of him in school, a guiding light whom my grandfather and his best friend, Ithiel, revered as boys before growing up themselves, going off to college, traveling together to Mexico as young men out of school for the summer, climbing Popocatépetl and hearing Trotsky speak—Ithiel was a communist then—at a meeting hall where attendees put their revolvers on a table by the door, this just a few years before Trotsky was shot and killed, returning at the end of the summer, my grandfather, to the musty lecture halls of New England from which he would emerge two years later engaged to my grandmother, a woman he would stay married to until her death

sixty years later and whose courtship had consisted of reading to
each other on a riverbank from *Ulysses*, that great eddy in the on-
flowing tide of entropy, a tide soon to wreck the world again in
bloodshed, a war my grandfather would spend at a research lab on
Long Island developing radar and where, on that fateful August
morning in 1945, he would do the math with a colleague to confirm
the lunatic destruction of which we were indeed now capable, a
datum central to reality henceforth, and so to the life of his newborn
daughter, my mother, and those of his children to follow and his
grandchildren, but then he *had* been the one to travel years before to
identify his uncle's body in the nowhere hills of western Pennsylva-
nia, a salesman who had died on the train to Chicago the very day
he and his wife adopted their first child, a cousin my grandfather
would never know, and perhaps he knew from this first lesson, or
should have known, the vicious derailments life has in store, things
that would ultimately know nothing of his inner weighing of compromise and possibility and hope, what the quality of love he had
for the people he loved was *like*—*felt* like—what pride or disappointment he felt in them or in himself, getting into bed at night
thinking he might have spoken up more bravely or loved more
fiercely, as we all do, or that he might have lived another life altogether, and why not; and if he had, would the white-capped waves
in the bay look different to him now, what does he see when they
catch the sun, can we know, or when he stood at the helm of his
sailboat named for an old slave munity, or sailed into prewar Europe
with his sister and caught that first glimpse of a foreign land, how
did the words of *Ulysses* strike him on the tongue of the woman he
would soon marry in secret two months before their wedding—as
confronting a fundamental uncertainty? as an insistent affirmative?—
and what did he see when he was left alone with the strange can-
dlelit faces of his children and grandchildren, arguing and laughing
at the dinner table, these people who were him and also not him
and destined to live lives mysterious to his own, what did he hope
the world might become as his life went on and finally extinguished,

trying to make more right decisions than wrong, trying to balance the love we owe one another with the inevitable and proper love we must save for ourselves?

And if I am to stay in the water of this skybound bay, looking for an anchor attached to nothing, I hope you will believe me that at a wedding by a pond, I was not a romantic or a sap to see in the consummatory kiss a flicker of the metanarrative's grandeur, or a straining into the absence that suggests it could still have a place, the first lone voice that rises up to answer the dithyramb, the bondage of our curiosity, *this*, *here*, after a moment's quiet for the life of the pond, the choral frogs and boatmen, the turtles and skimmers, the dragonflies that skitter, the vipers, the doves.

Acknowledgments

Thank you:

Ann Beattie, Georges, Anne, and Valerie Borchardt, Rachel Brooke, Deborah Eisenberg, the Fine Arts Work Center, Nina Frieman, Laird Gallagher, Elizabeth Gordon, Debra Helfand, Yuka Igarashi, Jonathan Lippincott, the MacDowell Colony, Matthew Neill Null, Andrew Palmer, Jon Parrish Peede, Sigrid Rausing, Sarah Scire, Peng Shepherd, Lorin Stein, Christopher Tilgham, the University of Virginia MFA Program, VCCA, Allison Wright.

This book owes a singular debt to the wisdom, labor, and encouragement of Eric Chinski, Bella Lacey, Alexis Schaitkin, Samantha Shea, and Deborah Treisman.

It is my great fortune to count you as readers and friends.

Keep in touch with
Granta Books:

Visit grantabooks.com to discover more.

GRANTA